POPULAR PUBLICATIONS   FACSIMILE EDITIONS

Famous Fantastic Mysteries #3
(December 1939)

Initially published by The Frank A. Munsey Company, *Famous Fantastic Mysteries* was dedicated to reprinting the rare science fiction and fantasy stories from the early years of *Argosy*, *The All-Story*, and *The Cavalier*. *Famous Fantastic Mysteries* is one of the most important science fiction pulps. The third issue contains classic stories by A. Merritt, Ralph Milne Farley, Homer Eon Flint, and Edison Marshall, among others.

Authors:

Ralph Milne Farley, Waldemar Kaempffert, Homer Eon Flint, Philip Fisher, A. Merritt, Edison Marshall, J. U. Giesy

Illustrators:

Frank R. Paul, Virgil Finlay

NOTE: We have attempted to restore the original page scans in this facsimile in order to provide an enjoyable reading experience. However, in some cases there can be text loss due to damage to the original pulp, tight bindings, or other reasons.

In answering advertisements it is desirable that you mention FAMOUS FANTASTIC MYSTERIES

 **Famous FANTASTIC Mysteries**

Patent Applied For

Vol. 1   DECEMBER, 1939   **No. 3**

THIS magazine is the answer to thousands of requests that we have received over a period of years, demanding a second look at famous fantasies which, since their original publication, have become accepted classics. Our choice has been dictated by *your* requests and our firm belief that these are the aces of imaginative fiction.

—*The Editors.*

THE FRANK A. MUNSEY COMPANY, Publisher, 280 Broadway, New York, N. Y.
WILLIAM T. DEWART, *President*

THE CONTINENTAL PUBLISHERS & DISTRIBUTORS, LTD.
3 La Belle Sauvage, Ludgate Hill, London, E.C., 4
Paris: HACHETTE & CIE, 111 Rue Reaumur

The January Issue Will Be On Sale December 6

CAUGHT by rising tide in SHARK-FILLED WATERS!

G. BROOKS TAYLOR
Pledger, Texas

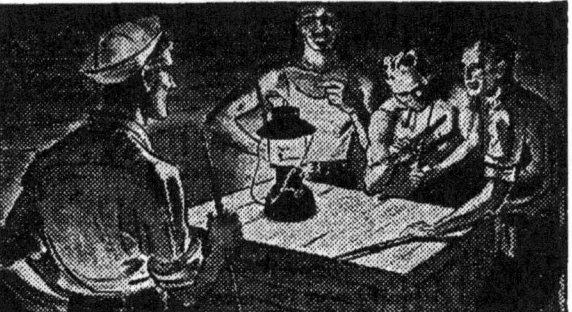

1 "**One night** a party of us started out to spear flounders in the warm, shallow Gulf coast waters," writes Mr. Taylor. "As the tide ebbs away, the flounder remains on the sandy bottom, often in only a few inches of water.

2 "**Enjoying the sport,** we wandered farther and farther from land, trusting the lantern left on the beach with one of our party to guide us safely back.

3 "**Suddenly,** we realized that the tide had turned! Then, our guiding light disappeared. We didn't know which way to run—trapped in shark-filled waters!

4 "**Panic stricken,** we scurried about madly. Then, a pin-point of light far away winked reassuringly! Unable to fix the disabled lantern, the man on shore had sensed our plight, and luckily had a flashlight in his dufflebag. It probably saved us. From now on we will sing the praises of 'Eveready' *fresh* DATED batteries—the kind you can *depend* upon in emergency. (*Signed*) *G Brooks Taylor*"

N⁰ 950
EVEREADY
EXTRA LONG LIFE BATTERY
A NATIONAL CARBON COMPANY PRODUCT

FRESH BATTERIES LAST LONGER... *Look for the* DATE-LINE

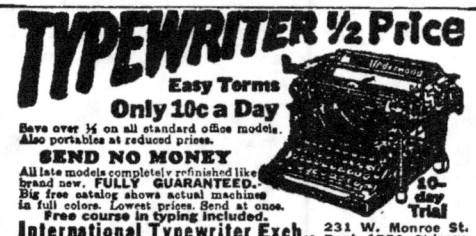
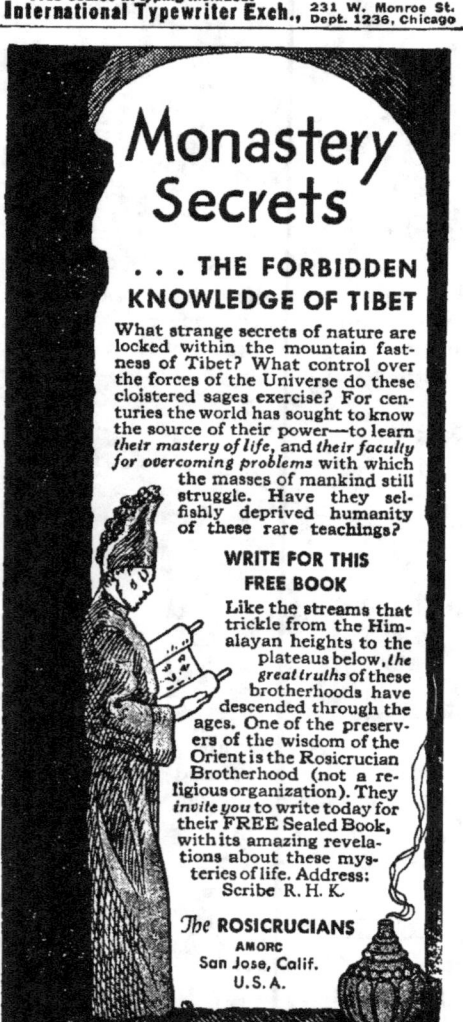
In answering advertisements it is desirable that you mention FAMOUS FANTASTIC MYSTERIES

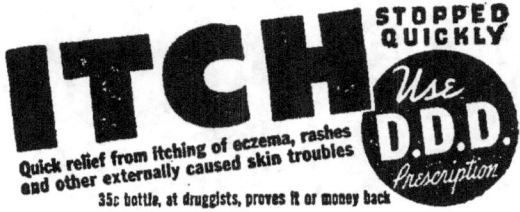
Since I took up writing for a hobby life is twice as much fun!...

*says well-known New York business man**

"When I leave the office at the end of the day I step into a thrilling new world! You see, spare-time writing gives you the tremendous fun of creating something—of building up your observations and ideas so they're as interesting to other people as to yourself! And there's that other big thrill—the thrill of *social recognition*. For I've acquired hosts of interesting and important new friends. The *profit* is worthwhile, too!" . . . Lucky fellow, you say. Yet like all the men and women who have made a success of this profitable hobby he has a very simple secret— *he learned how to write.*

Learn to Write by Writing

A recent survey conducted by a famous university shows that *journalistic training* has proved itself practical over all other methods of learning how to write. For the careers of the majority of authors questioned (including America's greatest writers) were built on experience gained under the Newspaper Copy Desk Method! And that's the method Newspaper Institute of America uses to teach you professional writing as a hobby. You learn to write by writing under skilled constructive criticism, sympathetically directed to help you with your individual writing problems.

Each week you receive a fascinating assignment. Your work is analyzed by men of long newspaper experience. As you write, profiting by their corrections and advice, you find yourself acquiring a distinctive style. You master the intricacies of story construction —learn how to write a story vigorously, dramatically. In short, you're learning to write the kind of things editors will buy.

Here's How to Get Started

Send the coupon for our Writing Aptitude Test—it tells you honestly and accurately what your native abilities at writing are. You'll enjoy this interesting test. There is absolutely no obligation. Get started—send the coupon now. Newspaper Institute of America, 1 Park Avenue, New York.

* Name on Request.

"Help! Help! I can't get my arm out. The plant is eating me!" he cried, as Doggo fussed about, trying to aid him

The Radio Man

PART I

By RALPH MILNE FARLEY
Author of "The Radio Beasts," "The Radio Planet," etc.

A blinding flash, and Myles Cabot finds himself in the strange Ant World of the planet Venus

CHAPTER I

THE MESSAGE IN THE METEOR

NEVER had I been so frightened in all my life! It was a warm evening late in August, and I was sitting on the kitchen steps of my Chappaquiddick Island farmhouse, discussing the drought with one of the farm hands. Suddenly there appeared in the sky over our heads a flaming fiery mass, rushing straight downward toward us.

"Here's where a shooting star gets me," I thought, as I instinctively ducked my head, just as though such a feeble move as ducking one's head could afford any possible protection from the flaming terror. The next instant there came a dull crash, followed by silence, which in turn was broken by the hired man dryly remarking: "I reckon she struck over to Cow Hill." Cow Hill was the slight elevation just back of our farmhouse.

So the meteor hadn't been aimed exactly as *me*, after all.

If that thing had hit me, some one else would be giving to the world this story.

We did nothing further about the meteor that night, being pretty well shaken up by the occurrence. But next morning, as soon as the chores were done, the hired man and I hastened to the top of Cow

The other ants stood uncertainly. Were they friendly, or would they leave him to his fate?

Hill, to look for signs of last night's fiery visitor.

And, sure enough, there were plenty of signs. Every spear of grass was singed from the top of the hill; the big rock on the summit showed marks of a collision; and several splinters of some black igneous material were lying strewed around. Leading from the big rock there ran down the steep side of the hill a gradually deepening furrow, ending in a sort of caved-in hole.

We could not let slip such a good opportunity to get some newspaper publicity for our farm. And so on the following Thursday a full account of the meteoric visita-

tion appeared in the Vineyard *Gazette,* with the result that quite a number of summer folks walked across the island from the bathing beach to look at the hole.

And there was another result, for early the following week I received a letter from Professor Gerrish, of the Harvard Observatory, stating that he had read about the meteor in the paper, and requesting that I send him a small piece—or, if possible, the whole meteor—by express, collect, for purposes of analysis.

Anything for dear old Harvard! Unfortunately all the black splinters had been carried away by tourists. So I set the men

7

to work digging out the main body. Quite a hole was dug before we came to the meteor, a black pear-shaped object about the size of a barrel. With rock tongs, chains and my pair of Percherons we dragged this out onto the level. I had hoped that it would be small enough so that I could send the whole thing up to Harvard and perhaps have it set up in front of the Agassiz Museum, marked with a bronze plate bearing my name; but its size precluded this.

My wife, who was present when we hauled it out, remarked: "It looks just like a huge black teardrop or raindrop."

And sure enough it did. But why not? If raindrops take on a streamline form in falling, why might not a more solid meteor do so as well? But I had never heard of one doing so before. This new idea prompted me to take careful measurements and to submit them to Professor O. D. Kellogg, of the Harvard mathematics department, who was summering at West Chop near by. He reported to me that the form was as perfectly streamlined as it was possible to conceive, but that my surmise as to how it had become so was absurd.

WHILE making these measurements I was attracted by another feature of the meteor. At one place on the side, doubtless where it had struck the big rock, the black coating had been chipped away, disclosing a surface of yellow metal underneath. Also there was to be seen in this metal an absolutely straight crack, extending as far as the metal was exposed, in a sidewise direction.

At the time the crack did not attract me so much as the metal. I vaguely wondered if it might not be gold. But, being reminded of Professor Gerrish's request for a sample of the meteor, I had one of the men start chiseling off some pieces.

The natural spot to begin was alongside of the place where the covering was already chipped. It was hard work, but finally he removed several pieces, and then we noticed that the crack continued around the

waist of the meteor as far as had been chipped. This crack, from its absolute regularity, gave every indication of being man-made.

Our curiosity was aroused. Why the regularity of this crack? How far did it go? Could it possibly extend clear way around? Was it really a threaded joint? And if so, how could such a phenomenon occur on a meteorite dropped from the sky?

Forgotten was the second crop mowing we had planned to do that day. Hastily summoning the rest of the help, we set to work with cold chisels and sledges, to remove the black coating in a circle around the middle of the huge teardrop. It was a long and tedious task, for the black substance was harder than anything I had ever chipped before. We broke several drills and dented the yellow metal unmercifully, but not so much so but what we could see that the threaded crack did actually persist.

The dinner hour passed, and still we worked, unmindful of the appeals of our womenfolk, who finally abandoned us with much shrugging of shoulders.

It was nearly night when we completed the chipping and applied two chain wrenches to try and screw the thing apart. But, after all our efforts, it would not budge. Just as we were about to drop the wrenches and start to chisel through the metal some one suggested that we try to unscrew it as a left-handed screw. Happy thought! For, in spite of all the dents which we had made, the two ends at last gradually untwisted.

What warrant did we have to suppose that there was anything inside it? I must confess, now it is all over, that we went through this whole day's performance in a sort of feverish trance, with no definite notion of what we were doing, or why; and yet impelled by a crazy fixed idea that we were on the verge of a great discovery.

And at last our efforts had met with success, and the huge teardrop lay before us in two neatly threaded parts. The inside was hollow and was entirely filled with something tightly swathed in silver colored felt tape.

Breathless, we unwound over three hundred feet of this silver tape, and finally came to a gold cylinder about the size and shape of a gingersnap tin—that is to say, a foot long and three inches in diameter —chased all around with peculiar arabesque characters. By this time Mrs. Farley and my mother-in-law and the hired girl had joined us, attracted by the shouts which we gave when the teardrop had come apart.

One end of the cylinder easily unscrewed—also with a left-handed thread— and I drew forth a manuscript, plainly written in the English language, on some tissue-thin substance like parchment.

Every one clustered around me, as I turned to the end to see who it was from, and read with astonishment the following signature: "Myles S. Cabot."

But this name meant nothing to anyone present except myself.

I heard one of the hands remark to another:

" 'Twarn't no shootin' star at all. Nothin' but some friend of the boss shootin' a letter to him out of one of these here long-range guns."

"Maybe so," said I to myself.

But Mrs. Farley was quivering with excitement.

"You must tell me all about it, Ralph," said she. "Who *can* be sending you a message inside a meteor, I wonder?"

My reply was merely: "I think that there is a clipping in one of my scrapbooks up in the attic which will answer that question."

There was! I found the scrapbook in a chest under the eaves, but did not open it until after chores and supper, during which meal I kept a provoking silence on the subject of our discovery.

WHEN the dishes were finally all cleared away, I opened the book on the table and read to the assembled household the following four-year-old clipping from the Boston *Post*.

CITIZEN DISAPPEARS

Prominent Clubman Vanishes from Beacon Street Home

Myles S. Cabot, of 162 Beacon Street, disappeared from his bachelor quarters late yesterday afternoon, under very mysterious circumstances.

He had been working all day in his radio laboratory on the top floor of his house, and had refused to come down for lunch. When called to dinner, he made no reply: so his butler finally decided to break down the door, which was locked.

The laboratory was found to be empty. All the windows were closed and locked, and the key was on the inside of the door. In a heap on the floor lay a peculiar collection of objects, consisting of Mr. Cabot's watch and chain, pocket knife, signet ring, cuff links and tie pin, some coins, a metal belt buckle, two sets of garter snaps, some safety pins, a gold pen point, a pen clip, a silver pencil, some steel buttons, and several miscellaneous bits of metal. There was a smell in the air like one notices in electric power houses. The fuses on the laboratory power line were all blown out.

The butler immediately phoned to police headquarters, and Detective Flynn was dispatched to the scene. He questioned all the servants thoroughly, and confirmed the foregoing facts.

The police are still working on the case.

WAS PROMINENT RADIO ENTHUSIAST

Myles S. Cabot, whose mysterious disappearance yesterday has shocked Boston society, was the only son of the late Alden Cabot. His mother was a Sears of Southboro.

The younger Cabot since his graduation from Harvard had devoted himself to electrical experimenting. Although prominent in the social life of the city, and an active member of the Union, University, New York Yacht, and Middlesex Hunt Clubs, he nevertheless had found time to invent novel and useful radio devices, among the best known of which is the Indestructo Vacuum Tube.

He had established at his Beacon Street residence one of the best equipped radio laboratories in the city.

His most recent experiment, according to professional friends, had been with television.

Mr. Cabot substituted two circuits for the usual television circuit, one controlling the vertical lines of his sending and receiving screens, and the other the horizontal, thus enabling him to enlarge his screen considerably, and also to present a continuous picture instead of one made up of dots. The effect of perspective he obtained by adding a third circuit.

The details of this invention had not been given out by Mr. Cabot prior to his disappearance.

His nearest relatives are cousins.

The last was a particularly gentle touch, it seemed to me. Well, his cousins hadn't yet inherited his property, although they had tried mighty hard; and perhaps this mysterious message from the void would prevent them from ever doing so. I hoped that this would be the case, for I liked Myles, and had never liked those cousins of his.

Myles had been a classmate of mine at Harvard, though later our paths drifted apart, his leading into Back Bay society and radio, and mine leading into the quiet pastoral life of a farm on Chappaquiddick Island off the coast of Massachusetts. I had heard little of him until I read the shocking account of his sudden disappearance.

The police had turned up no further clues, and the matter had quickly faded from the public sight. I had kept the *Post* clipping as a memento of my old college chum.

I was anxious to learn what had become of him these four years past. So I opened the manuscript and proceeded to read aloud.

In the following chapters I shall give the story contained in that manuscript—a story so weird, and yet so convincingly simple, that it cannot fail to interest all those who knew Myles Cabot. It completely clears up the mystery surrounding his disappearance. Of course, there will be some who will refuse to believe that this story is the truth. But those of his classmates and friends who knew him well will find herein unmistakable internal evidence of Myles Cabot's hand in this nar-

rative conveyed to me in the golden heart of a meteorite.

CHAPTER II

STRANDED IN SPACE

THUS wrote Myles Cabot:
My chief line of work, since graduating from Harvard, was on the subject of television. By simultaneously using three sending sets and three receiving sets, each corresponding to one of the three dimensions, any object which I placed within the framework of my transmitter could be seen within the framework of my receiver, just as though it stood there itself.

All that prevented the object from actually being made to stand there was the quite sufficient fact that no one had yet, so far as I was then aware, invented a means for dissolving matter into its well-known radiations, and then converting these radiations back into matter again.

But at just this time, by a remarkable coincidence, there came into my hands a copy of an unpublished paper on this subject by Rene Flambeau.

The prior experiments of De Gersdorff are well known; he had succeeded by means of radio waves, in isolating and distinguishing the electro-magnetic constituents of all the different chemical elements. Flambeau went one step further, and was able to transmit small formless quantities of matter itself, although for some reason certain metals, but not their salts, appeared to absorb the electrical energy employed by him, and thus be immune to transportation.

As I could already transmit a three-dimensional picture of an object, and as Flambeau had been able to transmit formless matter, then by combining our devices in a single apparatus I found I could transmit physical objects unchanged in form.

But this apparatus produced one unexpected phenomenon—namely, that whenever I employed excessive power my sending set would transmit objects placed slightly outside its normal range, and certain small quantities thereof would turn up in other portions of my laboratory than within my receiving set.

To test this phenomenon further, I secured some high voltage equipment and arranged with the Edison Company for its use.

On the afternoon when the installation was completed, I started to place a small blue china vase in position to send it. Something must have become short-circuited, for there came a blinding flash, and I knew no more.

HOW long the unconsciousness lasted, I have no means of telling. I was a long time regaining my senses, but when I had finally and fully recovered I found myself lying on a sandy beach, beside a calm and placid lake, and holding in my hand the small blue vase.

The atmosphere was warm, moist and fragrant, like that of a hothouse, and the lap-lapping of the waves gave forth such a pleasing musical sound that I lay where I was and dozed off and on, even after I had recovered consciousness.

I seemed to sense, rather than really to see, my surroundings. The sand was very white. The sky was completely over-clouded at a far height, and yet the clouds shone with such a silvery radiance that the day was as bright as any which I had ever seen with full sunlight on earth, but with a difference, for here the light diffused from all quarters, giving the shadowless effect which one always notes in a photographer's studio.

To my right lay the lake, reflecting the silvery color of the sky. Before me stretched the beach, unbroken save for an occasional piece of driftwood. To my left was the upland, covered with a thicket of what at first appeared to be dead trees, but on closer scrutiny were seen to be some gigantic species of the well-known branched gray lichen with red tips, which I used to find on rocks and sticks in the woods as a child.

No birds were flying overhead, I suppose because there were no birds to fly. I fell to wondering, vaguely and pleasantly, where I was and how I got there; but for the moment I remained a victim of complete amnesia.

Suddenly, however, my ears were jarred by a familiar sound. At once my senses cleared and I listened intently to the distant purring of a motor. Yes, there could be no mistake—an airplane was approaching. Now I could see it, a speck in the sky, far down the beach.

Nearer and nearer it came.

I sprang to my feet, and to my intense surprise found that the effort threw me quite a distance into the air. Instantly the thought flashed through my mind: "I must be on Mars!" But no, for my weight was not nearly enough lighter than my earthly weight to justify such a conclusion.

For some reason my belt buckle and most of the buttons which held my clothes together were missing, so that my clothing came to pieces as I arose, and I had to shed it rapidly in order to avoid impeding my movements. I wondered at the cause of this.

But my speculations were cut short by the alighting of the airplane a hundred yards down the beach. It seemed to land vertically, rather than run along the ground, but I could not be sure at that distance. What was my horror when out of it clambered not men but ants! Ants, six-footed and six feet high. Huge ants, four of them, running toward me over the glistening sands.

Gone was all my languor as I seized a piece of driftwood and prepared to defend myself as well as I could. The increase in my jumping ability, although slight, coupled with an added buoyancy, enabled me to prolong the unequal encounter.

The ants came slowly forward, four abreast, like a cavalry formation, while I awaited their onslaught, grasping the stick of driftwood firmly in my hand. When nearly upon me they executed right-by-troopers and started circling in an ever-narrowing circle.

Suddenly the ants wheeled and converged from all four points of the compass, clicking their mandibles savagely as they came. The whole movement had been executed with uncanny precision, without a single word of communication between the strange black creatures; in fact, without a single sound except the clicking of their mandibles and a slight rattling of their joints. How like a naval attack by a fleet of old-fashioned Ford cars, I thought.

When within about ten feet of me, they made a concerted rush; but I leaped to one side, at the same time giving one of my antagonists a crack with my club as they crashed together in the center. This denouement seemed to confuse them, for they slowly extricated themselves from their tangle and withdrew for a short distance, where they again formed and stood glaring at me for a few minutes, clicking their jaws angrily.

Then they rushed again, this time in close formation, but again I jumped to one side, dealing another blow with my club. Whereupon the fighting became disorganized, the ants making individual rushes, and I leaping and whacking as best I could.

I scored several dents in the armor of my opponents, and finally succeeded by a lucky stroke in beheading one of them. But at this the other three came on with renewed vigor. Although each ant wore some sort of green weapon slung in a holster at its side, they fought only with their mandibles.

The slight difference in gravity from that to which I had been accustomed finally proved my undoing; for, although it increased my agility, it also rendered me a bit less sure on my feet, and this was enhanced by the rapid disintegration of the soles of my shoes. The result was that at last I slipped and fell, and was immediately set upon and pinned down by my enemies. One of the ants at once deliberately nipped me in the side with his huge mandibles. An excruciating pain shot through my entire body; and then, for the second time that day, I lost consciousness.

WHEN I came to, I found myself lying in the cockpit of an airplane, speeding through the sky. One of my ant captors was standing on a slight incline at the bow of the ship, operating the control levers with his front feet; and the other two were watching the scenery. The dead ant was nowhere to be seen. No one was paying any attention to me.

I was not bound, and yet I was unable to move. My senses were unusually keen, and yet my body was completely paralyzed. I had no idea as to what sort of country we were flying over, for I could not raise my head above the edge of the cockpit. I didn't know where I was going, but I certainly was on my way all right. And not so all right, at that.

Overhead was the same silvery glare, without a patch of blue sky. No sound came from my sinister, indifferent captors. The only noise was the throbbing of the motors.

As to the time of day, or how long I had been on board, I had no idea; and what was more, I didn't particularly care. Rather a pleasant sort of a jag, if it were not for the intense pain of lickering-up.

After a while the pleasant sensation wore off, and my throat began to feel dry. I tried to call to the ants, but of course could not, because of the paralysis; and finally desisted even the attempt when I remembered that the ants were speechless and hence probably unable to hear.

By a coincidence, however, one of the creatures seemed to sense my needs, and brought me some water in a bowl, gently holding up my head with one of his forepaws so that I could drink. This action touched my heart, and also filled me with hope that the ants might not turn out to be such bad captors after all.

Then I fell to studying them. First of all, I noticed that each ant carried on the back of his thorax a line of peculiar white characters, somewhat like shorthand writting; and below it several rows of similar writing, only smaller in size.

The peculiar green-colored weapon, slung in a holster on the right-hand side of each ant, I had already noticed during the fight. But, apart from the white marks and the green weapons, my captors were absolutely naked; and so far as I could see they were exactly like the ordinary black ants to which I had been accustomed on earth, only of course magnified to an enormous size.

I studied the faces which the ants now occasionally turned toward me. These faces were sinister and terrifying. They recalled to my memory the fright which I had once had when, as a child, I attended an entomological movie and was suddenly confronted with a close-up of the head of some common insect.

But the ant who had brought me the water had a human look which relieved him of much of his terrible grimness. In fact, he struck me as vaguely familiar. Ah! Now I had it! A certain stolidity of movement, amounting almost to a mannerism, reminded me of one of my Harvard classmates, a homely, good-hearted boy whom we had all known by the nickname of "Doggo." And so, from then on, I instinctively thought of that particular ant as named Doggo.

Then, for the first time, it struck me as strange that these ants, instead of scuttling aimlessly over the ground, or having wings of their own to fly with, as in the mating season on earth, were utilizing a carefully and scientifically built airplane, apparently of their own make. And it struck me as even more strange that I had not wondered about this before.

But then the events of that day had occurred with such startling rapidity—from the flash in my Beacon Street laboratory, through my awakening beside that strange lake, the approach of the airplane, my fight with the ants, and my second lapse from consciousness, down to my present predicament—that I was to be excused for not considering any particular phase of my adventures as being more extraordinary than any other.

Now, however, that I had had time to draw my breath and collect my thoughts, it dawned on me with more and more force that here I was, apparently on some strange planet of which the ruling race, apparently of human or superhuman intelligence, were not men. And they were not even some other mammal, but were insects—ants, to be more specific. For all that I knew, I was the only mammal—or perhaps even vertebrate—on this entire planet.

Then I remembered a remark by Professor Parker in Zoology I in my freshman year at Harvard: "The two peaks of development, in the chain of evolution from the amoeba upward, are the order of hymenoptera (bees, wasps and ants) among insects, and the order of primates (men and monkeys) among mammals. In any other world it is probable that evolution would produce a ruling race, in much the same way that man has been produced upon the earth; and it is a toss-up whether this ruling race would develop along the lines of the hymenoptera, or in a form similar to the mammals; but one or the other seems inevitable."

"Well," said I to myself, "old Parker is certainly vindicated, at least with respect to *one* planet."

Thus I mused, as the airplane sped along. Then the purr of the motors lulled me to sleep, and for the third time that day I became unconscious.

WHEN I awoke the sky was losing its luminous silver quality. On one side it was faintly pink, and on the other the silver color merged into a duller gray. The airship still sped along.

Doggo brought me another bowl of water, and I found, to my joy, that I could now lift my head enough to drink without any further assistance than to have Doggo hold the bowl. At this sign of recovery, one of the other ants advanced menacingly as if to bite me again. But Doggo jumped between us, and after much snapping of mandibles and quivering of antenna by both, the other ant desisted.

This event decided me that Doggo was a friend worth cultivating, but I was at a loss how to make advances which would be understood. Finally, however, I determined to attempt stroking the huge ant in a way which I had found to be very effective in making friends with animals.

Accordingly, when Doggo came near enough, by a great effort I overcame my paralysis sufficiently to reach up and touch him on the side of his head just behind one of his great jaws. Apparently this pleased the ant, for he submitted to the caress, and finally lifted me to a sitting position, so that the patting could be continued with greater ease.

I later learned that this patting, to which I had resorted purely by accident, is a universal custom of this planet, corresponding to shaking hands on earth, and signifying greetings, friendship, farewell, bargain binding, and the like.

The other ant man occasionally would advance menacingly toward me with his head lowered, but each time Doggo would step between us, lower his own head and agitate his antenna, at which the other would desist. I nicknamed the other Satan, because of his diabolical actions.

In my new sitting position I was now able to see over the side of the airship. We were passing above gray woods, with occasional silver-green fields, in which were grazing some sort of pale green animals, too far below to be easily distinguishable. Through the woods and fields ran what appeared to be roads, but as nothing was moving on them, I could not tell for sure.

Suddenly my attention was distracted om the view by the frantic action of the t man who was steering the ship. He ned to be having difficulty with his rols. And then, so quickly that it gave warning, the ship reared up in the d made a complete loop. That is, ly suppose it made a complete one, the loop was half done, I dropped fell like a plummet through the

ber a momentary exultation at 'rom my captors, and a certain at the thought that I should

undoubtedly be dashed to pieces and thus rob them of their prey. Then I had just begun to wonder whether I shouldn't prefer captivity to death, when I struck—

And was *not* dashed to pieces.

I still lived, for I had been thrown slantwise into a net of some sort, and was now swaying gently back and forth like a slowing pendulum. Hooray! I was both free and safe.

But my joy was short lived, for I soon discovered that the fine silken strands of the net were covered with a substance like sticky fly paper, which held me firmly. The more I struggled, the more I drew other strands of the net toward me to entangle me. At last I paused for breath, and then the truth dawned on me: I was caught in a gigantic spider web! And, sure enough, there came the spider toward me from one corner of the web.

He wasn't a very large spider. That is to say, judging by the size of my previous captors, I should have expected that the spiders of this world would be as big as the Eifel Tower. He was quite large enough however, having a body about the size of my own, and legs fully ten feet long. I call him a "spider," for that is the earth word which comes closest to describing him.

With great assiduity he began wrapping me up into a cocoon, a process which he seemed to enjoy much more than I. But it did me no good to struggle, for any part of me which showed any indications of moving was immediately pinioned with a fresh strand of rope.

At last the job was finished, and I was completely enveloped with a layer of thick, coarse, sticky silk cloth, translucent, but not transparent.

CHAPTER III

OUT OF THE FRYING PAN

WHEN I had dropped from the airplane into the spider web, the time had been nearly evening. All night, off and on, I struggled, but to no avail. Finally, shortly after daylight, something startled me by falling—plop—into the net close beside me. Another victim, thought I. Well, at least I should have company.

But this other creature was not any more inclined to take its captivity calmly than I had been. It thrashed and struggled violently, until finally it tore a rent in the upper end of my shroud, so that I could see out.

My companion in misery was an orange-and-black-striped bee about the size of a horse. He was buzzing frantically and slashing about with his sting, while the spider hopped around him with great agility, dodging the thrusts of the sting, and applying a strand of silk here and there, whenever an opportunity offered. Thus gradually the bee's freedom of motion became less and less, as strand after strand were added to his bonds.

But the spider, getting bolder as his captive's struggles diminished, finally misjudged one thrust; and the imprisoned bee, putting all his effort into the stroke, drove his sting home. The spider toppled from the web, and the fight was unexpectedly at an end.

And now the bee and I were free, if we only could get free. Of the two of us, I had the easier task, for my cocoon had dried during the night and was now no longer sticky. But it was still very tough.

Slowly, inch by inch, biting, clawing, tearing, I gradually enlarged the hole near my head, until finally I was able to step out and jump to the ground, which was about ten feet away, a drop equivalent to a little less than eight feet on the earth; not much difference, it is true, but every little bit helped.

I now decided to assist my rescuer, the bee, to escape. A rash decision, one would say, and yet the bee seemed to realize that I was helping him, for not once did he strike at me. Picking up a tree branch, I hacked at the cords which bound him, until finally he was able to fly away, trailing a large section of the web after him.

As he left, I noticed that one of his hind legs was gone from the knee down, and that he bore a peculiar scarlike mark on the under side of his abdomen. I should know him, if ever I were to meet him again.

The web had been stretched between two large gray leafless trees of the sort I had observed near the beach, but without the red tips to the branches. Near by was a wood of similar but slightly smaller trees, bordering on a field of thickly matted silver-green grass, very similar to earth grass, except in color. In this field were grazing a herd of pale green insects a little larger than sheep with long trailing antenna.

These creatures swayed from side to side, lifting first one foot after another as they munched the matted grass. On the sides of some of them clung one or more bright red parasites, resembling lobsters in size and appearance; but their green hosts did not seem to mind or even notice them. Nor did they notice me, for that matter, as I passed between them across the field.

On the further side of the field was a road, built of concrete, resembling in every way such concrete roads as we have on the earth; and along it I set out, whither I knew not.

Now, I had had nothing to eat since I found myself on the sandy beach the previous morning. Also I had fought two battles on an empty stomach. The day was hot and moist, my feet were bare—as was the rest of me—and I felt discouraged and depressed. Still, I trudged along.

"Can it be true," said I, "that only yesterday I rejoiced at freedom from the ant men?"

Now I was alone and lost—lost on a strange planet. Oh, how I longed for the sight of my late captors. Better even captivity than this!

For a while the road ran between silver-green fields; then entered a wood. On the gaunt gray trees hung a tangle of tropical vines, and between the trees grew some kind of small shrub with large heart-shaped leaves, on each leaf of which there sat motionless one or more purple grasshoppers about four inches in length.

In the distance I occasionally caught

sight of some strange sort of bird—as I thought—flitting in tandem pairs from tree to tree. A multitude of tiny lizards, resembling miniature kangaroos, hopped about on the concrete and by the side of the road.

FOR a while the strange fauna and flora stimulated my curiosity and kept my mind off my troubles; but then I rapidly lost interest in everything. My stomach gnawed. My knees wabbled. My mind began to cloud. And from that time on, I wandered as in a dream, for I know not how many hours.

I vaguely remember falling on the roadway, and then crawling along for a while. Silly thoughts obsessed my brain, such as wondering whether my tail light was lit, and what made the weather so foggy. Finally I collapsed utterly, and had just strength enough to drag myself off the concrete lest I be run over by some passing car.

As I lay there in the bushes by the side of the road, there came to my nostrils a smell which partially revived me—a smell seemingly of griddle cakes and maple syrup. Opening my eyes again and following my nose, I discovered that this pleasant odor emanated from a large bowl-shaped leaf only a few feet away.

Upon dragging myself toward it, I discovered that in the bottom of the bowl there was a brown mass, looking very much like a stack of wheats, covered with some sticky substance. But unfortunately this delectable dish was quite obscured by little hopping lizards, now much bemired and hopping no more.

So I reached out my hand to brush them away, and instantly the leaf closed upon my arm like a steel trap.

My brain cleared at once, and I began a frantic struggle to extricate my hand; but it was too late, for with a gentle massaging motion the plant commenced to swallow my arm.

Inch by inch my arm descended into that rapacious maw. It was the steady slowness of the procedure that was so nerve-wracking, for without a pause my arm disappeared at a rate of about an inch a minute.

I braced my feet against the plant and pulled, but this cut off the circulation in my arm. Then I wiggled my fingers rapidly so as to keep my hand from going to sleep, whereupon the plant swallowed all the faster. Some ants stood watching.

The mouth of the plant had closed very much like a clam shell, so, just before my shoulder disappeared, I braced my body crosswise of the jaws, in the hope that this maneuver would prevent the swallowing process from proceeding any further.

But the plant merely opened its flexible lips, and closed them the other way, taking a firm grip on my chest, and just missing getting hold of my right ear. I craned my neck as far as I could to the left, and shrieked aloud with terror.

Was it for this that I had escaped the ant men and the spider—to be eaten alive by a plant?

The soft jaws now fastened on the back of my head and began gently drawing that in, too. At last only my nose was free. In a minute that, too, would be enveloped, then strangulation and death.

At this moment something fell upon me, and I felt the plant quiver and shake. The swallowing ceased. Then the soft lips were torn away from one side of my head, and I heard a familiar rattling sound.

A few seconds later the plant went limp, releasing my arm, and I lay upon my back, free once more, gazing upward into the eyes of my old friend and captor. "Doggo, Doggo!" I cried with joy, but he did not seem to hear me. Nevertheless he picked me up gently in his mandibles and trotted off with me down the road.

After about a quarter of a mile, we turned aside into a field, and there was Satan, the other ant man, standing beside a crumpled airship and the dead body of its pilot. Satan did not seem overjoyed to see me, but Doggo rummaged through the wreckage and finally produced a bowl, into which he put water and some medicine, which revived me greatly. Then he laid me on a pile of grass, covered me with leaves, and stood guard over me as the pink twilight deepened and the night fell.

As it began to grow dark I could hear an occasional tinkle like the sound of a Japanese wind bell, first on one side and then on another. This music gradually increased, until it assumed the volume of a fairy orchestra. I had never heard such dainty, bewitching tunefulness in my entire life. Many weeks later I learned that this was the song of the large purple grasshoppers I had seen; but even the knowledge of its source has never robbed the sound of its sweet mystery for me.

The fading silver radiance of the sky shed a moonlike light over all below. A faint breeze sprang up, gently fanning the moist, fragrant, hot-house air against my cheeks. The foliage around us waved like a sea of silver grain. And the tune of that elfin melody quickly lulled me into a soft and dreamless sleep, secure in the confidence that a faithful friend was watching near.

THE next morning I was awakened by Doggo stripping off my leafy coverlet. Satan was not to be seen, but grazing near us were some more of those peculiar large green insects, with long trailing antenna, which I had seen in my flight from the spider web.

As I sat up, Doggo presented me with a bowl of pale green liquid. But I was at a loss to know what to do with it. Was I supposed to wash in it, or to drink it, or to rub it in my hair?

My friend solved the question by lifting it to my mouth. So I drank, and found the taste to be sweetish and agreeable.

All morning we stayed by the wrecked machine, apparently waiting for something. Satan did not show up. Around noon, Doggo took the bowl and approached one of the green beasts grazing near. I followed with interest.

Two horns projected upwardly from the tail of the beast, one of which Doggo proceeded to stroke with his paw; and to my surprise, a green liquid spouted from the animal, quickly filling the bowl. So that is where my breakfast had come from! Green milk from green cows! Strange! And yet how much more logical than on earth, where a red cow eats green grass under a blue sky, and produces white milk, from which we get yellow butter.

Shortly after lunch I heard the hum of a motor, and presently Satan landed near us with a new plane. This strange plane of the ant men stopped abruptly, hovered for a moment, and then settled just where it was.

Doggo carried me aboard, and we started, Satan at the levers and Doggo standing guard over me. But whether this was to protect me from Satan, or to keep me from falling out again, I could not say.

We cruised along for several hours over much the same sort of country as I had seen before, except that we crossed several rivers, and once a small lake.

At last the ship hovered and landed on top of what seemed to be a helter-skelter pile of exaggerated toy building blocks, exactly in keeping with the size of the ants. As far as eye could see on all sides, these blocks were heaped. They were apparently of concrete, and resembled a group of Pueblo Indian dwellings.

Doggo and the fierce ant man whom I called Satan now picked me up in their jaws, the former gently and the latter not so gently, and carried me out of the airplane and down an inclined runway into the interior of the edifice. The passage was long, narrow, dark and winding, but presently we emerged into a room about thirty feet square by ten feet high, lighted by narrow windows opening toward the western sky. That is, I call it "western," for it was in this direction that the sky turned pink at eventide.

In this room I was laid on the floor. The unpleasant ant man departed, and Doggo placed himself on guard in the doorway.

Presently two strange ant men entered, carrying a couch, which they set down in one corner of the room. Then they walked several times around me, viewing me from all sides with evident interest, until, at a stiffening and quivering of Doggo's antenna, they hurriedly left the room. I noticed that Doggo no longer carried the green weapon, which seemed strange, as he was very evidently on guard.

Then I fell to wondering about the couch. It was a simple affair, and yet quite evidently intended for a bed. Upholstered with some kind of dark blue cloth, at that!

"What need have ants of a bed?" mused I. "Certainly they cannot lie down; and, even if they could, such a couch as this would be of little use to one of them, for this is only a man-size couch, whereas these ants are about ten feet in length!"

My perplexity was tinged with a hope that there might be human beings here.

My perplexity and my hope were both increased by the return of one of the ants who had brought the couch, this time bearing a sleeveless shirt or toga of white matted material, like very thin silk felt, reaching about to my knees, with a Grecian wave design in light blue around the bottom edge and around the neck and armholes. But what increased my perplexity still further, and at the same time destroyed most of my hope, was the presence of two vertical slits, with the same blue trimming, in the upper part of the back.

The two ant man watched with great interest while I put this toga on, and were evidently pleased to find that I knew how to do so. The messenger ant then withdrew, and presently returned with a bowl of green milk, which I drank as usual.

By this time it had become quite dark outside, but the room still remained light, due to two long glass bulbs, set in the ceiling, and containing some sort of incandescent substance. At that time I little guessed what a part those bulbs would come to play in my life! They resembled mercury vapor lamps; except that, instead of shining with a marked purple or green light, they gave forth a radiance indistinguishable from daylight, doubtless due to the substitution of some other gas for mercury vapor.

These lamps showed that the inhabitants of this planet were well advanced in electrical engineering. Was it not strange, then, that they had not developed radio and communicated with the earth? And yet not so strange, either, when one considers that they had no sense of hearing.

Dismissing these thoughts from my mind, I lay down on the couch. Then Doggo was relieved as sentinel by a new ant man, who carefully and inquisitively inspected me, but from a safe distance. This guard, too, was without any green weapon.

Finally the two lights went out, and I slept, my last thoughts being to wonder what was in store for me, and what was the significance of the couch and the strange blue-and-white article of clothing.

CHAPTER IV

GO TO THE ANT, THOU SLUGGARD

AS I slowly awakened the next morning, I vaguely remembered a terrible nightmare of the night before.

But no, it was no dream, for I opened my eyes upon the same plain concrete room with its slit windows. I was lying on the same couch. The same strange ant man was standing guard at the door. During the night some one had placed over me a blanket of some sort of light fleecy wool felt.

As I lay in bed I studied the walls of the room and noticed, what I had not seen before, three dials sunk in the opposite wall close to the ceiling. Each dial had twelve numbers or letters around the edge. and also a single pointer. The pointer of the right dial was slowly revolving left-handedly; the pointer of the middle dial was turning even more slowly; while that of the left dial appeared motionless. Absent-mindedly I started to time the right-hand pointer.

"One chim*panzee*. *Two* chim*panzee*. *Three* chim*panzee*," I counted in sing-song; that being a formula which I had been taught as a child, to count the time between a lightning flash and the resulting thunder, in order to estimate the distance of the stroke.

For, if carefully done, each chim*panzee* equaled one second of time, and each second meant one quarter-mile of distance. Of course the real object of the game was to distract the child's mind from his fear of the lightning.

I now found that it took about fifty chim*panzees* for the right pointer to move one of the twelve graduations. This fact I verified by several trials.

I fell to wondering what the device was for.

It looked and acted like a gas meter or electric meter.

Then I dismissed the meter from my mind, and considered my predicament. For some reason I thought of my father, Alden Cabot, now many years dead. The old man had been a stern puritanical character, abhorring sloth and frivolity.

How often had I heard him rebuke some act of laziness with his favorite Biblical quotation: "Go to the ant, thou sluggard; consider her ways and be wise."

"Wouldn't father be pleased," thought I, "for I have certainly gone to the ant. all right! But the big question now is how to get away from them."

By this time the sentinel noticed that I was awake, and immediately brought me my breakfast, consisting of a bowl of the sweet green liquid, and a bowl of dark reddish-brown paste, about the consistency of mashed beans, and having a rich flavor not unlike beef gravy.

After breakfast Doggo took his turn as guard. I patted his head, and then went over to the windows to see the view, if any.

The windows overlooked a courtyard completely enclosed by piled-up Pueblo buildings. In the yard was a fountain, surrounded by beds of plants quite unlike any that I had ever seen before. The prevailing color of the foliage was gray and silver green. Many of the twigs bore knobs of red or purple, and a few of the plants had brilliantly colored blue and yellow flowers somewhat similar to those of dandelions.

For a long time I aimlessly gazed upon this beautiful garden. The warm, moist, fragrant atmosphere was not conducive to hurry or to excitement. But finally even the beauties of the view palled upon me, and I returned to the blue couch.

Just then Doggo ushered into the room with great deference, four ant men slightly smaller than himself, but more refined looking than he, if one can appreciate such differences among ants. That is, they were more slender and delicate, like machines built for precision rather than for strength.

They evidently were a bit afraid of me, for after eying me furtively from the door they appeared to confer with Doggo, though not an audible word passed between them. To assure them that I was perfectly harmless, Doggo walked over to me and permitted himself to be patted; after which the committee drew near and inspected me carefully, agitating their antenna at each newly discovered peculiarity.

They appeared chiefly perplexed by my forehead and my back, to examine which, they lifted up my toga. They counted my fingers several times, and then counted my toes.

But the thing about me which amazed them the most was my ears. These they studied for a long time, with much inaudible consultation, as I judged by the motions of their antenna.

Finally they took their departure, and Doggo came to me bristling with excitement, and apparently having much important information to impart; but, alas, he did not know my language, and he had no language at all. I patted him again, but this time it did not soothe him, for he broke away from me impatiently and returned to his station by the door.

LEFT to myself, I fell to studying the meter again, watching the counterclockwise rotation of its hands. Even the *left* pointer had moved a bit since early morning.

Now I noticed, what I might have surmised on the analogy of an earthly gas meter, that each graduation of the central dial represented one complete revolution of the pointer on its right; and this principle presumably extended to the dial on its left. Then I counted chim*panzees* again, and found that the right hand pointer was still rotating counterclockwise at the rate of about fifty chim*panzees* per graduation. Counter*clock*wise! Why, perhaps this machine was a *clock!*

I made a hasty mental calculation: "One graduation equals fifty seconds. Twelve graduations—one complete rotation—equal six hundred seconds—ten minutes. Thus one graduation of the middle dial represents ten minutes, and its complete circuit, represents two hours. By the same token, a complete circuit of the left dial would represent twenty-four hours—one day!"

My guess was apparently correct.

At that time it did not occur to me as strange that a day on this planet should be twenty-four hours as on earth.

The figure to the left of the top of each dial was a single horizontal line, presumably standing for unity; for a single line, either horizontal or vertical, is the almost universal symbol for unity.

"Then," said I, "the next figure must be two, the next figure three, and so on around to twelve. Eureka! I can now count up to twelve with these creatures; thus establishing, in writing at least, the beginning of a possible basis of communication."

Eager to test my newfound knowledge, I beckoned to Doggo. He came to my side.

Scratching the ant figure five upon the floor with a small pebble which I found in a corner—for I could not reach the dials to point to their figures—I held up five fingers. The effect was electrical. Greatly excited, Doggo rushed to the door. But, pausing on the threshold, he returned; held up three legs, looking at me almost beseechingly, as I thought; and, when I wrote an ant figure three on the floor, his joy knew no bounds. He patted me on the side of my head for a moment, to show his appreciation, and then rushed once more from the room.

And now, for the first time, I was left unguarded, but I had no thought of escape; in the first place, because it would be unfair to my friend; and in the second, because escape merely from the room would be useless.

Presently Doggo returned with the committee of four, and put me through my paces. He would hold up a certain number of legs, and I would scratch the corresponding character upon the pavement. Finally, as a crowning stunt, I wrote down five and six, pointed to them, and then wrote down eleven. The committee were much impressed.

Then Doggo had me put on and take off my toga for them. Evidently he was trying to convince them I was a reasoning human being like themselves, though what the disrobing performance had to do with it I could not see for the life of me.

At last the committee left, and after that a very nice luncheon was served; more green milk, some baked cakes and honey. Real, honest to goodness honey, like we have on earth! You can't appreciate how these little touches of similarity to good old *terra firma* appealed to me, thoroughly homesick after three whole days' absence.

After luncheon, Doggo brought me a pad of paper and a pointed stick like a skewer, with its tip incased in some lead-like metal. This stick could thus be used as a pencil. He himself was similarly equipped, except that his pencil had a strap for attachment to his left front claw. The difference between the two pencils attracted my attention and excited my wonder, but I could not account for it.

Instruction began at once. I would point to some object; Doggo would make marks on his pad; and then I would copy them on mine, adding the name in English. These additions puzzled and annoyed my instructor; but I persisted, for otherwise I might early forget the meaning of his scratch marks.

When a vocabulary of about twenty concrete nouns had been accumulated, Doggo took away my sheet, and then pointed to the articles in turn, while I wrote down their ant names, as well as I could remember them. Fortunately I have a good visual memory, for I was no more able to invent sounds for the ant words, than I would have been able to read aloud a Chinese laundry ticket.

After several hours of this absorbing sport, Doggo produced a book! With rare presence of mind, I figure that as ant men wrote with their left hands and had counterclockwise clocks, their books would probably begin at the wrong end; so accordingly I opened at the back. And, sure enough, the last page was numbered one. This proof of my intelligence pleased my instructor greatly.

On page one was the picture of an ant man. Under it was printed the word which Doggo had given me as equivalent to himself. Next came the same word, followed by a strange word. Then these two words were repeated, followed by two others.

Reasoning by the analogy of my primary school days at home, I decided that these words were: "Ant man. An ant man. This is an ant man." But I was wrong, for on this basis, the next line made no sense; for, reading from right to left the next line would be: "An ant man is this."

Oh, I had it! "Ant man. The ant man. I see the ant man. The ant man sees me." To test it, I wrote down the word for "I," and pointed to myself. Doggo, who had been watching me intently as I studied the page, now showed unmistakable signs of pleasure at this evidence of my intelligence; and, departing, soon returned with a large, furry, beetlelike creature about two feet square, called a "buntlote"—so I learned later—which he set on the floor before me with every expectation of extreme gratitude on my part. I tried to appear grateful; but could not figure out what I was supposed to do with the beast!

The buntlote, however, had much more definite views on the subject, for he ambled over to me and patted me on the side with one of his front paws. I looked inquiringly at Doggo, who indicated that I was supposed to feed the buntlote with some of the remains of my luncheon, which was still sitting on the couch.

THE buntlote, after satisfying his hunger, curled up in a corner and went to sleep, whereupon I returned to my studies. Evidently ant men kept pets the same as humans; but whether this buntlote was supposed to be a dog, or a cat, or what, I did not know.

Doggo then taught me how to write "buntlote," and the words for food, mouth, and eat—my first verb, by the way—and so on.

By supper time I was in a position to carry on a very elementary conversation with my instructor, but only by pad and pencil, of course, for not a word or a sound had I ever heard him utter.

And since their speech was not articulate, their written language could not, of course, be phonetic. It must be ideographic, like the Chinese. The fact that each word consisted in but a single character lent color to this surmise.

And yet I noticed that all of the characters which I had so far learned could be decomposed into distinguishable parts, and that there were only about thirty of these parts in the aggregate. This fact certainly pointed to a *phonetic* alphabet of thirty *sounds*, for it was inconceivable that these highly cultivated animals possessed only thirty *ideas*. And yet how could an unspoken language be phonetic? I gave up the puzzle.

Supper came, the lights on, and my buntlote uncurled and ambled over to be fed. I decided to regard him as a cat, and so named him Tabby.

At this meal Doggo joined me, and as we ate, my attention was again attracted to the white marks on his back, which to my surprise I now noticed were exactly like those on the clock. They must be his license number: "334-2-18."

If the large figures represented his license number, I thought, what did the small figures stand for? The license numbers of the cars he had run into, perhaps? I little guessed how near this came to being the truth.

That night I went to bed well satisfied with my progress. But, alas, although Doggo proved to be an indefatigable teacher, I did not get on so well during the succeeding days.

But I did make progress in one thing, however; namely, in acquiring a beard. Although facilities for washing and bathing were provided in a little alcove off my room, and although a fresh toga was forthcoming from time to time, yet my captors did not furnish either a razor or a mirror. Of course ants have nothing to shave, and they cannot be blamed for not caring to look at themselves in the glass. I tried my best to explain to Doggo what I wanted, but it was no use.

If this manuscript is ever discovered, let the reader try to figure out how to explain by sign language to a person who has never seen either a razor or a looking glass, that you want them.

When the beard got well under way, the committee of four were recalled to view it. They were even more impressed with my beard than they had been with my ears, and made frequent visits to take notes on its growth.

This convinced me that they had never before seen any men, or at least any unneat ones, and so my hope for human companionship received another blow. Yet if there were no men on this planet, how account for the fact that when I drew a sketch of a table and a chair these were at once forthcoming, together with a written name for each?

Of course all my time was not spent in lessons. Sometimes I played with Tabby and sometimes I took long walks. Gradually I became more of a guest than a prisoner or even a curiosity, and so I was given the run of the entire city, which was built as one large connected house; a veritable jumble of rooms, passageways, ramps and courtyards.

But this freedom nearly proved my undoing.

One day when I had strolled unusually far from my own quarters, I met my old enemy, Satan, in one of the courtyards. Instinctively I shrunk back, but he gave every indication of wishing to be friendly, even to the extent of turning his head on one side to be patted. Distasteful as the act was to me, I decided that discretion was the better part of valor, and so patted him gingerly.

Apparently as a reward for this service, he beckoned me to follow him. And so I did, through many a winding corridor. Our way finally led to the outskirts of the city, to a grating guarded by a sentinel, whom Satan promptly relieved. When the old guard had gone, Satan, to my great surprise, opened the gate and motioned me to step out.

This was indeed a favor, for, although I had been able to get plenty of fresh air in the courtyard flower gardens and on the roofs, yet I had felt cramped and re-strained, and had longed for the freedom of a run in the open fields. So, patting him again, to show my gratitude, I rushed out and turned several handsprings for joy on the silver sward.

As I regained my feet, what should I see to my dismay but a squad of ant men issuing from the gate and rushing toward me at full speed, with Satan at their head, his savage jaws snapping with hate. I stood astounded for a moment, and then turned and fled.

At an earthly speed of running a man would have little hope of distancing one of these creatures, but the added buoyancy of this strange planet gave me a slight ad-vantage over them, until I had the mis-fortune to stub my toe on something and fall. Whereupon the pack closed over me.

The fall stunned me, and as my brain darkened, I felt the sharp mandibles of my enemy fasten upon my throat.

CHAPTER V

A VISION

THE full measure of Satan's perfidy was now evident. Under the guise of pretended friendship he had lured me to the city gate and had persuaded me to step outside. Then hastily calling a de-tachment of the guard, he had informed them that I had escaped. He had led them in pursuit of me, and my flight had furn-ished sufficient verification of his accusa-tion.

So now I was entirely in his power. He was free to kill me without fear of the con-sequences, for the whole squad would back up his story that I had fled and that he had been forced to slay me for the pur-pose of preventing my escape.

Why he did not bite me at once and end my life I do not know. Perhaps he wished first to gloat over me. At any rate, after I came out of my daze, he loosened his hold on my throat and, planting his front feet upon my prostrate body, threw his head aloft, as if singing a pean of vic-tory, although of course no sound came.

Then suddenly he sprang away from me entirely. And now I discovered the mean-ing and use of the peculiar green weapon which every ant man carried slung in a holster at his side when out of doors. These supposed weapons were nothing more nor less than green umbrellas which Satan and the others were now hastily putting up in very evident terror.

Sitting up weakly, I tried to figure out what had so frightened them as to cause them to desist abruptly from their at-tack on me. But I could discern nothing except a patch of sunlight, the very first I had seen, by the way, since my advent on the planet. My late antagonists were ap-parently watching this—to me—very pleasant sight, with every indication of extreme fear. Looking above, I saw a small bit of blue sky.

The patch of sunlight passed close by me and proceeded toward a small herd of green cows who were grazing near by. And, as it passed among them, the shift-ing of their feet stopped, and every cow on whom the light had rested shuddered, wilted and dropped in evident agony upon the ground.

Then I realized that this planet must be very close to the center of the solar system, and protected from the intense heat of the sun only by the dense, silvery clouds which surround it. I was now nearly certain, as I had surmised before from the prevailing silver-gray and the gravity slightly less than that on earth, that this must be the planet Venus.

I was still gazing abstractedly at the stricken cows in the wake of the solar heat, when I was rudely called to my senses by the ant pack closing over me once more. And once again the mandibles of Satan fastened on my throat.

But the best laid plans of mice and men —and even ant men—gang aft aglee. With all his clever scheming, Satan had made one fatal mistake: he had reckoned with-out the faithful Doggo. As Satan's jaws were about to pierce my jugular, again he dropped me, and stood at attention, as if in response to a peremptory command from a military superior. I looked up and saw that the rest of the guard were also standing at attention, while rapidly approaching us from the city gate came my old friend, Doggo, with antenna erect and quivering. Once more he had saved my life.

How I regretted the blows which I had struck him in the fight at the beach on my first day upon this planet, and how glad I was that his had not been the head which I had severed in that spirited encounter.

Presently, as if in response to another command, Satan slunk away, and the squad of ant soldiers returned to the city, while Doggo came and stood solicitously at my side. When I had rested sufficiently I rose to my feet, and together we returned to my quarters.

It was time for my lesson, but I was in no mood for study, so I gloomily pushed the books and papers to one side and went and stood by one of the windows, gazing aimlessly at the beautiful garden below.

It is always darkest before dawn. As I stood there at the window, with my spirits at a low ebb, there came to my eyes a vision which changed the entire course of my life.

For, crossing the courtyard below me, was what seemed to be a human being! Here at last was some one for me to talk to!

But was it a human being, after all? He, or she, or it, stopped just in front of my window, and began daintily to pluck a bouquet of flowers, so that I had ample opportunity to study the creature. It wore a blue and white toga, similar to the one which the ant man had furnished me. And now I saw the reason for the slits in the back, for through them protruded a pair of tiny rudimentary butterfly wings of iridescent pearly hue.

The complexion of this dainty creature was a softer pink and white than ever I had seen on any baby. Its hair was closely cropped and curly and brilliantly golden. But the most attractive thing about it was the graceful way in which it swayed and pirouetted, as if before a mirror, though there was no mirror there, unless in its own imagination. This pirouetting led me to suppose that the creature whether human or not, was probably feminine.

Is there any more beautiful sight in the world, or in any world for that matter, than a beautiful girl admiring herself and preening herself, and acting altogether natural and girlish, when she thinks that she is alone and unobserved?

But was this a girl? She was pretty enough to be an angel, or a fairy, and the little wings suggested something along that line.

But then I began to notice certain other things about her which puzzled me. In the first place, she had an extra little finger on each hand, and six toes on each of her bare little feet, yet this fact did not in the least detract from their dainty slimness. Then, too, there projected from her forehead two tiny antenna, such as one sees on pictures of elves. Also she apparently had no ears. Anyhow, the lack of ears was hardly noticeable, though the absence of the little pink tip just barely showing below the edge of short hair, did give a slightly unfinished look to that part of her head.

Antenna and wings! This must be either a fairy, or some new and beautiful kind of creature.

She bore such a close resemblance to a human being, that my lonely spirit was cheered by the thought that at last there was a possibility of speech and human companionship on this planet.

So intent had I been on drinking in this vision of beauty below my window that I had not noticed Doggo approach me and place himself at my side. I was terribly fearful lest the girl should go away without my finding out who she was and how I might see her again. So, forgetting my manners and even the fact that she was of an unknown race, I plucked up sufficient courage to address her.

"My dear young lady," began I; but I got no further, for without noticing me in the least, she picked up her flowers and left the courtyard. Then I turned, and there was Doggo standing beside me. So he, too, had seen the fairy!

Seizing my pad and paper I wrote: "What is that?"

And he replied: "It is a Cupian."

"Are there many Cupians?" I wrote.

"Yes," he answered.

"Am I a Cupian?" I asked.

His answer was: "We do not know. It puzzles us."

THAT afternoon I made more progress with my studies than I had made in weeks. For now I was no longer fitting myself merely for a bare existence in an ant civilization; but rather I was preparing for communication with—and I hoped, life among—creatures closely resembling my own kind.

The beautiful Cupian was evidently, like the ant men, devoid of hearing. Apparently she lived here in the ant city, and so undoubtedly understood the ant language.

But to make sure, I asked Doggo on my pad: "Do Cupians read and write this kind of writing?"

And he answered: "Yes."

At this I certainly did tackle my work with a vim. It was clear now that if I wished to communicate with her, I must perfect myself in the written language of the ants; and so I set myself assiduously to the task.

Every day at about the same hour she came and picked the blue and yellow flowers and the red and purple twig knobs of the garden below my window. And every day I sat in the window and watched her, and racked my brains for some tactful way in which to attract her attention.

Of course I raised the question with Doggo, but he kept putting me off by saying, in substance: "It is not yet time."

This I took to mean that I could not yet write fluently enough to converse with her, and so I redoubled my efforts at my studies.

So rapid was my progress now, under the spur of my desire for human companionship, that within a very few days I was able to graduate from my primers and read real books.

One of the first real books which they brought me was a history of their world; and this interested me greatly, as it furnished a setting for the experiences which shortly were to crowd upon me. The book confirmed my theory that this world was the silver planet, Venus.

Finally I reached a point where my interest was such that I could not wait to wade further through the voluminous pages; so, taking my pad and pencil, I asked Doggo: "Tell me briefly about the more recent events on Poros." For so they called the planet, though of course, I did not yet know the sound of this word, nor even whether it had a sound. "Tell me more particularly about the great war."

"Well," he replied, also in writing, of course: "A little over five hundred years ago the entire inhabited part of the planet Poros, that is to say the continent which is surrounded by the boiling sea, was divided up into twenty or more warring kingdoms of Cupians and one small queendom of ant men, namely Formia.

"The Formians, who were possessed of all the virtues, became more and more vexed with the increasing degeneracy of their neighbors, until, for purely altruistic reasons, the Formians began a conquest to extend their culture.

"When the first convenient excuse offered we declared war on one of the Cupian nations, which we proceeded to attack through the territory of a neutral state."

"But wasn't this wrong?" I interjected.

He admitted: "I suppose that you are right and that it really was in violation of all treaties and of the solemn customs of the planet. But it was all in a noble cause.

"The other nations did not have sense enough," he continued, "to rally to combat the common menace, and so the Formians gradually conquered them one by one, until at last Formia was mistress of all Poros.

"There must have been some very able statesmen in the Imperial Council at that time, judging by the terms imposed by our conquering nation. We erected a fence, or 'pale,' across the middle of the entire continent; and all the Cupians, regardless of their former boundaries, were organized into a single nation to the north of this pale. The nation was named Cupia, after the creatures who composed it, and Kew the First was made its king."

Kew, so I later gathered from the book, was a renegade Cupian, who had always greatly admired the conquerors, and had even gone so far as to assist them in their conquest.

"The ant men," Doggo went on, "took over all the territory to the south of the pale, and prospered greatly. We were naturally a more industrious race than the sport-loving Cupians, and now had in addition the services of slaves, for by the terms of the Treaty of Mooni, every male Cupian upon coming of age has to labor for two years in Formia.

"There have followed nearly five hundred years of peace, a peace of force, it is true, and yet a peace under which both countries had enjoyed prosperity; in recognition of which fact the anniversary of the signing of the treaty is annually celebrated throughout the continent.

"The present reigning monarch of Cupia is Kew the Twelfth, the first after a long line of docile kings to give us any trouble in the enforcement of the treaty, but even he keeps within the law.

"The statutes of Cupia are enacted by a popular Assembly, while those of Formia are promulgated by an appointive Council of Twelve; but the laws of both countries must receive the approval of the Queen of Formia."

Such were the salient features of the recent history of Poros.

EVERY day I watched for the fair Cupian at the appointed hour. I learned to know her every feature and every curve of her supple, girlish body. I noted that her eyes were azure blue. I noticed the dainty way in which the tip of her little pink tongue just touched each edible red twig knob which she placed between her lips, and many another individual mannerism.

A great many beautiful girls have I met in the source of my brief existence. Boston society need yield the palm to none on this score. Yet I had gone to all the teas and dinners and dances perfunctorily, merely because it was done; and had always regarded women as an awful bore.

How few women are interested in radio engineering, for instance, or even have a sympathetic feeling for it!

But now all was changed, and I didn't in the least care whether or not *this* girl was interested in radio engineering, or *what* she was interested in; provided I could eventually interest her in me. For I longed for human companionship.

Of course on days when tropical thunderstorms swept the city, as happened frequently, I did not expect her. But on such days I missed this, my one contact with humanity, and felt vaguely uneasy.

Yet I did not fully realize how much even these daily visits of hers to my garden had come to mean to me, until one perfectly pleasant day, when the Cupian girl failed to show up at the expected hour.

I waited and waited, and fretted and fretted, but still she did not come. Doggo was unable to offer any consolation, and my lessons went very badly.

The next day the committee of four made one of their visits of inspection. I had now progressed far enough in my mastery of their language so that Doggo was able to explain to me the reason for the existence of this committee.

"These four," wrote he, "are the professors of biology, anatomy, agriculture, and eugenics from the University of Mooni, the center of education of all Poros. Immediately upon your capture, this committee was speedily dispatched by the university authorities to make a thorough study of you. They were to determine whether you are a Cupian or some new and strange kind of beast, and whether your particular breed could be put to any good use."

"How interesting," I wrote on my pad. "And have they reached any conclusions?"

"It is for *them* to question *you,*" he replied. "Come, I will write down, for you to answer, the things they wish to know."

So then, through the medium of Doggo's pad, they questioned me at length about myself, the earth, how I had come to Poros, and my progress since landing. But their procedure mystified me. How did Doggo know what they wanted him to say? Was he a mind reader?

When they had asked me all they cared, they gathered together in a corner, apparently holding an inaudible conference on the results.

It was evident that there was something of great moment in the air.

And so there was, for presently they withdrew and returned with the young girl, the girl whose presence on this planet had inspired me to master at last the ant language!

Eagerly I sprang forward with my stylus and paper, anxious to start a conversation with this fair creature. And then I was halted by the sight of her face.

To my dying day nothing can ever wipe from my memory the deeply engraved picture of the look of absolute horror and loathing which she gave me, as she recoiled from the contamination of my presence. Then she swooned and was carried out by the four professors.

Oh, how I longed for her, the one human-like creature that I had seen on Poros, and yet what an impassable gulf separated us! The gulf between the understandings and mentalities and means of communication of two distinct worlds! I was determined, nevertheless, to see her again. But how? Ah, that was the question!

TO BE CONTINUED IN THE NEXT ISSUE

Coming in the January Issue—On Sale December 6
THE "V" FORCE
By Fred Smale

An astounding story of a strange supernatural entity which caused havoc wherever it went

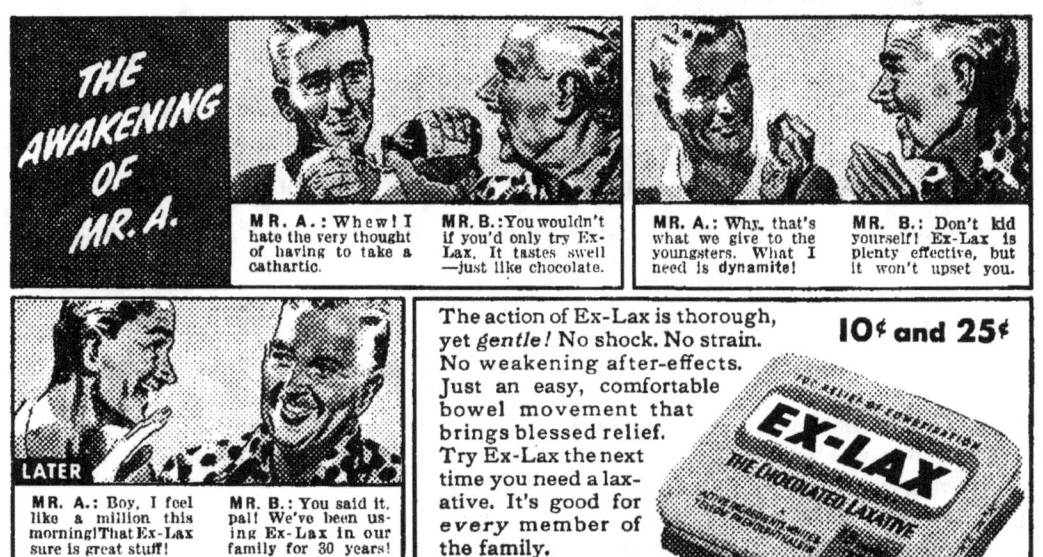

My Jeanne had turned into a little statuette of wondrous beauty!

The Diminishing Draft

By WALDEMAR KAEMPFFERT

Author of "Science Today and Tomorrow," just published

Frivolous fingers play with Science's secrets in a perilous game of hide-and-seek

"WELL, I've engaged an assistant," I announced to my wife one day at luncheon.

"I am glad of that. You have been working much too hard. Who is he?"

"It isn't a 'he,'" I replied as carelessly as I could. "It's Jeanne Briand."

"But why Jeanne Briand? What qualifications has she? What does she know of biochemistry?" she inquired, too searching. I thought, in that high-pitched, staccato voice of hers which latterly had grated on me.

"She's taken her master's degree," I

explained as best I could, "and besides, she had a course in biology under Calhoun."

The wife of a university professor may not be versed in the subject with which his name is identified, but she knows that academic standards are high. Knows that a vivacious, copper-haired, laughing-eyed girl who has dabbled in a few text-books and chased butterflies with a net is not ordinarily given an important post in a famous biochemical laboratory.

"I think you might have taken young Mitchel or some other postgraduate in your department."

That was all we said. She suspected something. There was no question of it.

And so Jeanne was duly installed in my home laboratory. I made it very plain to her that she must keep regular hours, also that she must conduct herself as my assistant and not as the woman whom I loved and whom I hoped to wed.

FROM the first I had my misgivings. It was Jeanne who conceived the idea of working in the laboratory with me— not I. She was as out of place among my instruments and reagent bottles as a wood nymph.

It is needless to dwell on the circumstances that swayed us, needless to recount here how difficult it was to part whenever we had passed an hour together, needless to picture the dreamy longing that hung over us both until our hands and lips touched again. That is a characteristic of every week-old love.

"Please let me help you in your work," she pleaded over and over again. "I want to be near you always. Let me do anything—anything. I can keep the instruments clean. I can write down your notes. It is unbearable to see you only like this, once in a long while. Let me work with you in the laboratory."

"But you forget," I reasoned, "that the laboratory where I do most of my work is in my own house. And I am married. Some day we shall be together always. Think of the risks that we would run. We can't have a scandal. Sooner or later we would be discovered."

I had intended to make a clean breast of the whole affair to my wife and free myself from my marital ties in the conventional way, even though it meant the end of my university career. But Jeanne could not and would not wait. A man of stronger will than mine would have yielded. The desire to have her ever near me, to see the winsome smile on her face, to sense her presence in the same room, moved me more than her arguments. In short, I yielded.

Scientifically speaking, she was all but useless in the laboratory. She had some talent for drawing, and so I employed her in making diagrams for my treatise on "Experimental Evolution."

She radiated femininity. She had an elfish way of interrupting me in my work. At the most critical stage in dissecting the head of an insect under the glass, she would come up and stroke my hair or kiss the nape of my neck. If I reproved her, she wept, which meant much kissing away of her tears and mollifying her with the endearments that all lovers automatically invent on the spur of the moment. And yet, she honestly tried to help me, simply because of her slavish devotion to me.

Although she needed constant supervision, her drawings were excellent. Indeed, they soon justified her presence in my laboratory in the eyes of the entire university.

It was about a fortnight after she became my nominal assistant that I assigned to her the task of making a series of sketches to demonstrate the effect of baroturpinol on parameba.

I may mention in passing that parameba is a microscopic animal—a mere cell— found in stagnant ponds, and that in a dilute solution of baroturpinol the whole structure of the creature undergoes a remarkable change. It was I who discovered the effect of baroturpinol on microorganisms of the parameba class. Immersed in baroturpinol the few cells of which parameba is composed dwindle and dwindle under the microscope until finally the organism, still keeping its own shape, disappears.

I had completely misinterpreted this disappearance of microorganisms under the action of baroturpinol. I thought that they merely disintegrated. It was Jeanne who taught me otherwise.

One day, while she was engaged in making the drawings which would show the progressive disappearance of parameba, Jeanne exclaimed:

"They've come back again!"

"Who has?" I questioned, thinking that she was talking of people whom we knew. Besides, I was engrossed in correcting the proofs of a scientific paper.

"Why, the parameba. I can't understand it!"

A glance convinced me that she was right. In less than a minute I saw a specimen literally grow under my eyes into a full-fledged parameba. I can liken the proceeding only to the coming of an object toward one, with all the attendant increase in size that the movement implies.

PERHAPS I may make myself clearer if I say that the restoration of parameba, as I saw it then and many times after, was like a railway train traveling toward one from the distance. At first a far speck is visible; then the outline of a locomotive engine can be distinguished; and at last a huge machine and thundering cars threaten to crush one out of existence.

But that was not all. *Parameba came back alive!* Every biologist and chemist supposed that baroturpinol was a deadly poison. At all events, I had noticed that when any microorganism was brought into contact with even a trace of baroturpinol, all activity ceased. Death seemed necessarily to precede the process of shrinking. I could hardly believe my eyes when I saw my resuscitated parameba moving about with that characteristic tumbling motion by which it is so well known.

"What have you been doing?" I asked.

"Just what you told me to do."

"Dear, dear Jeanne," I said, taking her two hands in mine. "Do you know that you have made what may prove to be a very important discovery in biology? Do you know that you may have upset the whole theory of life?"

She clapped her hands. But at the time the wonderful scientific significance of what she had seen was lost to her. She saw that I approved of her, and she was happy.

But what did this astonishing revival of parameba mean? Over and over again I watched for the return of specimens under the microscope. Parameba would not return. I questioned Jeanne closely; I even watched her prepare a few slides herself, hoping that she had unconsciously departed from the routine that I had prescribed and had contaminated the baroturpinol in a way that would explain everything.

At last she remembered. She had touched the slide with a little glass rod in order to shift it on the stage of the instrument. The rod did not seem clean. She thought to improve matters by wiping it. A painstaking and conscientious laboratory worker would have used a piece of sterile cotton. Jeanne used her pocket handkerchief. It was clear enough that that little piece of linen was strangely linked with the accidental revivification of parameba.

My deduction was confirmed when I, too, experimented with the handkerchief. I deposited a single drop of stagnant water on a clean glass slide. Under the powerful lens I saw parameba tumbling about. Then I added a drop of baroturpinol (one gram of barturpinol to a cubic centimeter of distilled water is the proportion, as every one knows), and at once all activity ceased. Apparently killed, the specimens of parameba began to shrink in that curious manner upon which I had already dilated. I took a glass rod and wiped it on Jeanne's handkerchief. First making sure that parameba had quite disappeared, I touched the little drop of moisture on the slide.

My guess was right. It was Jeanne's handkerchief. Parameba came rushing back to life as startlingly as at first.

The handkerchief had been definitely linked with the phenomenon, but I was in the dark as much as ever. What mysterious properties had this little piece of fabric that it should thus divert the whole course of modern biochemistry?

"Tell me, Jeanne," I said, "did your handkerchief touch anything here—some solution?"

"No, I'm sure."

"But you must have done something with it. Feel. It's a little damp."

"I wiped my eyes with it," she admitted reluctantly. "I had been crying at something that you said."

I did not stop to inquire what it was that I had said. A light dawned on me. Her tears had so uncannily brought back parameba to life! And tears—what are they, when stripped of all sentiment, but salt water?

A spectroscopic analysis of Jeanne's handkerchief convinced me that common salt had the property of bringing back parameba to life.

Dozens of experiments showed that almost any solution of salt would answer; the stronger it was the more quickly did life triumph over death.

AND now began an investigation which was a strange mixture of scientific research and love-making. To Jeanne it was like a play. She was very much bored when I would repeat tests perhaps twenty-five or fifty times simply to be sure of my results. But when we experimented with a new organism, she was all eagerness, all dancing eyes and clapping hands.

It was Jeanne who made the discovery in the first place, and Jeanne who developed its full possibilities. She had no well-considered plan of work: she simply allowed her impulses, her girlish whims to sway her.

"I want things to happen," she would say, as I tried to explain to her how time-wasting was this unscientific, haphazard, blind plunging into a new and unexplored field. And yet, through her insatiable desire for excitement, her dramatic interest, we found out what really happened when higher organisms were subjected to the action of baroturpinol.

As for me, I confined myself entirely to simple-celled organisms, all so small that they cannot be seen with the naked eye. Here, I thought, was enough work to engage me for years. But that was too tame for Jeanne. She had the imagination and the daring that seem to accompany scientific ignorance.

I kept a little aquarium in one corner of the laboratory—a spawning glass jungle of fresh-water life. It was a never-ending source of entertainment for her. I have known her to sit for an hour at a time watching crayfish crawl lazily along on the bottom, or a school of tiny goldfish fighting for a crumb that she had mischievously tossed in.

One day—it was about two months after she came to me—she ran to me all radiant, holding a bowl at the bottom of which were two or three tiny golden flakes. They were so small that I had to hold the bowl against the window and view them by transmitted light.

"What have we here?" I asked, wondering what new fancy had seized her.

"Goldfish," she said.

"Nonsense," I retorted.

"Yes, they are," she insisted. "I took some Japanese goldfish from the aquarium and dropped them into baroturpinol, and they all shrank up like this."

If the original discovery of parameba's disappearance and return had startled me, how shall I describe the stupefaction that this announcement called forth? I saw at once what I had only guessed at before. Parameba had shrunk beyond the limits of visibility under the microscope, which accounted for its utter disappearance. But the goldfish, being much larger, had shrunk until each became perhaps the size of a dot on the letter "i."

I gazed at the girl with increasing wonder. Never would it have occurred to me to leap at once from simple microscopic organisms to so high a form of life as a fish. On the other hand I must say that it was my academic timidity, if I may so call it: my systematic way of proceeding stepwise from one experiment to another, that had led to the original misconception of baroturpinol's effect.

To every physician and every biologist in the world, baroturpinol was simply a germicide. True, Tilden, who had discovered it, had noticed that it had a curious puckering effect on living tissue, for which reason it had been condemned as quite useless as a substitute for mercury bichloride, phenol, and similar agents, and had been adopted simply as a convenient and cheap hospital sterilizer. And now comes my Jeanne, my capricious, dancing, playful Jeanne, a mere trifler in science, and at once uncovers the hidden possibilities of a completely misunderstood compound, not because she is a biologist, but because she simply wants to be amused.

Obviously it was my business to find out whether, like the microscopic organisms that I had thus far examined, the baroturpinoled goldfish would be revivified by a solution of common salt. I decanted the liquid in the bowl, washed the inanimate, shimmering flakes in distilled water, and then filled the bowl with a solution of salt.

The drama of parameba's return to life was repeated on a more striking scale. Very slowly the dead creatures began to expand. Soon they assumed their normal shapes—not, I repeat, that they had lost them by shrinking, but simply that the curves of their bodies were developed. It was not until they had regained their full size that life itself returned.

To me the thing was as startling as if a man, who had been poisoned by prussic acid, and who had been pronounced dead, were to open his eyes, get up, and walk. I took some pains to explain all this to the intensely amused Jeanne, and I repeated the experiment with a particularly large goldfish which I abstracted from the aquarium. I made no impression whatever upon her. She promptly christened the fish "Lazarus" when he came back to life, and adopted him as a pet.

This impulsiveness of hers, this reckless disregard of all system and plan, could this be a form of mental activity which I had been wrong in regarding rather lazily as showing only an average order of intellect? Some one has defined intuition as a swift deduction from present facts. If that be so—I am no psychologist —then we must reckon with intuition as well as with the slower and more deliberate methods of reasoning in scientific research.

If Jeanne was anything she was intuitive. I felt that I must credit her with powers that were denied me. After all it was she, and not I, who had stumbled upon the amazing action of baroturpinol. I had done little beyond repeating her fanciful experiments under rigorous scientific control. She showed me the stars, as it were: I merely counted them.

THE possession of a common secret strengthened the tie between Jeanne and myself. It was as if we had found some beautiful, priceless gem which we had decided to keep for ourselves and never to show to the world. We lost all self-control. In the beginning we had maintained a semblance of formality. She kept regular laboratory hours, coming in the morning at nine and leaving at about five in the afternoon. It was always "Professor Hollister" and "Miss Briand" when we spoke to each other before others.

But in truth the hours that we spent together in the laboratory each day heightened our love for each other, made us more and more indispensable to each other. It became so difficult for us to leave each other out of our sight that we even went into the woods together for specimens to be experimented with in the laboratory. These specimens she could easily have gathered for me quite alone. The university students and the villagers began to talk about us.

It was my wife, of course, who imparted that information to me.

"You are making yourself ridiculous," she announced.

"Indeed? How?"

"Every one is talking about you."

I pretended not to understand. An attempt of mine to divert her attention from a topic which it made me uneasy to discuss, failed ignominiously.

"Even the postmaster in the village comments on your conduct with Jeanne Briand. Every one stopped talking when I came to the regular sewing-circle yesterday, and looked at me in a pitying sort of way. If you have no consideration for yourself, at least consider me."

I got up and stalked out of the room. I was neither polite nor brave.

The time had come for action. I could not go on in this way. A scandal was inevitable, and the best that I could now do was to mitigate it in some way. Jeanne and I must separate until such time as I could free myself with the aid of the divorce courts. I must tell her.

She read in my face that something was wrong when I stepped into the laboratory late that afternoon.

"You are in trouble, dear," she said. "What is it? Tell me."

And then I told her of the conversation with my wife, of the utter impossibility of concealing our true relations much longer.

"We must separate, Jeanne, if it's only for a little while—until I am free. And then we shall come back to each other again, and we will work together in the laboratory not as professor and assistant, but as man and wife."

She burst into tears. Never before had I seen a human being in such distress. She was convulsed with anguish, so that her whole body shook. I took her in my arms and did my best to soothe her.

"It will only be for a little while," I repeated over and over again. It was all that I could think of, all that I could say.

The sun had long since set, and the laboratory was soon quite dark. We sat together on the couch in the corner in close embrace, Jeanne's head on my shoulder.

"You must rest," I said, and laid her on the couch and sat beside her.

She half-murmured, half-moaned something and let me do with her as I would.

How long she lay there I did not realize at the time. Hour after hour slipped by. At last it struck me that we could not stay thus all night—that I must take Jeanne home.

"Come," I admonished her, "we must go now. It is very late."

I helped her to her feet, pressed a button, and turned on the electric light. She was as limp as a drooping flower, all numb and listless. I walked to the closet and took her hat from its peg.

As I did so I heard footsteps in the corridor leading to the laboratory. Who could this be?

Completely unnerved as I was, distracted by Jeanne's despair, I was incapable of thinking clearly. It was one in the morning by the laboratory clock. Jeanne never stayed in the laboratory later than six. No one must find her here now.

In my ordinary senses the fall of a footstep in the corridor would not have disturbed me. Now I acted automatically and with cowardly absurdity. I ran to the door and locked it instead of flinging it open wide.

There came a knock.

If some one had leveled a pistol at me and threatened to shoot me, I could not have been more alarmed. Jeanne, too, was frightened. We looked at each other questioningly, two helpless lovers.

"Let me in," shrilled a voice outside. It was my wife's. From what she had told me earlier in the day, I inferred that she must have been watching Jeanne like a cat, and that she carefully noted when the girl came and went. Where to find her now she knew only too well.

Concealment was useless.

"What do you want?" I asked.

A flood of impassioned accusations followed, in which Jeanne was referred to as "that woman," with much incoherent repetition of the phrase "wrecked home." The situation was damning.

MONTHS ago I had decided that the divorce proceedings should be free from the usual scandal. But what a ghastly story this would make in the newspapers! I could read the suggestive headlines and the salaciously worded account of the manner in which my wife had trapped me—a university professor. The sensational newspapers in particular would rejoice in the opportunity of pilloring the supposedly academic scientist and of exposing him as if he were a libertine in cap and gown.

It was Jeanne who saved us. I stood like one paralyzed, not knowing what to do. It was the rustle of her skirt that brought me to my senses. I turned around just in time to see her raise a beaker of baroturpinol to her lips and pour it down.

I know that I cried out: for there was a sudden cessation of the clamor outside the door. I rushed to Jeanne's side. Good Heavens! What would the effect be?

Never had we experimented with baroturpinol on anything higher than a fish. She lost consciousness in my arms. I thought she was dead. She was pallid and stiff, as if *rigor mortis* had set in. Then came over her that change which I had observed under the microscope and in the test tube. Her form dwindled and dwindled in my arms as if it were slipping from me, until at last I held nothing but her limp clothes.

It was as if both her soul and her body had drifted away from the room. As if she had slipped out of her earthly fabric like a butterfly from its chrysalis. I dropped the bundle on the floor and began to grope within it. Somewhere within these folds I knew must be the shrunken body of my Jeanne.

At last I found it—a little white form. I slipped it into my pocket. The clothes and hat I stuffed into a chest.

My courage had returned now. I stepped to the door, unlocked it and flung it wide open. My wife entered, and with her a maid whom she evidently brought as a witness. Her lips were tightly drawn; her eyes were mere slits. If ever there was an infuriated woman bent on vengeance, it was she.

She looked about her. Under other circumstances her astonishment would have been comical. All this furtive watching, all these clamorous accusations—all for nothing? She darted to the closet in which Jeanne would hang her hat and coat and I my laboratory aprons, convinced that Jeanne was hidden there. She threw back the door with such violence that the knob indented the plaster wall.

"Where is she? What have you done with her?" she screamed.

"You see that you are mistaken; there is no one here."

She saw that further inquiry would be useless. Outwitted but not deceived, she swept angrily out of the room. I locked the door after her.

I sat down at the laboratory table, took out of my pocket the thing that had once been my Jeanne, and placed it before me. My eyes were blurred with tears. So this was all that was left to me of Jeanne. This was the price of my weakness and my cowardice! She was dead now, and I felt as if I had been an accomplice in her suicide.

There comes an interval in every grief, an interval of calm, during which all mundane affairs seem trivial and even one's own misery becomes petty. It is as if one had passed out of a long, dark, narrow passageway into a vast open twilight beyond. In one of those intervals of calm I regained sufficient control of myself to examine the white remnant of Jeanne.

The thing that to my fevered touch had felt like a mere shapeless mass when I hastily thrust it into my pocket, revealed itself as a little statuette of wondrous beauty. It seemed carved out of ivory, this exquisite miniature, frozen Jeanne. What would not Cellini have given if he could have shaped a figure so beautiful?

Everything was white except the hair, her eyebrows, and the lashes of her closed eyes. The lips were delicately tinted like a budding rose, but they had not the rich color of pulsating life. As for her hair, it still lay in tiny coils about her hair, a mass of twisted, coppery brown. Jeanne must have been in the act of falling when I caught her in my arms. One foot of the little figure was raised, and it seemed as if she were about to sink down on one knee.

A sculptor would have marveled at the mere material of which this rare work of art had been fashioned. It seemed like wax; yet it had nothing of the oiliness of wax to the touch. Could it be ivory? It was too exquisitely white.

And then the wonderful perfection of its detail! I was afraid to touch the lashes of the eyes, lest I should break them. And the little ears, how finely they were modeled! The little hands and feet, how scrupulously every curve and line and hollow had been preserved! And the dear body of her, how plastic for all its lifeless rigidity!

For the first time in my life I understood the ecstatic ravings of artists when they endeavored to reveal to others the beauty that is so evident to them. Beauty such as this left one inarticulate.

The face perplexed me—or rather its expression. Jeanne was all gaiety and animation. But this reduction of herself suggested nothing of that. How could it? Jeanne was motion personified, flitting hither and thither like a butterfly. These placid features, with no trace of the smile that lit up the dearest face in the world, were still and cold.

The aspect of this precious, pallid beauty, all that was left to me of Jeanne, overcame me. I know that I sobbed and I am not ashamed to own it. I vowed to myself that I would preserve this remnant of her, this visible evidence of her self-sacrifice, as a thing to be worshiped. I would enshrine it in some secret, fitting way: it would be my holy of holies.

Dawn was breaking. I washed my hot, fevered face and held a water soaked towel to my swollen eyes for a few minutes. Fresh air and a long walk would do me good, I thought. I wrapped the white figure tenderly in cotton, dropped it into my pocket, and then walked out into the open.

I must have wandered about in a stupor. For the life of me I cannot now tell where I went or how I returned. I know that the sun was well up in the heavens when I found myself in and went to my room. In the afternoon I had to give a lecture on Mendel's laws to the senior class in biology. I flung myself down on the bed, dressed as I was, hoping that I might snatch an hour's sleep, so that I might not appear too manifestly beside myself with grief.

I MUST have dozed for I was awakened by a knock at the door. It was the maid. I was wanted at the telephone.

"Say that I can't be disturbed," I directed her.

"She says it's very important," was the reply.

"Who does?"

"Miss Briand's landlady."

My state of mind can be imagined when I say that I could not divine why Jeanne's landlady wished to speak to me on the telephone. I found out quickly enough when I answered.

Did I know where Miss Briand was? asked the voice over the telephone. She had not been at home all night, and it was now past noon. Was she at the laboratory yesterday? When did she leave? Should her disappearance be reported to the police?

I could tell from her voice that the woman was concerned more about herself than about Jeanne. She ran a respectable house, she insisted again and again. She did hope nothing had happened which would compromise her or her establishment. I reassured her as best I could and promised her that I would look into the matter of Jeanne's disappearance and communicate with her again.

Her reference to the police startled me. It brought me to my senses. It had not occurred to me before that a human being cannot step out of existence, as it were, unchallenged. Suppose the police were to descend on the laboratory and investigate!

What could I say? No one would believe me, of course, if I told the truth. About the experiments with parameba and how they had led step by step to Jeanne's undoing. Even if I summoned the best experts, even if they confirmed my discoveries, what biologist would be bold enough to administer baroturpinol to a human being and prove that even the highest forms of life yielded to the strange influence of that mysterious compound? And what human being, short of a madman could be found who would willingly sacrifice himself? Good Heavens!

And then there were Jeanne's clothes. They would surely be found in the chest.

I sank into a chair. My whole body was bathed in a perspiration of fright. Suppose that I were accused of murder? A divorce scandal was bad enough, but a murder, a murder—

Lecturing was out of the question. I telephoned to the university that illness would prevent me from attending and that the class was to be dismissed. I had to think this out; I must gain time. My case was clearly desperate.

All at once a ray of hope flashed upon me. Why not try salt? If parameba, a sea-urchin, a goldfish—and a fish is, after all, not so very low in the scale of evolution—can be restored to their natural proportions and to life, why not a human being? Yes, perhaps the salt solution would save me and bring back my Jeanne to me.

But what reason had I to suppose that because a few animals could be reduced and expanded at will, I might bring Jeanne back to life? Suppose that the little statuette should return to life, but to remain a mere miniature of Jeanne? That was too horrible!

Worse still, suppose that the figure should reassume the girl's natural shape, but that no spark of life would reanimate the body? What then? I should be worse off than ever. The white remnant of her that I carried with me could be hidden. The clothes in the chest, too, could be disposed of. No one could prove that Jeanne was really dead.

But a lifeless body—

I fled into the laboratory. If ever a man was on the verge of madness, it was I. Tormented by grief at the loss of Jeanne and stricken with terror at the prospect of arrest, I felt like a wild beast at bay.

I longed for some simple-minded, practical, unscientific friend to whom I could turn for counsel in my need. I knew the difference between a holothurian and a jellyfish, but in the cloistered university I had lost track of human hearts and problems. However, my problem was my problem; I alone could solve it.

It came to me very clearly at last that I owed it to Jeanne to make some effort at resuscitating all that was left of her. The resolution was more easily made than carried out. Where should I conduct this momentous experiment?

The laboratory naturally suggested itself first. I dismissed the thought almost at once. There was no vessel large enough to hold a human body, and suspicion might be aroused if I had one brought in. I might go to a hotel and engage a room and bath; the bathtub would surely serve the purpose.

But suppose that the little figure of Jeanne should swell and magnify, and suppose that life should not return. I would have to explain the presence of a corpse in my room—the corpse of a woman who had played a part in my life and for whom the police were searching. That would help neither Jeanne nor me. Better a thousand times that she should remain in my pocket than that!

Finally I came to the conclusion that I must go to some lonely place by the sea. Had we not discovered early in our investigations that any solution of salt, even seawater, performed the miracle of bringing back to life organisms which had been diminished by baroturpinol? Besides, would it not be easy to dispose of the corpse if life did not return?

I looked at my watch. It was just half past three. Glaston-by-the-Sea was three hours' distant by the railway. If I left this afternoon, by night all my doubts and fears would be dispelled.

I had not slept in twenty-four hours. Some rest I must have. My nerves were so unstrung that I could feel my eyelids quivering; I could hardly touch a book or an implement without dropping it.

So I went into my room, and bathed, and threw myself down on the bed to catch what little sleep I could.

GLASTON-BY-THE-SEA is a fishing village comprising nothing more than a dozen houses. In front of it lies the ocean; in back tower cliffs of limestone. The sand stretches on either side of the village for miles and miles. Walk ten minutes away from the village and you might as well be in the Desert of Sahara for any signs of human life that you can see.

I knew the coast well; many a specimen had I collected among the rocks as the tide went out.

It was dark when I alighted from the train, four miles from Glaston. The full moon was rising in the east—a great round, yellow topaz that crept higher and higher in the sky. I had not counted on a bright night.

To carry out a hazardous experiment in the aspect of that cold, luminous disk seemed too public. It was so like a round, inscrutable face that looked down at me in benignant curiosity. Then it occurred to me how strangely fascinated Jeanne had always been by the full moon. How she had longed for the time when we might watch it rise together in some such lonely place as this, shut off from the strife and the clamor and the prying eyes of the world. I am not superstitious, but it did seem as if that great ball in the sky might be a good omen.

At about ten o'clock I reached the shore two miles above Glaston; for I had care-fully avoided the village. It was flood tide. The sea was dappled with opalescent ripples. Now and then a swelling wave would roll up on the sands and the water would tumble reluctantly back again in a vast expanse of foam. Only the rhythmic wash of a smooth sea broke the silence of that moonlit solitude.

Jeanne's clothes and hat I had brought with me in a traveling-bag. I took them out and spread them on the beach just as I imagined she would have arranged them herself in her chamber.

Now that I thought of it, this idea of coming to Glaston and making an heroic attempt to bring Jeanne back to life seemed like a stroke of genius. What if the experiment did fail? What if the reduced image of herself did resume its normal shape, but without coming back to life? I could leave the corpse on the sands. It would seem as if she had died in some inexplicable way.

Here were her clothes all neatly arranged, testifying mutely in my behalf. There was no sign of violence.

One by one I took off my own clothes and laid them down beside Jeanne's. Very, very carefully I unwrapped the parcel in which I had carried her about. I feared that I might break off a strand of hair or nick a foot or hand.

Holding the figure in my outstretched hands as if it were a sacred image, I walked into the sea straight toward the moon, my face uplifted. This was more than a scientific experiment. Human life, human happiness, human love were at stake.

Now that I look back at the events of that unforgettable night, the whole proceeding must have seemed more like a religious ceremony than a frantic man's desperate effort to save the thing that he held most precious. Surely no worshiper who had ever entered an ancient Egyptian temple was more reverentially hopeful than I, nor more innocently expectant of a miracle that would sweep away all earthly doubts and reveal the hand of destiny itself pointing toward the light.

Slowly the water rose to my knees, to my waist, and at last to my breast. It lapped the frail figure in my hand. I clutched the thing lest it should slip from my grasp. How long I stood thus, shoulder-high in the waves, I do not know. Perhaps it was only five minutes, perhaps as long as a quarter of an hour.

I know that I was stricken with terror for a time; for the figure in my hands might have been made of stone for any change that I could feel.

Was I to fail? Was Jeanne hopelessly, irretrievably dead?

Then a moment came when the figure seemed to slip in my hands. I grasped it tighter lest I should lose it. Still it slipped —slipped as a fish slips in the hands. Now I realized what was happening. Jeanne was growing, literally growing in my crooked fingers! I almost swooned.

Even if the swelling miniature were not the most precious thing in the world to me, even if it did not mean happiness and life itself, I would have found it difficult to retain my self-control. Very, very slowly the figure grew to the size of a child. I had to hold it in my arms now; it was not only larger, but perceptibly heavier.

A doubt assailed me. Would it stop growing? I prayed that it might keep on.

Presently it grew so large that I could no longer hold it in my arms alone. I walked back a few steps and lowered the figure so that its feet touched the bottom. But I saw to it that it was completely immersed, fearful lest some monstrous effect might be produced if even a shoulder were dry and could not grow with the rest.

In half an hour, I should judge, what had been apparently an exquisite statuette, something that I could carry in my pocket, had become the full-sized form of my Jeanne. But it was still hard. There was no feeling of yielding flesh—nothing but the rigidity of so much clay.

For that I had been prepared by the observation that I had made in my laboratory. Life returned to a shrunken organism slowly, almost hesitantly.

At last I felt Jeanne soften in my arms.

She was a thing of flesh now. Her form had become supple and flexible; I could feel it as so much tissue.

And then the miracle of miracles happened! Her bosom heaved; she sighed; her eyes opened. She moaned, and stared at me, utterly bewildered. Her mind could not orient itself at first. In a dim way she seemed to realize who I was.

I could feel her arms tighten about my neck, and so I carried her to the beach, in the most ecstatic and exalted state in which I have ever been.

I TOLD my wife everything—everything of the initial experiments with parameba and the goldfish, everything except Jeanne's bold swallowing of the baroturpinol in a critical situation and of her subsequent miraculous reanimation. Jeanne meant all to me; and my wife had ceased to be, if I may say so, what she never was. I wanted a divorce, and I said so frankly.

"So this is to be the end?" she sobbed bitterly.

"I see no other way. To remain as we are, and to pretend that all is as it should be between us, would mean misery for both of us. It is better that we should part."

"But what if I should refuse? Is it right that you should begin a new and happy life and that I, after all these years, should drift about aimlessly and wretchedly? This home is mine as much as yours. I made it what it is, and shall I give up everything for a woman whom I hate?"

There was much more in the same vein. I had not counted on this. It was partly bitter hatred of Jeanne that swayed her and partly wounded pride.

It had never occurred to me before that marriage means more to a woman than the building of a nest and the gratification of the mating instinct. In her scheme of existence the conventions or vanities of married life are enormously important. Her conjugal rights, the social status brought about by the mere act of marriage are to her what his patent of nobility is to a duke—something not to be relinquished without a struggle.

My wife refused point-blank to divorce me.

"But that is senseless," I argued. "If I stay here, our life will be a mere travesty; if I leave you and go my own way you will not be unhappier. What do you gain by refusing?"

"You can't marry a woman who has ruined my life, and whom I hate. By refusing to divorce you I destroy her. No decent man or woman will befriend her, knowing what she is to you."

With that she flounced out of the room.

This turn of events I had not foreseen. I knew that divorce meant the end of my university career, and for that I was fully prepared. But to have the finger of scorn pointed at the woman I loved—

I am a social being. Companionship means much to me, and it meant as much to Jeanne. For a few months we might be sufficient to ourselves. Then would come a time when I would wish to spend an evening with congenial friends, and Jeanne with women who give teas and form organizations for the uplift of the poor and unenlightened.

What then? I could hardly venture to cross the thresholds of those temples of purity and virtue whither I would eventually be drawn, and on my arm a woman whose relations to me were regarded as scandalous.

And she—she would undoubtedly be rebuffed if she sought to enter the circle within which she now moved so freely.

You see that a scientist can be far more practical in his reasoning than the world supposes. After all, his whole training teaches him how to deal with facts.

I was to meet Jeanne that evening in a dense grove, near a little farmhouse about half a mile from the end of the trolley-line. Ever since her astonishing restoration we had arranged to see each other there three times a week. Her return to the laboratory was out of the question for the time being.

There she was at the appointed time and place, looking very demure in a neat white dress which she had made herself. She saw that I was troubled, and I told her at once the outcome of the afternoon's parley.

Either she would not or she could not see the situation in its true light. Was I not everything in her life? She was more than willing to forego ordinary social intercourse if she could only work and live with me. A thousand reasons she advanced to prove how unnecessary the outer world must be to us.

She was a born romanticist, living perpetually in a fairy castle on a mountaintop capped with silvery clouds. In that atmosphere there is no time; Jeanne lived only in the present. I could hope for no practical assistance from her. I must reason this problem out for myself.

So I changed the topic at the first opportunity, and we passed the rest of the evening in the usual lighthearted way.

During these meetings we talked chiefly of the romantic possibilities of baroturpinol.

"How simple and cheap it would be for us to travel," she would ramble on. "You could carry me in your pocket just as you did to Glaston; or I could pack you away in my handbag and take you with me. If I had a friend, I might even have myself sent to you by parcel-post. Salt water you can get everywhere."

Of course I smiled at this, but I'm not so sure that Jeanne was not serious.

That was the last I ever saw of her.

TWO days later I was to keep my tryst with Jeanne for the third time that week. I was in the grove at the appointed hour. She did not come. Was she detained? Or was she ill? I fretted and fumed, hoping that each figure that loomed up in the darkness (for the grove was near the road) might be Jeanne. At eleven o'clock I gave up all hope of seeing her that night.

My wife met me as I opened the door of my house.

"May I speak to you a moment?" she asked.

I hung up my hat and followed her into her own room. She took from her safe a little box and laid it on her dressing-table. Next she raised a window which opened on a paved court below. It was clear she was following a well-thought-out plan of action.

"I believe you wish to say something to me," I said to relieve my suspense.

"Yes." Nothing more.

She untied the box, concealed it from me as she did so. Presently she turned around, holding in her hand an envelope.

"Read this," she said. "It came yesterday."

The envelope had been steamed open. It was addressed to me in Jeanne's handwriting.

"And so you open and read my letters?" I queried angrily.

"When I suspect that they concern me, I do," she retorted coolly.

I reproduce it here. That letter and a lock of hair that she once gave me are all that I have of Jeanne.

Dearest Dick:

I have been thinking so much of that wonderful night on the beach at Glaston—the night when I was born again on the bosom of the sea, just as if I were another Aphrodite. How beautiful it was to awaken and find myself looking at you by the light of the moon! I want to live all that over again, to come back from oblivion and find myself clinging to you.

If I were to ask you, I know that you would never consent to my becoming a dead image of myself again. You would suspect my motive if I were to ask you for some baroturpinol. So I have bought what I need. If you will come to meet me in the grove beyond the farm at the usual time on Friday, you will find only a little white Jeanne in the midst of her clothes.

Put her in your pocket and take her with you to Glaston next Monday. The moon will then be full.

Jeanne

WAS I frightened? I can hardly say. It was as if some one had struck me a blow. I was stunned.

Intuitively I sensed the diabolical thing that my wife had done. I had told her enough of my first experiments; the rest Jeanne's letter made sufficiently plain.

"When I read this," she explained, all the while standing, "I understood everything. I know now what happened in the laboratory that afternoon when I knocked at the door.

"Now, listen carefully to what I say. I have told you that I hate this woman, that I will not permit her to take from me what is rightfully mine. Late this afternoon I went to the place that she mentions in her letter. I did not know just when she was to meet you, and I didn't care. It was merely a matter of waiting. I hid myself behind some bushes and watched.

"A little while after sunset I saw her down the road. She came into the grove and sat down on the grass. Then she took off her hat and laid it beside her. She sat very quietly, looking down the road through the trees. At first I thought that she was afraid and that she would not take the solution at all. Then I realized why she did nothing. She was waiting for you.

"She was clever! She was not going to run the risk of leaving a heap of clothes in a grove an hour before you came, with the chance of arousing the curiosity of some boy who might wander into the grove. She would wait until she saw you far away. You would reach her just at the right moment. So it proved. I could see you myself fully a quarter of a mile away; it was still quite light. She never took her eyes off the road. I think she must have seen you before I did. She opened her handbag and took out a bottle before I caught my first glimpse of you.

"The next I knew, she had placed the bottle to her lips and drained it off. I turned away. I didn't want to see her shrivel up before my very eyes. A quarter of a minute, I thought, would be about long enough for her to shrink. So I counted fifteen and turned around. Where she had sat was only a heap of clothes.

"There was not a second to lose now. You were almost at the grove. I crawled

out of the bushes and gathered up everything, clothes, hat, and all. Then I ran
away from the place just as you were about
to enter."

All the while she had been handling the
box. I knew what it contained, and my
brain was feverishly busy devising and
rejecting, over and over again, plans to get
it away from her; by stealth if possible,
by force if necessary. I should have leaped
from my seat at once and seized her, but I
sat still dazed, as if in a kind of hypnotic
trance.

"And here is your Jeanne," she almost
screamed as she took out a white, sitting
figure. "You will never, never have her

again. I take her so, and this—*this* is what
I do to her!"

This time I did act. I leaped to my feet,
knocked over the table that she had so
ingeniously placed to obstruct me, and
rushed at her.

But I was too late.

She was at the open window.

She raised her hand high above her
head, posed there for a fraction of a second. the very incarnation of hate and
vengeance. Then she dashed the white
thing upon the stone pavement of the
court below.

I heard it break into a hundred pieces
as it struck.

Write and tell us how you like this issue. Address your letter to The
Letter Editor, Famous Fantastic Mysteries, 280 Broadway, New York.

The Lord of Death

By HOMER EON FLINT

Author of "The Planeteer," etc.; co-author of "The Blind Spot"

A Complete Novelet

Part I
The Discovery

CHAPTER I

THE SKY CUBE

THE doctor, who was easily the most musical of the four men, sang in a cheerful baritone:

"The owl and the pussy-cat went to sea
In a beautiful, pea-green boat."

The geologist, who had held down the lower end of a quartet in his university days, growled an accompaniment under his breath as he blithely peeled the potatoes. Occasionally a high-pitched note or two came from the direction of the engineer; he could not spare much wind while clambering about the machinery, oil-can in hand. The architect, alone, ignored the famous tune.

"What I can't understand, Smith," he insisted, "is how you draw the electricity from the ether into this car without blasting us all to cinders."

The engineer squinted through an opal glass shutter into one of the tunnels, through which the anti-gravitation current was pouring. "If you don't know any more about buildings than you do about machinery, Jackson," he grunted, because of his squatting position, "I'd hate to live in one of your houses!"

The architect smiled grimly. "You're living in one of 'em right now, Smith," said he; "that is, if you call this car a house."

Smith straightened up. He was an unimportant-looking man, of medium height and build, and bearing a mild, good-humored expression. Nobody would ever look at him twice, would ever guess that his skull concealed an unusually complete knowledge of electricity and mechanisms.

"I told you yesterday, Jackson," he said, "that the air surrounding the earth is chock full of electricity. And—"

"And that the higher we go, the more juice," added the other, remembering. "As much as to say that it is the atmosphere, then, that protects the earth from the surrounding voltage."

The engineer nodded. "Occasionally it breaks through, anyhow, in the form of lightning. Now, in order to control that current, and prevent it from turning this machine, and us, into ashes, all we do is to pass the juice through a cylinder of highly compressed air, fixed in this wall. By varying the pressure and dampness within the cylinder, we can regulate the flow."

The builder nodded rapidly. "All right. But why doesn't the electricity affect the walls themselves? I thought they were made of steel."

The engineer glanced through the deadlight at the reddish disk of the earth, hazy and indistinct at a distance of forty million miles. "It isn't steel; it's a non-magnetic alloy. Besides, there's a layer of crystalline sulphur between the alloy and the vacuum space."

"The vacuum is what keeps out the cold, isn't it?" Jackson knew, but he asked in order to learn more.

Copyrighted, 1919, by The Frank A. Munsey Co.

"Look out!" cried Jackson, as the sides of the glass case fell away, and the gigantic monster sat
glaring furiously, as if about to rise and spring

"Keeps out the sun's heat, too. The outer shell is pretty blamed hot on that side, just as hot as it is cold on the shady side." Smith seated himself beside a huge electrical machine, a rotary converter which he next indicated with a jerk of his thumb. "But you don't want to forget that the juice outside is no use to us, the way it is. We have to change it.

"It's neither positive nor negative; it's just neutral. So we separate it into two parts; and all we have to do, when we want to get away from the earth or any other magnetic sphere, is to aim a bunch of positive current at the corresponding pole of the planet, or negative current at the other pole. Like poles repel."

"Listen easy," commented Jackson. "Too easy."

"Well, it isn't exactly as simple as all that. Takes a lot of apparatus, all told." And the engineer looked about the room, his glance resting fondly on his beloved machinery.

All powerful Strokor, the iron-voiced dictator of Mercury when the Earth was young, wanted Ave, the girl who was different, to be his wife and mother a new race. Edam, the dreamer, the man who looked like Ave, Strokor feared not—and that was his fatal mistake

The big room, fifty feet square, was almost filled with machines; some reached nearly to the ceiling, the same distance above. In fact, the interior of the "cube" had very little waste space. The living quarters of the four men who occupied it had to be fitted in wherever there happened to be room. The architect's own berth was sandwiched in between two huge dynamos.

He was thinking hard. "I see now why you have such a lot of adjustments for those tunnels," meaning the six square tubes which opened into the ether through the six walls of the room. "You've got to point the juice pretty accurately."

"I should say so." Smith led the way to a window, and the two shaded their eyes from the lights within while they gazed at the ashy glow of Mercury, toward which they were traveling. "I've got to adjust the current so as to point exactly toward his northern half." Smith might have added that a continual stream of repelling current was still directed toward the earth, and another toward the sun, away over to their right; both to prevent being drawn off their course.

"And how fast are we going?"

"Four or five times as fast as mother earth; between eighty and ninety miles per second. It's easy to get up speed out here, of course, where there's no air resistance."

Another voice broke in. The geologist had finished his potatoes, and a savory smell was already issuing from the frying pan. Years spent in the wilderness had made the geologist a good cook, and doubly welcome as a member of the expedition.

"We ought to get there tomorrow, then," he said eagerly. Indoor life did not appeal to him, even under such exciting circumstances. He peered at Mercury through his binoculars. "Beginning to show up fine now."

THE builder improved upon Van Emmon's example by setting up the car's biggest telescope, one of unusual excellence. All three pronounced the planet, which was three-fourths "full" as they viewed it, as having pretty much the appearance of the moon.

"Wonder why there's always been so much mystery about Mercury?" pondered the architect invitingly.

"Mercury is so close to the sun," answered the scientist, "that he's always been hard to observe. For a long time the astronomers couldn't even agree that he always keeps the same face toward the sun, like the moon toward the earth."

"Then his day is as long as his year?"

"Eighty-eight of our days; yes."

"Continual sunlight! He can't be inhabited, then?" The architect knew very little about the planets, but he possessed remarkable ability as an amateur antiquarian.

Dr. Kinney shook his head. "Not at present, certainly."

Instantly Jackson was alert. "Then perhaps there were people there at one time?"

"Why not?" the doctor put it lightly. "There's little or no atmosphere there now, of course, but that's not saying there never has been. Even if he is such a little planet—less than three thousand, smaller than the moon—he must have had plenty of air and water at one time, the same as the earth."

"What's become of the air?" Van Emmon wanted to know. Kinney eyed him in reproach. He said:

"You ought to know. Mercury has only two-fifths as much gravitation as the earth; a man weighing a hundred and fifty back home would be only a sixty-pounder there. And you can't expect stuff as light as air to stay forever on a planet with no more pull than that, when the sun is on the job only thirty-six million miles away."

"About a third as far as from the earth to the sun," commented the engineer. "By George, it must be hot!"

"On the sunlit side, yes," said Kinney. "On the dark side it is as cold as space itself—four hundred and sixty below, Fahrenheit."

They considered this in silence for some minutes. After a while the builder came back with another question.

"If Mercury ever was inhabited, then his day wasn't as long as it is now, was it?"

"No," said the doctor. "In all probability he once had a day the same length as ours. Mercury is a comparatively old planet, you know; being smaller, he cooled off earlier than the earth, and has been more affected by the pull of the sun. But it's been a mighty long time since he had a day like ours. Before the earth was cool enough to live on, probably."

"But since Mercury was made out of the same batch of material—" prompted the geologist.

"No reason, then, why life shouldn't have existed there in the past!" exclaimed the architect, his eyes sparkling with the instinct of the born antiquarian. He glanced up eagerly as the doctor coughed apologetically and said:

"Don't forget that, even if Mercury is part baked and part frozen, there must be a region in between which is neither." He picked up a small globe from the table and ran a finger completely around it from pole to pole. "So. There must be a narrow band of country where the sun is only partly above the horizon, and where the climate is temperate."

"Then"—the architect almost shouted in his excitement, an excitement only slightly greater than that of the other two —"then if there were people on Mercury at one time—"

The doctor nodded gravely. "There may be some there now!"

CHAPTER II

A DEAD CITY

FROM a height of a few thousand miles Mercury, instead of the craters, which always distinguished the moon, showed ranges of bona fide mountains.

The sky-car was rapidly sinking nearer and nearer the planet; already Smith had stopped the current with which he had attracted the cube toward the little world's northern hemisphere, and was now using negative voltage. This, in order to act as a brake, and prevent them from falling to destruction.

Suddenly, Van Emmon, the geologist, whose eyes had been glued to his binoculars, gave an exclamation of wonder. "Look at those faults!" He pointed toward a region south of that for which they were bound; what might be called the planet's torrid zone.

At first it was hard to see; then, little by little, there unfolded before their eyes a giant, spiderlike system of chasms in the strange surface beneath them. From a point almost directly opposite the sun, these cracks radiated in a half-dozen different directions; vast, irregular clefts, they ran through mountain and plain alike. In places they must have been hundreds of miles wide, while there was no guessing as to their width. For all that the four in the cube could see, they were bottomless.

"Small likelihood of anybody being alive there now," commented the geologist skeptically. "If the sun has dried it out enough to produce faults like that, how could animal life exist?"

"Notice, however," prompted the doctor, "that the cracks do not extend all the way to the edge of the disk." This was true; all the great chasms ended far short of the "twilight band" which the doctor had declared might still contain life.

But as the sky-car rushed downward their attention became fixed upon the surface directly beneath them, a point whose latitude corresponded roughly with that of New York on the earth. It was a region of low-lying mountains, decidedly different from various precipitous ranges to be seen to the north and east. On the west, or left-hand side of this district, a comparatively level stretch, with an occasional peak or two projecting, suggested the ancient bed of an ocean.

By this time they were within a thousand miles. Smith threw on a little more current; their speed diminished to a safer point, and they scanned the approaching surface with the greatest of care.

"Do either of you fellows see anything green?" demanded the engineer, a little later. They were silent; each had noticed, long before, that not even near the poles was there the slightest sign of vegetation.

"No chance unless there's foliage," muttered the doctor, half to himself. The builder asked what he meant. He explained: "So far as we know, all animal life depends upon vegetation for its oxygen. Not only the oxygen in the air, but that stored in the plants which animals eat. Unless there's greenery—"

He paused at a low exclamation from Smith. The engineer's eyes were fixed, in wonder and excitement, upon that part of the valley which lay at the joint of the "L" below them. It was perhaps six miles across; and all over the comparatively smooth surface jutted dark projections. Viewed through the glasses, they had a regular uniform appearance.

"By Jove!" exclaimed the doctor, almost in awe. He leaned forward and scrubbed the deadlight for the tenth time. All four men strained their eyes to see.

It was the architect who broke the silence which followed. The other three were content to let the thrill of the thing have its way with them. Such a feeling had little weight with the expert in archeology.

"Well," he declared jubilantly in his boyish voice, "either I eat my hat or that's a city!"

AS SWIFTLY as an elevator drops, and as safely, the cube shot straight downward. Every second the landscape narrowed and shrunk, leaving the remaining details larger, clearer, sharper. Bit by bit the amazing thing below them resolved itself into a real metropolis.

Within five minutes they were less than a mile above it. Smith threw on more current, so that the descent stopped; and the cube hung motionless in space.

For another five minutes the four men studied the scene in nervous silence. Each knew that the others were looking for the same thing—some sign of life. A little spot of green, or possibly something in motion—a single whiff of smoke would have been enough to cause a whoop of joy.

But nobody shouted. There was nothing to shout about. Nowhere in all that locality apparently was there the slightest sign that any save themselves were alive.

Instead, the most extraordinary city that man ever laid eyes upon was stretched directly beneath. It was grouped about what seemed to be the meeting-point of three great roads, which led to this spot from as many passes through the surrounding hills. And the city seemed thus naturally divided into three segments, of equal size and shape, and each with its own street system.

For they undoubtedly were streets. No metropolis on earth ever had its blocks laid out with such unvarying exactness. This Mercurian city contained none but perfect equilateral triangles, and the streets themselves were of absolutely uniform width.

The buildings, however, showed no such uniformity. On the outskirts the blocks seemed to contain nothing save odd heaps of dingy, sun-baked mud. On the extreme north, however, lay five blocks grouped together, whose buildings, like those in the middle of the city, were rather tall, square-cut and of the same dusty, cream-white hue.

"Down-town" were several structures especially prominent for their height. They towered to such an extent, in fact, that their upper windows were easily made out. Apparently they were hundreds of stories high!

Here and there on the streets could be seen small spots, colored a darker buff than the rest of that dazzling landscape. But not one of the spots was moving.

"We'll go down further," said the engineer tentatively, in a low tone. There was no comment. He gradually reduced the repelling current, so that the sky-car resumed its descent.

They sank down until they were on a level with the top of one of those extraordinary sky-scrapers. The roof seemed perfectly flat, except for a large, round, black opening in its center. No one was in sight.

When opposite the upper rows of windows, at a distance of perhaps twenty feet, Smith brought the car to a halt, and they peered in. There were no panes; the windows opened directly into a vast room. But nothing was clearly visible in the blackness save the outlines of the openings in the opposite walls.

They went down further, keeping well to the middle of the space above the street. At every other yard they kept a sharp lookout for the inhabitants; but so far as they could see, their approach was entirely unobserved.

When within fifty yards of the surface, all four men made a search for cross-wires below. They saw none; there were no poles, even. Neither, to their astonishment, was there such a thing as a sidewalk. The street stretched unbroken by curbing, from wall to wall and from corner to corner.

As the cube settled slowly to the ground, the adventurers left the deadlight to use the windows. For a moment the view was obscured by a swirl of dust; raised by the spurt of the current. Then this cloud vanished, settling to the ground with astounding suddenness, as though jerked down by some invisible hand.

Directly ahead of them, perhaps a hundred yards, lay a yellowish-brown mass of unusual octagonal shape. One end contained a small oval opening, but the men from the earth looked in vain for any creature to emerge from it.

The doctor silently set to work with his apparatus. From an air-tight double-doored compartment he obtained a sample of the ether outside the car; and with the aid of previously arranged chemicals, quickly learned the truth.

There was no air. Not only was there no oxygen, the element upon which all known life depends, but there was no nitrogen, no carbon dioxid. Not the slightest trace of water vapor or of the other less known elements which can be found in small amounts in our own atmosphere. Clearly, as the doctor said, whatever air the astronomers had observed must exist on the circumference of the planet only, and not in this sun-blasted, north-central spot.

On the outer walls of the cube, so arranged as to be visible through the windows, were various instruments. The barometer showed no pressure. The thermometer, a specially devised one which used gas instead of mercury, showed a temperature of six hundred degrees, Fahrenheit.

No air, no water, and a baking heat; as the geologist remarked, how could life exist there? But the architect suggested that possibly there was some form of life, of which men knew nothing, which could exist under such circumstances.

They got out three of the suits. These were a good deal like those worn by divers, except that the outer layer was made of non-conducting aluminum cloth, flexible, air-tight and strong. Between it and the inner lining was a layer of cells, into which the men now pumped several pints of liquid oxygen. The terrific cold of this chemical made the heavy flannel of the inner lining very welcome; while the oxygen itself, as fast as it evaporated, revitalized the air within the big, glass-faced helmet.

Once safely locked within the clumsy suits. Jackson, Van Emmon, and Smith took their places within the vestibule; while the doctor, who had volunteered to to stay behind, watched them open the outer door. With a hiss all the air in the vestibule rushed out; and the doctor earnestly thanked his stars that the inner door had been built very strongly.

The men stepped out on to the ground. At first they moved with great care, being uncertain that their feet were weighted heavily enough to counteract the reduced gravitation of the tiny planet. But they had been living in a very peculiar condition, gravitationally speaking, for the past three days; and they quickly adapted themselves.

After a little shifting about, the three artificial monsters gave their telephone wires another scrutiny. Then, keeping always within ten feet of each other, so as not to throw any strain on the connections, they strode in a matter-of-fact way toward the nearest doorway.

For a moment or two they stood utside the queer, peaked archway, their glimmering suits standing out oddly in the blinding sunlight. Then they advanced boldly into the opening. In a flash they vanished from the doctor's sight, and the inklike blackness of the opening again stared at him from that dazzling wall.

CHAPTER III

THE HOUSE OF DUST

THE geologist, strong man that he was, and by profession an investigator of the unknown—Van Emmon—took the lead. He stalked straight ahead into a vast space which, without any preliminary hallway, filled the entire triangular block.

Before their eyes were accustomed to the shadow—"Pretty cold," murmured the architect into the phone transmitter. It was fastened to the inside of the helmet, directly in front of his mouth, while the receiver was placed beside his ear. All three stopped short to adjust each other's electrical heating apparatus. To do this, they did not use their fingers directly; they manipulated ingenious non-magnetic pliers attached to the ends of fingerless, insulated mittens.

Before they had finished, the builder, who had been puzzling over the extraordinary suddenness with which that cloud of dust had settled received an inspiration. He was carrying note-book and camera. With his pliers he tore out a sheet from the former, and holding book in one hand and the leaf in the other, he allowed them to drop at the same instant.

They reached the ground together.

"See?" The architect repeated the experiment. "Back home, where there's air, the paper would have floated down. It would have taken three times as long for it to fall as the book."

Smith nodded, but he had been thinking of something else. He said gravely: "Remember what I told you—it's air that insulates the earth from the ether. If there's no air here"—he glanced out into the pitiless sunlight—"then I hope there's no flaw in our insulation. We're walking in an electrical bath."

They looked around. Objects were pretty distinct now. They could easily see that the floor was covered with what appeared to be machines, laid out in orderly fashion. Here, however, as outside, everything was coated with that fine, cream-colored dust. It filled every nook and cranny; it stirred about their feet with every step.

The geologist led the way down a broad aisle, on either side of which towered immense machinery. Smith was for stopping to examine them one by one; but the others vetoed the engineer's passion, and strode on toward the end of the triangle. More than anything else, they looked for the absent population to show itself.

Suddenly Van Emmon stopped short. "Is it possible that they're all asleep?" He added that, even though the sun shone steadily the year around, the people must take times for rest.

But Smith stirred the dust with his foot and shook his head. "I've seen no tracks. This dust has been lying here for weeks, perhaps months. If the folks are away, then they must be taking a community vacation."

At the end of the aisle they reached a small, railed-in space, strongly resembling what might be seen in any office on the earth. In the middle of it stood a low, flat-topped desk, for all the world like that of a prosperous real-estate agent, except that it was about half a foot lower. There was no chair. For lack of a visible gate in the railing, the explorers stepped over, being careful not to touch it.

There was nothing on top of the desk

save the usual coat of dust. Below, a very wide space had been left for the legs of whoever had used it. And flanking this space were two pedestals, containing what looked to be a multitude of exceedingly small drawers. Smith bent and examined them; apparently they had no locks. He unhesitatingly reached out, gripped the knob of one, and pulled.

Noiselessly, instantaneously, the whole desk crumbled to powder.

Startled, Smith stumbled backward, knocking against the railing. Next instant it lay on the floor, its fragments scarcely distinguishable from what had already covered the surface. Only a tiny cloud of dust arose, and in half a second this had settled.

The three looked at each other significantly. Clearly, the thing that had just happened argued a great lapse of time since the user of that desk officiated in that enclosure. It looked as though Smith's guess of "weeks, perhaps months," would have to be changed to years, perhaps centuries.

"Feel all right?" asked the geologist. Jackson and Smith made affirmative noises; and again they stepped out, this time walking in the aisle along the outer wall. They could see their sky-car plainly through the ovals.

Here the machinery could be examined more closely. They resembled automatic testing scales, said Smith. The kind that are used in weighing complicated metal products after finishing and assembling. Moreover, they seemed to be connected, the one to the other, with a series of endless belts. These, Smith thought, indicated automatic production. To all appearances, the dust-covered apparatus stood just as it had been left when operations ceased, an unguessable length of time before.

SMITH showed no desire to touch the things now. Seeing this, the geologist deliberately reached out and scraped the dust from the nearest machine. To the vast relief of all three, no damage was done. The dust fell straight to the floor, exposing a streak of greenish-white metal.

Van Emmon made another tentative brush or so at other points, with the same result. Clean, untarnished metal lay beneath all that dust. Clearly it was some non-conducting alloy. Whatever it was, it had successfully resisted the action of the elements all the while that such presumably wooden articles as the desk and railing had been steadily rotting.

Emboldened, Smith clambered up on the frame of one of the machines. He examined it closely as to its cams, clutches, gearing, and other details significant enough to his mechanical training. He noted their adjustments, scrutinized the conveying apparatus, and came back carrying a cylindrical object which he had removed from an automatic chuck.

"This is what they were making," he remarked, trying to conceal his excitement. The others brushed the dust from the thing, a huge piece of metal which would have been too much for their strength on the earth. Instantly they identified it.

It was a cannon shell.

Again Van Emmon led the way. They took a reassuring glance out the window at the familiar cube, then passed along the aisle toward the farther corner. As they neared it they saw that it contained a small enclosure of heavy metal scrollwork, within which stood a triangular elevator.

The men examined it as closely as possible, noting especially the extremely low stool which stood upon its platform. The same unerodable metal seemed to have been used throughout the whole affair.

When they returned to the heap of powdered wood which had been the desk, Smith spied a long work-bench under a near-by window. There they found a very ordinary vise, in which was clamped a piece of metal. But for the dust, it might have been placed there ten minutes before. On the bench lay several tools, some familiar to the engineer and some entirely strange. A set of screw-drivers of various sizes caught his eye. He picked them up, and again experienced the sensation of having wood turn to dust at his touch. The blades were whole.

Still searching, the engineer found a square metal chest of drawers, each of which he promptly opened. The contents were laden with dust, but he brushed this off and disclosed a quantity of exceedingly delicate instruments. They were more like dentists' tools than machinists', yet plainly were intended for mechanical use.

One drawer held what appeared to be a roll of drawings. Smith did not want to touch them; with infinite care he blew off the dust with the aid of his oxygen pipe. After a moment or two the surface was clear, but it offered no encouragement; it was the blank side of the paper.

There was no help for it. Smith grasped the roll firmly with his pliers—and the next second gazed upon dust.

In the bottom drawer lay something that aroused the curiosity of all three. These were small reels, about two inches in diameter and a quarter of an inch thick, each incased in a tight-fitting box. They resembled measuring tapes to some extent, except that the ribbons were made of marvelously thin material. Van Emmon guessed that there were a hundred yards in a roll. Smith estimated it at three hundred. They seemed to be made of a metal similar to that composing the machines. Smith pocketed them all.

Under the bench they discovered a very small machine, decidedly like a stock ticker, except that it had no glass dome, but possessed at one end a curious metal disk about a foot in diameter. Apparently it had been undergoing repairs; it was impossible to guess its purpose. Smith's pride was instantly aroused; he tucked it under his arm, and was impatient to get back to the cube, where he might more carefully examine this find with the tips of his fingers.

It was when they were about to leave the building that they thought to inspect walls and ceiling.

"Look at that dust again! How'd it get there?" Van Emmon paused while the others, the thought finally getting to them, felt a queer chill striking at the backs of their necks. "Men—there's only one way

for the dust to settle on a wall! It's got to have air to carry it! It couldn't possibly get there without air!

"That dust settled long before life appeared on the earth, even! It's been there ever since the air disappeared from Mercury!"

CHAPTER IV

THE LIBRARY

"I THOUGHT you'd never get back," complained the doctor crossly, when the three entered. They had been gone just half an hour.

Next moment he was studying their faces, and at once he demanded the most important fact. They told him, and before they had finished he was half-way into another suit. He was all eagerness; but somehow the three were very glad to be inside the cube again, and firmly insisted upon moving to another spot before making further explorations.

Within a minute or two the cube was hovering opposite the upper floor of the building the three had entered. With only a foot of space separating the window of the sky-car and the dust-covered wall, the men from the earth inspected the interior at considerable length. They flashed a search-light all about the place, and concluded that it was the receiving room, where the raw iron billets were brought via the elevator, and from there slid to the floor below. At one end, in exactly the same location as the desk Smith had destroyed, stood another, with a low and remarkably broad chair beside it.

So far as could be seen, there were neither doors, window-panes, nor shutters through the structure. "To get all the light and air they could," guessed the doctor. "Perhaps that's why the buildings are all triangular; most wall surface in proportion to floor area, that way."

A few hundred feet higher they began to look for prominent buildings.

"We ought to learn something there," the doctor said after a while, pointing out a particularly large, squat, irregularly built affair on the edge of the "business district." The architect, however, was in favor of an exceptionally large, high building in the isolated group previously noted in the "suburbs." But because it was nearer, they maneuvered first in the direction of the doctor's choice.

The sky-car came to rest in a large plaza opposite what appeared to be the structure's main entrance.

The doctor was impatient to go. Smith was willing enough to stay behind; he was already joyously examining the strange machine he had found. Two minutes later Kinney, Van Emmon, and Jackson were standing before the portals of the great building.

There they halted, and no wonder. The entire face of the building could now be seen to be covered with a mass of carvings; for the most part they were statues in bas relief. All were fantastic in the extreme, but whether purposely so or not, there was no way to tell. Certainly any such work on the part of an earthly artist would have branded him either as insane or as an incomprehensible genius.

Directly above the entrance was a group which might have been labeled, "The Triumph of the Brute." An enormously powerful man, nearly as broad as he was tall, stood exulting over his victim, a less robust figure, prostrate under his feet. Both were clad in armor.

The victor's face was distorted into a savage snarl, startlingly hideous by reason of the prodigious size of his head, planted as it was directly upon his shoulders; for he had no neck. His eyes were set so close together that at first glance they seemed to be but one. His nose was flat and ape-like in type, while his mouth, devoid of curves, was revolting in its huge, thick-lipped lack of proportion. His chin was square and aggressive; his forehead, strangely enough, extremely high and narrow, rather than low and broad.

His victim lay in an attitude that indicated the most agonizing torture; his head was bent completely back, and around behind his shoulders. On the ground lay two battle-axes, huge affairs almost as heavy as the massively muscled men who had used them.

But the eyes of the explorers kept coming back to the fearsome face of the conqueror. From the brows down, he was simply a huge, brutal giant; above his eyes, he was an intellectual. The combination was absolutely frightful. The beast looked capable of anything, of overcoming any obstacle, mental or physical, internal or external, in order to assert his apparently enormous will. He could control himself or dominate others easily.

"It can't be that he was drawn from life," said the doctor, with an effort. It wasn't easy to criticize that figure, lifeless though it was. "On a planet like this, with such slight gravitation, there is no need for such huge strength. The typical Mercurian should be tall and flimsy in build, rather than short and compact."

But the geologist differed. "We want to remember that the earth has no standard type. Think what a difference there is between the mosquito and the elephant, the snake and the spider! One would suppose that they had been developed under totally different planetary conditions, instead of all right on the same globe.

"No; I think this monster may have been genuine." And with that the geologist turned to examine the other statuary.

Without exception, it resembled the central group; all the figures were neckless, and all much more heavily built than any people on earth. There were several female figures; they had the same general build, and in every case were so placed as to enhance the glory of the males. In one group the woman was offering up food and drink to a resting worker. In another she was being carried off, struggling, in the arms of a fairly good-looking warrior.

Dr. Kinney led the way into the building. As in the other structure, there was no door. The space seemed to be but one story in height, although that had the effect of a cathedral. The whole of the ceiling, irregularly arched in a curious, pointed manner, was ornamented with grotesque figures. The walls were also partially formed of squat, semihuman statues, set upon huge, triangular shafts. In the spaces between these outlandish pilasters there had once been some sort of 'decorations. A great many photos were taken here.

As for the floor, it was divided in all directions by low walls. About five and a half feet in height, these walls separated the great room into perhaps a hundred triangular compartments, each about the size of an ordinary living-room. Broad openings, about five feet square, provided free access from one compartment to any other. The men from the earth, by standing on tiptoes, could see over and beyond this system.

"Wonder if these walls were supposed to cut off the view?" speculated the doctor. "I mean, do you suppose that . the Mercurians were such short people as that?" His question had to go unanswered.

They stepped into the nearest compartment, and were on the point of pronouncing it bare, when Jackson, with an exclamation, excitedly brushed away some of the dust and showed that the presumably solid walls were really chests of drawers. Shallow things of that peculiar metal, these drawers numbered several hundred to the compartment. In the whole building there must have been millions.

ONCE more the dust was carefully removed, revealing a layer of those curious rolls or reels, exactly similar to what had been found in the tool chest in the shell works. A careful examination of the metallic tape showed nothing whatever to the naked eye, although the doctor fancied that he made out some strange characters on the little boxes themselves.

His view was shortly proved. Finding drawer after drawer to contain a similar display, varying from one to a dozen of of the diminutive ribbons, Van Emmon adopted the plan of gently blowing away the dust from the faces of the drawers before opening them. This revealed the fact

that each of the shallow things was neatly labeled.

Instantly the three were intent upon the fresh clue. The markings were very faint and delicate, the slightest touch being enough to destroy them. To the untrained eye, they resembled ancient Egyptian hieroglyphics. To the archeologist, they meant that a brand-new system of ideographs had been found.

Suddenly Jackson straightened up and looked about with a new interest. He went to one of the square doorways and very carefully removed the dust from a small plate on the lintel. He need not have been so careful; engraved in the solid metal was a single character, plainly in the same language as the other ideographs.

The architect smiled triumphantly into the inquiring eyes of his friends. "I won't have to eat my hat," said. he. "This is a sure-enough city, all right, and this is its library!"

Smith was still busy on the little machine when they returned to the cube. He said that one part of it had disappeared, and was busily engaged in filing a bit of steel to take its place. As soon as it was ready, he thought, they could see what the apparatus meant.

The three had brought a large number of the reels. They were confident that a microscopic search of the ribbons would disclose something to bear out Jackson's theory that the great structure was really a repository for books, or whatever corresponded with books on Mercury.

"But the main thing," said the doctor enthusiastically, "is to get over to the 'twilight band.' I'm beginning to have all sorts of wild hopes."

Jackson urged that they first visit the big "mansion" on the outskirts of this place; he said he felt sure, somehow, that it would be worth while. But Van Emmon backed up the doctor, and the architect had to be content with an agreement to return in case their trip was futile.

Inside of a few minutes the cube was being drawn steadily over toward the left or western edge of the planet's sunlit face. As it moved, all except Smith kept close watch on the ground below. They made out town after town, as well as separate buildings. And on the roads were to be seen a great many of those octagonal structures, all motionless.

After several hundred miles of this, the surface abruptly sloped toward what had clearly been the bed of an ocean. No sign of habitation here, however. So, apparently, the water had disappeared after the humans had gone.

This ancient sea ended a short distance from the district they were seeking. A little more travel brought them to a point where the sun cast as much shadow as light on the surface. It was here they descended, coming to rest on a sunlit knoll which overlooked a small, building-filled valley.

According to Kinney's apparatus, there was about one-fortieth the amount of air that exists on the earth. Of water vapor there was a trace; but all their search revealed no human life. Not only that, but there was no trace of lower animals; there was not even a lizard, much less a bird. And even the most ancient-looking of the sculptures showed no creatures of the air; only huge, antediluvian monsters were ever depicted.

They took a great many photos as a matter of course. Also, they investigated some of the big, octagonal machines in the streets, finding them to be similar to the great "tanks" used in war, on earth, except that they did not have the caterpillar tread. Their eight faces were so linked together that the entire affair could roll, after a jolting, slab-sided, flopping fashion. Inside were curious engines, and sturdy machines designed to throw the cannon-shells the visitors had seen. No explosive was employed, apparently, but centrifugal force generated in whirling wheels. Apparently these cars, or chariots, were universally used.

The explorers returned to the cube, where they found that Smith, happening to look out a window, had spied a pond not far off. The three visited it and found,

on its banks, the first green stuff they had seen; a tiny, flowerless salt grass, very scarce. It bordered a slimy, bluish pool of absolutely still fluid. Nobody would call it water. They took a few samples of it and went back.

And within a few minutes the doctor slid a small glass slide into his microscope, and examined the object with much satisfaction. What he saw was a tiny, gelatin-like globule; among scientists it is known as the amoeba. It is the simplest form of life—the so-called "single cell." It had been the first thing to live on that planet, and apparently it was also the last.

CHAPTER V

THE CLOSED DOOR

AS THEY neared Jackson's pet "mansion" each man paid close attention to the intervening blocks. For the most part these were simply shapeless ruins; heaps of what had once been, perhaps, brick or stone.

Apparently the locality they were approaching had been set aside as a very exclusive residence district for the elite of the country. Possibly it contained the homes of the royalty, assuming that there had been a royalty. At any rate the conspicuous structure Jackson had selected was certainly the home of the most important member of that colony.

When the three, once more in their helmets and suits, stood before the low, broad portico which protected the entrance to that edifice, the first thing they made out was an ornamental frieze running across the face. In the same bold, realistic style as the other sculpture, there was depicted a hand-to-hand battle between two groups of those half savage, half cultured monstrosities. And in the background was shown a glowing orb, obviously the sun.

"See that?" exclaimed the doctor. "The size of that sun, I mean! Compare it with the way old Sol looks now!"

They took a single glance at the great ball of fire over their heads; nine times the size it always seemed at home, it contrasted sharply with the rather small ball shown in the carvings.

"Understand?" the doctor went on. "When that sculpture was made, Mercury was little nearer the sun than the earth is now!"

The builder was hugely impressed. He asked, eagerly: "Then probably the people became as highly developed as we?"

Van Emmon nodded approvingly, but the doctor was opposed. "No; I think not, Jackson. Mercury never did have as much air as the earth, and consequently had much less oxygen. And the struggle for existence," he went on, watching to see if the geologist approved each point as he made it, "the struggle for life is, in the last analysis, a struggle for oxygen.

"So I would say that life was a pretty strenuous proposition here, while it lasted. Perhaps they were—" He stopped, then added: "What I can't understand is, how did it happen that their affairs came to such an abrupt end? And why don't we see any—er—indications?"

"Skeletons?" The architect shuddered. Next second, though, his face lit up with a thought. "I remember reading that electricity will decompose bone in time." And then he shuddered again as his foot stirred that lifeless, impalpable dust.

As they passed into the great house the first thing they noted was the floor, undivided, dust-covered, and bare, except for what had perhaps been rugs. The shape was the inevitable equilateral triangle. And, here, with a certain magnificent disregard for precedent, the builders had done away with a ceiling entirely, and instead had sloped the three walls up till they met in a single point, a hundred feet overhead.

In one corner a section of the floor was elevated perhaps three feet above the rest, and directly back of this was a broad doorway, set in a short wall. The three advanced at once toward it.

Here the electric torch came in very handy. It disclosed a poorly lighted stairway, very broad, unrailed, and preposterously steep. The steps were each over three feet high.

"Difference in gravitation," said the doctor, in response to Jackson's questioning look. "Easy enough for the old-timers, perhaps." They struggled up the flight as best they could, reaching the top after over five minutes of climbing.

Perhaps it was the reaction from this exertion; at all events each felt a distinct loss of confidence as, after regaining their wind, they began to explore. Neither said anything about it to the others; but each noted a queer sense of foreboding, far more disquieting than either of them had felt when investigating anything else. It may have been due to the fact that, in their hurry, they had not stopped to eat.

The floor they were on was fairly well lighted with the usual oval windows. The space was open, except that it contained the same kind of dividing walls they had found in the library. Here, however, each compartment contained but one opening, and that not uniformly placed. In fact, as the three noted with a growing uneasiness, it was necessary to pass through every one of them in order to reach the corner farthest from the ladderlike stairs. Why it should make them uneasy, neither could have said.

WHEN they were almost through the labyrinth, Van Emmon, after standing on tiptoes for the tenth time, in order to locate himself, noted something that had escaped their attention before. "These compartments used to be covered over," he said, for some reason lowering his voice. He pointed out niches in the walls, such as undoubtedly once held the ends of heavy timbers. "What was this place, anyhow? A trap?"

Unconsciously they lightened their steps as they neared the last compartment. They found, as expected, that it was another stairway. Van Emmon turned the light upon every corner of the place before going any further; but except for a formless heap of rubbish in one corner, it was bare as the rest of the floor.

Again they climbed, this time for a much shorter distance; but Jackson, slightly built chap that he was, needed a little help on the steep stairs. They were not sorry that they had reached the uppermost floor of the mansion. It was somewhat better lighted than the floor below, and they were relieved to find that the triangular compartments did not have the significant niches in their walls. Their spirits rose perceptibly.

At the corner farthest from the stairs one of the walls rose straight to the ceiling, completely cutting off a rather large triangle. The three paid no attention to the other compartments, but went straight to what they felt sure was the most vital spot in the place. And their feelings were justified with a vengeance when they saw that the usual doorway in this wall was protected by something that had, so far, been entirely missing everywhere else.

It was barred by a heavy door.

For several moments the doctor, the geologist, and the architect stood before it. Neither would have liked to admit that he would just as soon leave that door unopened. All the former uneasiness came back. It was all the more inexplicable, with the brilliant sunlight only a few feet away, that each should have felt chilled by the place.

"Wonder if it's locked?" remarked Van Emmon. He pressed against the dust-covered barrier, half expecting it to turn to dust; but evidently it had been made of the time-defying alloy. It stood firm. And it seemed nearly airtight.

"Well!" said the doctor suddenly, so that the other two started nervously. "The door's got to come down; that's all!" They looked around; there was no furniture, no loose piece of material of any kind. Van Emmon straightway backed away from the door about six feet, and the others followed his example.

"All together!" grunted the geologist; and the three aluminum-armored monsters charged the door. It shook under the impact; a shower of dust fell down; and they saw that they had loosened the thing.

"Once more!" This time a wide crack showed all around the edge of the door, and the third attempt finished the job. Noiselessly—for there was no air to carry the sound—but with a heavy jar which all three felt through their feet, the barrier went flat on the floor beyond.

At that same instant a curious, invisible wave, like a tiny puff of wind, floated out of the darkness and passed by the three men from the earth. Each noticed it, but no one mentioned it at the time. Van Emmon was already searching the darkness with the torch.

Apparently it was only an anteroom. A few feet beyond was another wall, and in it stood another door, larger and heavier than the first. The three did not stop; they immediately tried their strength on this one also.

After a half dozen attempts without so much as shaking the massive affair—"It's no use," panted the geologist, wishing that he could get a handkerchief to his forehead. "We can't loosen it without tools."

Jackson was for trying again, but the doctor agreed with Van Emmon. They reflected that they had been away from Smith long enough, anyhow. The cube was out of sight from where they were.

Van Emmon turned the light on the walls of the anteroom, and found, on a shelf at one end, a neat pile of those little reels, eleven in all. He pocketed the lot. There was nothing else.

Jackson and Kinney started to go.

"Look here," Van Emmon said in a low, strained voice. They went to his side, and instinctively glanced behind them before looking at what lay in the dust.

It was the imprint of an enormous human foot!

THE first thing that greeted the ears of the explorers upon taking off their suits in the sky-car, was the exultant voice of Smith. He was too excited to notice anything out of the way in their manner. He was almost dancing in front of his bench, where the unknown machine, now reconstructed, stood belted to a small electric motor.

"It runs!" he was shouting. "You got here just in time!" He began to fumble with a switch.

"What of it?" remarked the doctor in the bland tone which he kept for occasions when Smith needed calming. "What will it do if it does run?"

The engineer looked blank. "Why—" Then he remembered, and picked up one of the reels at random. "There's a clamp here just the right size to hold one of these," he explained, fitting the ribbon into place and threading its free end into a loop on a spool which looked as though made for it. But his excitement had passed; he now cautiously set a small anvil between himself and the apparatus. And then, with the aid of a long stick, he threw on the current.

For a moment nothing happened, save the hum of the motor. Then a strange, leafy rustling sounded from the mechanism. Next, without any warning, a high-pitched voice, nasal and plaintive but distinctly human, spoke from the big metal disk.

The words were unintelligible. The language was totally unlike anything ever heard on the earth. And yet, deliberately if somewhat cringingly, the voice proceeded with what was apparently a recitation.

As the thing went on the four men came closer and watched the operation of the machine. The ribbon unrolled slowly; it was plain that, if the one topic occupied the whole reel, then it must have the length of an ordinary book chapter. And as the voice continued, certain dramatic qualities came out and governed the words, utterly incomprehensible though they were. There was a real thrill to it.

After a while they stopped the thing. "No use listening to this now," as the doctor said. "We've got to learn a good deal more about these people before we can guess what it all means."

And yet, although all were hungry, on Jackson's suggestion they tried out one of the "records" that was brought from that baffling room. Smith was very much interested in that unopened door, and he and Van Emmon were in the midst of discussing it when Jackson started the motor.

The geologist's words stuck in his throat. The disk was actually shaking with the vibrations of a most terrific voice. Prodigiously loud and powerful, its booming, resonant bass smote the ears like the roll of thunder. It was irresistible in its force, compelling in its assurance, masterful and strong to an overpowering degree. Involuntarily the men from the earth stepped back.

On it roared and rumbled, speaking the same language as that of the other record; but whereas the first speaker merely used the words, the last speaker demolished them. One felt that he had extracted every ounce of power in the language, leaving it weak and flabby, unfit for further use. He threw out his sentences as though done with them. Not boldly, not defiantly, least of all, tentatively. He spoke with a certainty and force that came from a knowledge that he could compel, rather than induce his hearers to believe.

It took a little nerve to shut him off; Van Emmon was the one who did it. Somehow they all felt immensely relieved when the gigantic voice was silenced; and at once began discussing the thing with great earnestness. Jackson was for assuming that the first record was worn and old, the last one, fresh and new; but after examining both tapes under a glass, and seeing how equally clear cut and sharp the impressions all were, they agreed that the extraordinary voice they had heard was practically true to life.

They tried out the rest of the records in that batch, finding that they were all by the same speaker. Nowhere among the ribbons brought from the library was another of his making, although a great number of different voices was included. Neither was there another talker with the volume, the resonance, the absolute power of conviction of this unknown colossus.

This is not place to describe the laborious process of interpreting these documents, records of a past which was gone before earth's mankind had even begun. The work involved the study of countless photos, covering everything from inscriptions to parts of machinery, and other details which furnished clue after clue to that superancient language. It was not deciphered, in fact, until several years after the explorers had submitted their find to the world's foremost lexicographers, antiquarians and paleontologists. Even today some of it is disputed.

But right here is, most emphatically, the place to insert the tale told by that unparalleled voice. And incredible though it may seem, as judged by the standards of the peoples of this earth, the account is fairly proved by the facts uncovered by the expedition. It would be only begging the question to doubt the genuineness of the thing. And if, understanding the language, one were to hear the original as it fell, word for word from the iron mouth of Strokor the Great (in the Mercurian language, *strok* means iron, or heart)—hearing that, one would believe; none could doubt, nor would.

And so it does not do him justice to set it down in ordinary print. One must imagine the story being related by Strokor himself; must conceive of each word falling like the blow of a mammoth sledge. The tale was not told—it was bellowed; and this is how it ran:

Part II
The Story

CHAPTER I

THE MAN

I AM Strokor, son of Strok, the armorer. I am Strokor, a maker of tools of war; Strokor, the mightiest man in the world; Strokor, whose wisdom outwitted the hordes of Klow; Strokor, who has never feared, and never failed. Let him who dares, dispute it. I—I am Strokor!

In my youth I was, as now, the marvel of all who saw. I was ever robust and daring, and naught but much older, bigger lads could outdo me. I balked at nothing, be it a game or a battle; it was, and forever shall be, my chief delight to best all others.

'Twas from my mother that I gained my huge frame and sound heart. In truth, I am very like her, now that I think upon it. She, too, was indomitable in battle, and famed for her liking for strife. No doubt 'twas her stalwart figure that caught my father's fancy.

Aye, my mother was a very likely woman, but she boasted no brains. "I need no cunning," I remember she said. She was a grand woman, slow to anger and a match for many a good pair of men. Often, as a lad, have I carried the marks of her punishment for the most of a year.

And thus it seems that I owe my head to my father. He was a marvelously clever man, dexterous with hand and brain alike. Moreover, he was no weakling. Perchance I should credit him with some of my agility, for he was famed as a gymnast, though not a powerful one. 'Twas he who taught me how to disable my enemy with a mere clutch of the neck at a certain spot.

But Strok, the armorer, was feared most because of his brain, and his knack of using his mind to the undoing of others. And he taught me all that he knew; taught me all that he had learned in a lifetime of fighting for the emperor. Of mending the complicated machines in the armory, of contact with the chemists who wrought the secret alloy, and the chiefs who led the army.

When I became a man he abruptly ended his teaching. I think he saw that I was become as dexterous as he with the tools of the craft, and he feared lest I know more than he. Well he might; the day I realized this I laughed long and loud. And from that time forth he taught me, not because he chose to, but because I bent a chisel in my bare hands, before his eyes, and told him his place.

Many times he strove to trick me, and more than once he all but caught me in some trap. He was a crafty man, and relied not upon brawn, but upon wits. Yet I was ever on the watch, and I but learned the more from him.

"Ye are very kind," I mocked him one morning. When I had taken my seat a huge weight had dropped from above and crushed my stool to splinters, much as it would have crushed my skull had I not leaped instantly aside. "Ye are kinder than most fathers, who teach their sons nothing at all."

He foamed at his mouth in his rage and discomfiture. "Insolent whelp!" he snarled. "Thou art quick as a cat on thy feet!"

But I was not to be appeased by words. I smote him on the chest with my bare hand, so that he fell on the far side of the room.

The time came when I saw that my father was reconciled to his master. I saw that he genuinely admitted my prowess; and where he formerly envied me, he now took great pride in all I accomplished, and claimed that it was but his own brains acting through my body.

I must admit, too, that I owe a great deal to that gray-beard, Maka, the star-gazer.

I MET Maka on the very morn that I first laid eyes on the girl, Ave.

I was returning from the northland at the time. A rumor had come down to Vlama that one of the people in the snow country had seen a lone specimen of the mulikka. Now these were but a myth. No man living remembers when the carvings on the House of Learning were made, and all the wise men say that it hath been ages since any being other than man roamed the world. Yet, I was young. I determined to search for the thing anyhow; and 'twas only after wasting many days in the snow that I cursed my luck, and turned back.

I was afoot, for the going was too rough for my chariot. I had not yet quit the wilderness before, from a height, I spied a group of people ascending from the valley. Knowing not whether they be friends or foes, I hid beside the path up which they must come; for I was weary and wanting no strife.

Yet I became alert enough when the three—they were two ditch-tenders, one old, one young, and a girl—came within earshot. For they were quarreling. It seemed that the young man, who was plainly eager to gain the girl, had fouled in a try to force her favor. The older man chided him hotly.

And just when they came opposite my rock, the younger man, whose passion had got the better of him, suddenly tripped the older, so that he fell upon the ledge and would have fallen to his death on the rocks below had not the girl, crying out in her terror, leaped forward and caught his hand.

At once the ditch-tender took the lass about the waist, and strove to pull her away. For a moment she held fast, and in that moment I, Strokor, stood forth from behind the rock.

Now, be it known that I am no champion of weaklings. I was but angered that the ditch-tender should have done the trick so clumsily, and upon an old man, at that. I cared not for the gray beard, nor what became of the chit. I clapped the trickster upon the shoulder and spun him about.

"Ye clumsy coward!" I jeered. "Have ye had no practice that ye should trip the old one no better than that?"

"Who are ye?" he stuttered, like the coward he was. I laughed and helped the chit drag Maka—for it was he—up to safety.

"I am a far better man than ye," I said, not caring to give my name. "And I can show ye how the thing should be done. Come; at me, if ye are a man!"

At that he dashed upon me; and such was his fear of ridicule—for the girl was laughing him to scorn now—he put up a fair, stiff fight. But I forgot my weariness when he foully clotted me on the head with a stone. I drove at him with all the speed and suddenness my father had taught me, caught the fellow by the ankle, and brought him down atop me.

The rest was easy. I bent my knee under his middle, and tossed him high. In a flash I was upon my feet, and caught him from behind. And in another second I had rushed him to the cliff, and when he turned to save himself, I tripped him as neatly as father himself could have done it. So that the fellow will guard the ditch no more, save in the caverns of Hofe.

I laughed and picked up my pack. My head hurt a bit from the fellow's blow, but a little water would do for that. I started to go.

"Ye are a brave man!" cried the girl. I turned carelessly, and then, quite for the first time, I had a real look at her.

She was in no way like any woman I had seen. All of them had been much like the men; brawny and close-knit, as well fitted for their work as are men for war. But this chit was all but slender; not skinny, but prettily rounded out, and soft like. I cannot say that I admired her at first glance; she seemed fit only to look at, not to live. I was minded of some of the ancient carvings, which show delicate, lightly built animals that have long since been killed off; graceful trifles that rested the eye.

As for the old man: "Aye, thou art brave, and wondrous strong, my lad," said he, still a bit shaky from his close call. I was pleased with the acknowledgment, and turned back.

"It was nothing," I told them; and I recounted some of my exploits, notably one in which I routed a raiding party of men from Klow, six in all, carrying in two alive on my shoulders. "I am the son of Strok, the armorer."

"Ye are Strokor!" marveled the girl, staring at me as though I were a god. Then she threw back her head and stepped close.

"I am Ave. This is Maka; he is my uncle, but best known as a star-gazer. My father was Durok, the engine-maker."

"Durok?" I knew him well. My father had said that he was quite as brainy as himself. "He was a fine man, Ave."

"Aye," said she proudly. She stepped closer; I could not but see how like him she was, though a woman. And next second she laid a hand on my arm.

"I am yet a free woman, Strokor. Hast thou picked thy mate?" And her cheeks flamed.

Now, 'twas not my first experience of the kind. Many women had looked like that at me before. But I had always been a man's man, and had ever heeded my father's warning to have naught whatever to do with women. "They are the worst trick of all," he told me; and I had never forgot. Belike I owe much of my power to just this.

But Ave had acted too quickly for me to get away. I laughed again, and shook her off.

"I will have naught to do with ye," I told her, civilly enough. "When I am ready to take a woman, I shall take her; not before."

At that the blood left her face; she stood very straight, and her eyes flashed dangerously. Were she a man I should have stood on my guard. But she made no move; only the softness in her eyes gave way to such a savage look that I was filled with amaze.

And thus I left them; the old man calling down the blessing of Jon upon me for having saved his life, and the chit glaring after me as though no curses would suffice.

A right queer matter, I thought at the time. I guessed not what would come of it; not then.

CHAPTER II

THE VISION

'TWAS a fortnight later, more or less, when next I saw Maka. I was lumbering along in my chariot, feeling most uncomfortable under the eyes of my friends; for one foot of my machine had a loose link, and 'twas flapping absurdly. And I liked it none too well when Maka stopped his own rattletrap in front of mine, and came running to my window. Next moment I forgot his impertinence.

"Strokor," he whispered, his face alive with excitement, "thou art a brave lad, and didst save my life. Now, know you that a party of the men of Klow have secreted themselves under the stairway behind the emperor's throne. They have killed the guards, and will of a certainty kill the emperor, too!"

" 'Twould serve the dolt right," I replied, for I really cared but little. "But why have ye come to me, old man? I am but a lieutenant in the armory; I am not the captain of the palace guard."

"Because," he answered, gazing at me very pleasingly, "thou couldest dispose of the whole party single handed—there are but four—and gain much glory for thyself."

"By Jon!" I swore, vastly delighted; and without stopping to ask Maka whence he had got his knowledge, I went at once to the spot. However, when I got back, I sought the star-gazer. I ought to mention that I had no trouble with the louts, and that the emperor himself saw me finishing of the last of them. I sought the star-gazer and demanded how he had known.

"Hast ever heard of Edam?" he inquired in return.

"Edam?" I had not; the name was strange to me. "Who is he?"

"A man as young as thyself, but a mere stripling," quoth Maka. "He was a pupil of mine when I taught in the House of Learning. Of late he has turned to prophecy; and it is fair remarkable how well the lad doth guess. At all events, 'twas he, Strokor, who told me of the plot. He saw it in a dream."

"Then Edam must yet be in Vlama," said I, "if he were able to tell ye. Canst bring him to me? I would know him."

And so it came about that, on the eve of that same day, Maka brought Edam to my house. I remember it well; for 'twas the same day that the emperor, in gratitude of my little service in the anteroom, had relieved me from my post in the armory and made me captain of the palace guard. I was thus become the youngest captain, also the biggest and strongest; and, as will soon appear, by far the longest-headed.

I was in high good humor, and had decided to celebrate with a feast. So when my two callers arrived, I sat them down before a magnificent meal.

Edam was a slightly built lad, not at all the sturdy man that I am, but of less than half the weight. His head, too, was unlike mine. His forehead was wide as well as tall, and his eyes were mild as a slave's.

"Ye are very young to be a prophet," I said to him, after we were filled, and the slaves had cleared away our litter. "Tell me, hast foretold anything else that has come to pass?"

"Aye," he replied, not at all boldly, but what some call modestly. "I prophesied the armistice which now stands between our empire and Klow's."

"Is this true?" I demanded of Maka. The old man bowed his head gravely and looked upon the young man with far more respect than I felt. He added:

"Tell Strokor the dream thou hadst two nights ago, Edam. It were a right strange thing, whether true or not."

The stripling shifted his weight on his stool, and moved the bowl closer. Then he thrust his pipe deep into it, and let the liquid flow slowly out his nostrils. (A curious custom among the Mercurians, who had no tobacco. There is no other way to explain some of the carvings. Doubtless the liquid was sweet-smelling, and perhaps slightly narcotic.)

"I saw this," he began, "immediately before rising, and after a very light supper; so I know that it was a vision from Jon, and not of my own making.

"I was standing upon the summit of a mountain, and gazing down upon a very large, fertile valley. It was heavily wooded, dark green and inviting. But what first drew my attention was a great number of animals moving about in the air. They were passing strange affairs, some large, some small, variously colored, and they were all covered with the same sort of fur, quite unlike any hair I have ever seen."

"In the air?" I echoed, recovering from my astonishment. Then I laughed mightily. "Man, ye must be crazy! There is no animal can live in the air! Ye must mean in the water or on land."

"Nay," interposed the star-gazer. "Thou hast never studied the stars, Strokor, or thou wouldst know that there be a number of them which, through the enlarging tube, show themselves to be round worlds, like unto our own.

"And it doth further appear that these other worlds also have air like this we breathe, and that some have less, while others have even more. From what Edam has told me," finished the old man, "I judge that his vision took place on Jeos (the Mercurian word for earth), a world much larger than ours, according to my calculations, and doubtless having enough air to permit very light creatures to move about in it."

"Go on," said I to Edam, good humoredly. "I be ever willing to believe anything strange when my stomach is full."

THE dreamer had taken no offense. He went on, "Then I bent my gaze closer as I am always able, in visions. And I saw the greenery was most remarkably dense, tangled and luxuriant to a degree not ever seen here. And moving about in it was the most extraordinary collection of beings that I have ever laid these eyes upon.

"There were some huge creatures, quite as tall as thy house, Strokor, with legs as big around as that huge chest of thine. They had tails, as had our ancient mulikka, save that these were terrific things, as long and as big as the trunk of a large tree. I know not their names. (Probably the dinosaur.)

"But nowhere was there a sign of a man. True, there was one hairy, grotesque creature which hung by its hands and feet from the tree-tops, very like thee in some way, Strokor. But its face and head were those of a brainless beast, not of a man. Nowhere was there a creature like me or thee.

"And the most curious thing was this: Although there were ten times as many of these creatures, big and little, to the same space as on our world, yet there was no great amount of strife. In truth, there is far more combat and destruction among we men than among the beasts.

"And," he spoke almost earnestly, as though he would not care to be disbelieved, "I saw fathers fight to protect their young!"

I near fell from my stool in my amaze. Never in all my life had I heard a thing so far from the fact. "What!" I shouted. "Ye sit there like a sane man, and tell me ye saw fathers fight for their young?"

He nodded his head, still very gravely.

"Faugh!" I spat upon the ground. "Such softness makes me ill! I'll be glad I were born in a man's world, where I can take a man's chances. I want no favoring. If I am strong enough to live, I live; if not, I die. What more can I ask?"

"Aye, my lad!" said Maka approvingly. "This be a world for the strong. There is no room here for others; there is scarce enough food for those who, thanks to their strength, do survive." He slipped the gold band from off his wrist, and held it up for Jon to see. "Here, Strokor, a pledge! A pledge to—the survival of the fittest!"

"A neat, neat wording!" I roared, as I took the pledge with him. Then we both stopped short. Edam had not joined us.

"Edam, my lad," spake the old man, "ye will take the pledge with us?"

"I have no quarrel with either of ye." Edam got to his feet, and started to the door. "But I cannot take the pledge with ye.

"I have seen a wondrous thing, and I love it. And, though I know not why, I feel that Jon has willed it for Jeos to see a new race of men, a race even better than ours."

I leaped to my feet. "Better than ours! Mean ye to say, stripling, that there can be a better man than Strokor?"

I fully expected him to shrink from me in fear; I was able to crush him with one blow. But he stood his ground; nay, stepped forward and laid a hand easily upon my shoulder.

"Strokor—ye are more than a man; ye are two men in one. There is no finer— I say it fair. And yet, I doubt not that there can be, and will be, a better!"

And with that such a curious expression came into his face, such a glow of some strange kind of warmth, that I let my hand drop and suffered him to depart in peace. Such was my wonder.

Besides, any miserable lout could have destroyed the lad.

Maka sat deep in thought for a time, and when he did speak he made no mention of the lad who had just quit us. Instead, he looked me over, long and earnestly, and at the end he shook his head sorrowfully and sighed:

"Thou art the sort of a son I would have had, Strokor, given the wits of thy father to hold a woman like thy mother. And thou didst save my life."

He mused a little longer, then roused himself and spake sharply:

"Strokor, thou hast everything needful to tickle thy vanity. Thou hast the envy of those who note thy strength, the praise of them who love thy courage, and the respect of they who value thy brains. All these thou hast, and yet ye have not that which is best!"

I thought swiftly and turned on him with a frown: "Mean ye that I am not handsome enough?"

"Nay, Strokor," quoth the star-gazer. "There be none handsomer in this world, no matter what the standard on any other, such as Edam's Jeos.

"It is not that. It is, that thou hast no ambition."

I considered this deeply. At first

thought it was not true; had I not always made it a point to best my opponent? From my youth it had been ever my custom to succeed where bigger bodies and older minds had failed. Was not this ambition?

But before I disputed the point with Maka, I saw what he meant. I had no final ambition, no ultimate goal for which to strive. I had been content from year to year to outdo each rival as he came before me. And now, with mind and body alike in the pink of condition, I was come to the place where none durst stand before me.

"Ye are right, Maka," I admitted. Not because I cared to gratify his conceit, but because it were always for my own good to own up when wrong, that I might learn the better. "Ye are right; I need to decide upon a life-purpose. What have ye thought?"

The old man was greatly pleased. "Our talk with Edam brought it all before me. Know you, Strokor, that the survival of the fittest is a rule which governs man as well as men. It applies to the entire population, Strokor, just as truly as to me or thee.

"In fine, we men who are now the sole inhabitants of this world, are descended from a race of people who survived solely because they were fitter than the mulikka, fitter than the reptiles, the fittest, by far, of all the creatures.

"That being the case, it is plain that in time either our empire, or that of Klow's, must triumph over the other. And that which remains shall be the fittest!"

"Hold!" I cried. "Why cannot matters remain just as they now are?"

"That," he said rapidly, "is because thou knowest so little about the future of this world. It is now known that the sun is a very powerful magnet, and that he is constantly pulling upon our world and bringing it nearer and nearer to himself. That is why it hath become slightly warmer during the past hundred years; the records show it plain. And the same influence has caused the lengthening of our day."

He stopped and let me think. Soon I saw it clearly enough; a time must come when the increasing warmth of the sun would stifle all forms of vegetable life, and that would mean the choking of mankind. It might take untold centuries. Yet, plainly enough, the world must some day become too small for even those who now remained upon it.

Suddenly I leaped to my feet and strode the room in my excitement. "Ye are right, Maka!" I shouted, thoroughly aroused. "There cannot always be the two empires. In time one or the other must prevail; Jon has willed it. And"—I stopped short and stared at him—"I need not tell ye which it shall be!"

"I knew thou wouldst see the light, Strokor! Thou hast thy father's brains."

I sat me down, but instantly leaped up again, such was my enthusiasm. "Maka," I cried, "our emperor is not the man for the place! It is true that he was a brave warrior in his youth; he won the throne fairly. And we have suffered him to keep it because he is a wise man, and because we have had little trouble with the men of Klow since their defeat two generations gone.

"But he, today, is content to sit at his ease and quote platitudes about 'live and let live.' Faugh! I am ashamed that I should even have given ear to him!"

I stopped short and glared at the old man. "Maka, hark ye well! If it be the will of Jon to decide between Klow and the men of Vlamaland, then it is my intent to hasten this decision!"

"Aye, my lad," he said tranquilly. And then he added, quite as though he knew what my answer must be: "How do ye intend to go about it?"

"Like a man! I, Strokor, shall become the emperor!"

CHAPTER III

THE THRONE

A SMALL storm had come up while Maka and I were talking. Now, as he was about to quit me, the clouds were clearing away and an occasional stroke of lightning came down. One of these, however, hit the ground such a short distance away that both of us could smell the smoke.

My mind was more alive than it had ever been before. "Now, what caused that, Maka? The lightning, I mean; we have it nearly every day, yet I have never thought to question it before."

"It is no mystery, my lad," quoth Maka, dodging into his chariot, so that he was not wet. "I myself have watched the thing from the top of high mountains, where the air is so light that a man can scarce get enough to fill his lungs. And I say unto you that, were it not for what air we have, we should have naught save the lightning. The space about the air is full of it."

He started his engine, then leaned out into the rain and said softly: "Hold fast to what thy father has taught thee, Strokor. Have nothing to do with the women. 'Tis a man's job ahead of thee, and the future of the empire is in thy hands.

"And," as he clattered off, "fill not thy head with wonderings about the lightning."

I slept not at all that night, but sat till the dawn came, thinking out a plan of action. By that time I was fairly convinced that there was naught to be gained by waiting; waiting makes me impatient as well. I determined to act at once; and since one day is quite as good as the next, I decided that this day was to see the thing begun.

I came before the emperor at noon and received my decorations. Within the hour I had made myself known to the four and ninety men who were to be my command. A picked company, all of a height and weight, with bodies that lacked little of my own perfection. Never was there a finer guard about the palace.

My first care was to pick a quarrel with the outgoing commander. 'Twas easy enough; he was green with envy, anyhow. And so it came about that we met about mid afternoon, with seconds, in a well-frequented field in the outskirts.

Before supper was eaten my entire troop knew that their new captain had tossed his ball-slinger away without using it, had taken twenty balls from their former commander's weapon, and while thus wounded had charged the man and despatched him with bare hands! Needless to say, this exploit quite won their hearts. None but a blind man could have missed the respect they showed me when, all bandaged and sore, I lined them up next morning. Afterward I learned that they had all taken a pledge to "follow Strokor through the gates of Hofe itself!"

'Twas but a week later that, fully recovered and in perfect fettle, I called my men together one morn as the sun rose. By that time I had given them a sample of my brains through ordering a rearrangement of their quarters such as made the same much more comfortable. Also, I had dealt with one slight infraction of the rules in such a drastic fashion that they knew I would brook no trifling. All told, 'tis hard to say whether they thought the most of me or of Jon.

"Men," said I, as bluntly as I knew, "the emperor is an old man. And, as ye know, he is disposed to be lenient toward the men of Klow; whereas, ye and I well know that the louts are blackguards.

"Now I will tell ye more. It has come to me lately that Klow is plotting to attack us with strange weapons. Of course I have told the emperor of it; yet he will not act. He says to wait till we are attacked."

I stopped and watched their faces. Sure enough; the idea made them ache. Each of these men was spoiling for a fight.

"Now, tell me; how would ye like to become the emperor's bodyguard?" I did not have to wait long; the light that flared in their faces told me plainly. "And —how would ye like to have me for your emperor?"

At that their tongues were loosed, and I hindered them not. They yelled for pure joy, and pressed about me like a pack of children. I saw that the time was ripe for action.

"Up, then!" I roared, and led the way. We met the emperor's guard on the lower stairs; and from that point on we fairly hacked our way through.

Well, no need to describe that fight. For a time I thought we were gone; the guards had a cunningly devised labyrinth on the second floor, and attacked us from holes in a false ceiling, so that we suffered heavily at first.

But I saw what was amiss, and shouted to my men to clear away the timbers; and after that it was clear work. I lost forty men before the guard was disposed of. The emperor I finished myself; he dodged right spryly for a time, but at last I caught him and tossed him to the foot of the upper stairs. And there he still lies, for none of my men would touch him, nor would I. We covered him with quick-lime and some earth.

Then we all feasted on the emperor's store, and soon were feeling like ourselves.

"Men," I said impressively, "I am proud of ye. Never did an emperor have such a dangerous gang of bullies!"

At that they all grinned happily, and I added: "And 'tis a fine staff of generals that ye'll make!"

Need I say more? Those men would have overturned the palace for me had I said the word. As it was, they obeyed my next orders in such a spirit that success was assured from the first.

First, using the dead emperor's name, I caused the various chiefs to be brought together at once to the court chamber. At the same time I contrived to prevent any word of our action from getting abroad. So, when the former staff faced me the next morning, they learned that they were to be executed. I could trust not one; they were all friends of the old man.

With the chiefs out of the way, and my own men taking their commands, the whole army fell into my hands. True, there were some insurrections here and there; but my men handled them with such speed and harshness that any further stubbornness turned to admiration. By this time the fame of Strokor was spread throughout the empire.

And thus it came about that, within a week of the night that old Maka first put the idea into my head, Strokor, son of Strok, reigned throughout Vlamaland. And to make it complete, the army celebrated my accession by taking a pledge before Jon:

"To Strokor, the fittest of the fit!"

CHAPTER IV

THE ASSAULT

NOW, out of a total population of perhaps three million, I had about a quarter-million first-class fighters in my half of the world. Klow, by comparison, had but two-thirds the number; his land was not a rich one.

Shortly my spies reported that his armories were devising a new type of weapon. 'Twas a strange verification of my own fiction to my men. I could learn nothing, however, about it.

Meanwhile, I caused a vast number of flat-boats to be built, all in secret. Each of them was intended for a single fighter and his supplies. And each was so arranged, with side paddle wheels, that it could be driven by the motor in the soldier's chariot, and thus give each his own boat.

Discarding all precedent, I packed not all my forces together, as had been done in the past, but scattered them up and down the coast fronting the land of Klow. At a prearranged time my quarter-million men set out, a company in each tiny fleet. Just as I had planned, we all arrived at a certain spot on Klow's coast at practically the same hour.

'Twas a brilliant stroke. The enemy looked not for a fleet of water-ants, ready to step right out of the sea into battle. Their fleet was looking for us, true, but not in that shape. And we were all safely ashore before they had ceased to scour the seas for us.

I immediately placed my heavy machines, and just as all former expeditions had done, opened the assault at once with a shower of the poison shells. I relied, it will be seen, upon the surprise of my attack to strike terror into the hearts of the louts.

But apparently they were prepared for anything, no matter how rapid the attack. My bombardment had not proceeded many moments before, to my dismay, some of their own shells began to fall among us. Soon they were giving as good as we.

I had placed Maka in my cabinet as soon as I had reached the throne.

The old man stroked his beard gravely. "Perchance it had been wrong to come to the old landing. They simply began shelling it as a matter of course."

"Ye are right again," I told him; and forthwith moved my pieces over into another triangle. Previously, of course, all my charioteers had gone on toward the capital. However, I took care to move my machines, one at a time, so that there was no let-up in my bombardment.

But scarce had we taken up the new position before the enemy's shells likewise shifted, and began to strike once more in our midst. I swore a great oath and whirled upon Maka in wrath.

"Can ye explain this thing? My men have combed the land about us. There are none of the scouts secreted here. And, even so, they could not have notified Klow so soon. Besides, 'tis pitch dark." I was sorely mystified.

All we could do was to fling our shells as fast as our machines would work and dodge the enemy's hail as best we could. Thus the time passed, and it was near dawn when the first messengers returned.

"They have stopped us just outside the walls of the city," was the report. It pleased me that they should have pushed so far at first; I climbed at once into my chariot.

"Now is the time for Strokor to strike!" I gave orders for the staff to remain where it was. "I will send ye word when the city is mine."

But before I started my engine I

glanced up at the sky, to see if the dawn were yet come; and as I gazed I thought I saw something come between me and a star. I brushed the hair away from my eyes, and looked again. To my boundless surprise I made out, not one, but three strange objects moving about swiftly in the air!

"Look!" I cried, and my whole staff craned their necks. In a moment all had seen, and great was their wonder.

'Twas Maka who spoke first. "They are much too large to be creatures of Jon," he muttered. "They must be some trick of the enemy.

"Dost recall Edam's vision of the creatures in the air of Jeos?" he went on, knowing that I would not hinder him. "Now, as I remember it, he said they flew with great speed. Were it not possible, Strokor, for suitable engines to propel very light structures at such high speed as to remain suspended in the air, after the manner of leaves in a storm? I note these strangers move quite fast."

It was even so; and at that same instant one of them swung directly above our heads, so close that I could hear the hum of a powerful engine. So it was only a trick! I shook myself together.

"Attention!" My staff drew up at the word. "They are but few; fear them not! We waste no more time here! Pack up the machines, and follow!"

And thus we charged upon Klow.

I found that my men had entirely surrounded the city. Klow's men were putting up a plucky fight, and showing no signs of fearing us. Seeing this, I blew a blast on my engine's whistle, so that my bullies might know that I had come.

Immediately the word ran up and down the line, so that within a few minutes Klow was facing a roaring crowd of half-mad terrors. I myself set the example by charging the nearest group of the enemy. They were mounted within the rather small and perfectly circular chariots which they preferred. They were quick and slippery, but they could not stand before a determined rush.

I ran them down, and toppled them over, and dropped suffocation bombs into their little cages with such vigor and disregard of their volleys that my men could not resist the example. We charged all along that vast circular line, and we cheered mightily when the whole front broke, turned tail, and ran before us.

BUT scarce had they got away before a queer thing happened. A flock of those great air-creatures, some eight altogether, rose up from the middle of the city. It was now fairly light, and we could see well. They came out to the battleline and began to circle the city.

As they did so they dropped odd, misshapen parcels, totally unlike materials of war; but when they struck they gave off prodigious puffs of a greenish smoke, of so terribly pungent a nature that my men dropped before it like apples from a shaken tree. 'Twas a fearful sight; lucky for us that the louts had had no practise, else few of us should be alive to tell the tale.

And so they swept around the great circle, many triangles in area; and everywhere the unthinkable things smote the hearts of my men with a fear they had never known. Only one of the devices suffered; it was brought down by a chance fling of a poison shell. The rest, after loosing their burdens, returned to the city for more.

I am no fool. I saw that we could do nothing against such weapons.

"Return!" I commanded, and instantly my staff whistled the code. The men obeyed with alacrity, making off at top speed with the men of Klow in hot pursuit, although able to do little damage.

Aye, it was a sorrowful thing, that retreat. I was mainly angry that Klow had not showed himself.

By the time I had reached the seashore, most of my men were in their boats. I stayed till the last, although I could see the enemy's fleet bearing down hard upon us from the north. In truth we would have all been lost, had we come in the manner of former campaigns, all together in big transports. But because we could scatter every which way, the fleet harmed us little; and four-fifths of us got safely back.

Happily, none of the air-machines had range enough to reach Vlamaland. As soon as I could get my staff together, I gave orders such as would insure discipline. Then, reminding my hearties that Klow, knowing our helplessness, would surely attack as soon as fully equipped, I made this offer:

"To the man who shall suggest the best way of meeting their attack, I shall give the third of my empire!"

So they knew that the case was desperate. As for myself, I slept not a bit, but paced my sleep-chamber and thought deeply.

Now, a bit of a shell, from an enemy slinger, had penetrated my arm. Till now, I had paid no attention to it. But it began to bother me, so I pulled the metal from my arm with my teeth. And quite by chance I placed the billet on the table within a few inches of the compass I had carried on my boat.

To my intense surprise the needle of the compass swung violently about, so that one end pointed directly at the fragment of metal. I moved them closer together; there was no doubt that they were strongly attracted. The enemy's shells were made of mere iron!

The moment I fully realized this, I saw clearly how we might baffle the men of Klow. I instantly summoned some men, gave the orders much as though I had known for years what was to be done, and in a few moments had the satisfaction of seeing my messengers hurrying north and south.

And so it came about that, within three days of our shameful retreat, a tenth of my men were at work on the new project. As yet there was no word from my spies across the sea; but we worked with all possible haste. And this, very briefly, is what we did:

We laid a gigantic line of iron clear across the empire. From north to south, from snow to snow; one end was bedded in the island of Pathna, where the north magnetic-pole is found, while the other stopped on the opposite side of the world, in a hole dug through the ice into the solid earth of the South Polar Plain. And every foot of that enormous rod—'twas as big around as my leg—was insulated from the ground with pieces of our secret non-magnetic alloy!

Not for nothing had our chemists sought the metal which would resist the lightning. And not for nothing did my bullies piece the rod together, all working at the same time, so that the whole thing was complete in seven days. That is, complete save for the final connecting link. And that lay, a loglike roll of iron, at the door of my palace, ready to be rolled into place whenever I was ready.

And on the morrow Klow reached our shores.

CHAPTER V

THE VICTORY

MY first intent was to let them advance unhampered; but Maka pointed out that such a policy might give them suspicions, and so we disputed their course all the way. I gave orders to show no great amount of resistance. Thus the louts reached Vlama in high feather, confident that the game was theirs.

I stood at the door of the palace as Klow himself rolled up to the edge of the parade-ground. My men, obeying orders, had given way to him; his crew swarmed the space behind and on all sides of him, while my own bullies were all about and behind the palace. Never did two such giant armies face one another in peace; for I had caused my banner to be floated wrong end to, in token of surrender.

First, a small body of subordinates waited upon me, demanding that I give up the throne. I answered that I would treat with none save Klow himself. And shortly the knave, surrounded by perhaps fifty underlings, stepped up before me.

"Hail, Strokor!" he growled, his voice shaking a bit with excitement; not with fear, for he were a brave man. "Hail to thee and to thine, and a pleasant stay in Hofe for ye all!"

"Hail, Klow!" replied I, glancing up meaningly at the air monsters wheeling there. "I take it that ye purpose to execute us."

"Aye," he growled savagely. "Thou didst attack without provocation. Thy life is forfeit, and as many more as may be found needful to guarantee peace."

"Then," I quoth, my manner changing, "then ye have saved me the trouble of deciding what shall be thy fate. Execution, say you? So be it!"

And I strode down to the great log of iron which lay ready to fill the gap. Klow looked at me with a peculiar expression, as though he thought me mad. True, it looked it; how could I do him harm without myself suffering?

But I kicked the props which held the iron, and gave it a start with my foot. The ends of the pole-to-pole rod lay concealed by brush, perchance fifty yards away. In ten seconds that last section had rolled completely between them; and only a fool would have missed seeing that, the last ten feet, the iron was fair jerked through the air.

As this happened we all heard a tremendous crackling, like that of near-by lightning, while enormous clouds of dust arose from the two concealed ends, which were now become connections. And at the same time a loud, steely click, just one and no more, sounded from the intruding host.

For a moment Klow was vastly puzzled. Then he snarled angrily: "What means this foolery, Strokor? Advance, and give us thy ax!"

For answer I turned me about, so as to face my men, and held up my hand in signal. Instantly the whistles sounded, and my hearties came bounding into the field.

"Treachery!" shouted Klow; and his officers ran here and there, shouting: "To arms! Charge and destroy! No quarter!"

But I paid little attention to the hubbub. I was gazing up at those infernal creatures of the air; and my heart sang within me as I saw them, circling erratically but very surely down to the earth. And as they came nearer, my satisfaction was entire; for their engines were silent!

At the same time consternation was reigning among our visitors. Not a man of all Klow's thousands was able to move his car or lift a weapon. Every slinger was jammed, as though frozen by invisible ice. All their balls and shells were stuck together, like the work of a transparent glue. Even their side arms were locked in their scabbards; and all their tugging could budge them not!

But none of my men were so handicapped. Each man's chariot was running as though nothing had happened. They thundered forward, discharging their balls and shells as freely as they had across the sea. Their charge was a murderous one. Not a man of Klow's was able to resist, save with what force he could put into his bare hands.

Klow saw all this from the middle of his group of officers. None were able to more than place his body 'twixt us and their chief. In a very few moments they saw that the unknown magic had made them as children in our hands. They were utterly lost; and Klow turned away from the sight with a black face. Again he faced me.

"What means this, ye huge bundle of lies? What mean ye by tricking us with yon badge of surrender, only to tie our hands with thy magic of Hofe? Is this the way to fight like a man?"

I had stood at ease in my door since rolling the iron. Now, I looked about me still more easily; my men were running down the louts who had jumped from their useless chariots and taken to their heels. 'Twas but a matter of time before the army of Klow would be no more, at that rate.

"Klow," I answered him mildly; "ye are right; this is not the way to fight like a man. Neither," I pointed out one of the fallen air-cars; "neither is that the way, flitting over our heads like shadows, and destroying us with filthy smoke! Shame on ye, Klow, for stooping to such! And upon thy own head be the blame for the trick I have played upon ye!"

"You attacked us without provocation," he muttered, sourly.

"Aye, and for a very good reason," I replied. "Yet I see thy view-point, and shalt give thee the benefit of the doubt." I turned to my whistlers and gave an order; so that presently the great slaughter had stopped. My men and Klow's alike struggled back to see what might be amiss.

I handed Klow an ax. "Throw away thine own, scabbard and all," I told him. "It is useless, for 'tis made of iron. Ours, and all our tools of war, are formed of an alloy which is immune from the magic."

He took the ax in wonderment. "What means it, Strokor?" asked he again, meanwhile stripping himself in a businesslike fashion that was good to see.

"It means," said I, throwing off my robe, "that I have unchained the magnetism of this world. Know you, Klow, that all of the children of the sun are full of his power. It is like unto that of the tiny magnet which ye give children for to play. But it is mighty, even as our world is mighty."

"Good Jon!" he gasped; for his was not a daring mind. "What have ye done, ye trifler?"

"I have transformed this empire into one vast magnet," I answered coolly. Then I showed him a boulder on the summit of a distant hill; through the tube, Klow could see some of my men standing beside it.

"Place one of thy own men on the roof of the palace," I told Klow, "and give him orders to lower my banner should ye give him the word.

"For upon the outcome of this fight 'twixt me and thee, Klow, hinges the whole affair! If thou dost survive, down comes my banner. Then my men on the hill shall topple the boulder, which shall rush down the slope and burst the iron rod and break the spell. Stand, then, and defend thyself!"

And it did me good to see the spirit fly into his eyes. He saw that his empire lived or died as he lived or died, and he fought as he had never fought before. Small man that he was, beside myself, he was wondrous quick and sure in his motions. Before I knew it, he had bit his ax deep into my side.

And in another moment or two it was over. For, as soon as I felt the pain of that gash, I flung my own blade away. With a roar such as would have shaken a stouter heart than his, I charged the man. I took a second fearful blow full on my chest, and heeding it not at all I snatched the ax from his hands. Then, as he turned to run, I dropped that tool also.

And I ran him down, and felled him, and broke his head with my hands.

(An unfortunate accident of Mr. Smith's, before he was thoroughly familiar with the machine, mutilated a large portion of the tape so badly that it was made worthless. This explains why something appears to be missing from the account, and why the next chapter begins in the middle of a sentence.)

CHAPTER VI

THE FITTEST

SLAVES; but the most were slain. Neither could we bother with their women and others left behind.

Now, by this time the empire was as one man in its worship of me. I had been emperor but a year, and already I had made it certain that only the men of Vlamaland, and no others, should live in the sight of Jon. So well thought they of me, I might fair have sat upon my reputation, and have spent my last days in feasting, like the man before me.

But I was still too young and full of energy to take my ease. I found myself more and more restless; I had naught to do now. At last I sent for old Maka

"Ye put me up to this, ye old fraud," I told him, pretending to be wrathful. "Now set me another task, or I'll have thy head!"

He knew me too well to be affrighted. He said that he had been considering my case of late.

"Strokor, thy father was right when he told thee to have naught to do with women. That is to say, he was right at the time. Were he alive today he would of a certainty say that it was high time for thee to pick thy mate.

"Remember, Strokor; great though thou art, yet when death taketh thee thy greatness is become but a memory. Methinks ye should leave something more substantial behind."

It took but little thought to convince me that Maka was right once more. As soon as I thought upon it, it was a woman that I was restless for.

"Jon bless thee!" I told the old man. "Ye have named both the trouble and the remedy. I will attend to it at once. The best in the world shall be mine, of course. But as for which one, hast any notion thyself?"

"Aye," he quoth. " 'Tis my own niece I have in mind. Perchance ye remember her; a pretty child, who was with me when thou didst save my life up there on the mountainside."

"But she is not a vigorous woman. Maka. Think you she is fit for me?"

"Aye, if any be," he replied, earnestly. "Ave is not robust, true, but her muscles are as wires. It is because of what lies in her head, however, that I commend her. I have taught her all I know."

"So!" I exclaimed, much pleased. "Then she is indeed fit to be the empress. And as I recall her, she was exceedingly good to look at."

"Say no more. Ave shall be the wife of Strokor!" And so it was arranged.

There ye have the story of Strokor, the mightiest man in the world, and the wisest. More than this I shall not tell with my own lips. I shall have singers recite my deeds until half the compartments in the House of Words is filled with the records thereof.

My ambition is fulfilled. Let the hand of Jon descend upon our world, if it may. I care not if the sun comes nearer, and the water dry up, and the days grow longer and longer, till the day and the year become of the same length. I care not; my people, such as be left of them, shall own what there is, and shall live as long as life is possible.

I shall leave behind no race of weaklings. Every man shall be fit to live, and the fittest of them all shall live the longer. And he, no matter how many cycles hence, shall look back to Strokor, and to Ave, his wife, and shall say:

"I am what I am, the last man on the world, because Strokor was the fittest man of his time!"

Aye; my fame shall live as long as there be life. Tonight, as I speak these things into the word machine, my heart is singing with the joy of it all. Thank Jon, I was born a man, not a woman!

Tomorrow I go to fetch Ave. The more I think of her, the more I see that mine whole life hath been devised for this one moment. I see that, insignificant though she be, Ave is a needed link in the chain.

Here is the place to stop. There is no more I can say, the story is done; the story of Strokor, the greatest man in the whole world!

CHAPTER VII

THE GOING

'TIS several years since last I faced this machine, many and many a day since I said that my story was done, and placed the record on the shelf of my anteroom, my heart full of satisfaction. And today I must needs add another record, perhaps two, to the pile.

When I set out for the highlands on the morn following what I last related I took with me but two or three men; not that I had any need for guards, but because it looketh not well for the emperor to travel without retainers, however few.

I reached the locality as the sun went down. The sky was a brilliant color; I remember it well. Darkness would come soon, though not as quickly as farther south. Commonly, I think not upon such trifles; but I was nearing my love, and tender things came easily to my mind.

My chariot kept to the road which lay alongside the irrigating flume, a stone trough which runs from the snow-covered hills to the dry country below. I had already noted this flume where it emptied into the basin in the valley below; for it had had a new kind of a spillway affixed to it. A broad, smooth platform with a slightly upward curve, over which the water was shooting. I saw no sense in the arrangement, and made up my mind to ask Maka about it; for the empire prized this trough most highly. It ran straight and true, over expensive bridges where needed, with scarce a bend to hold back the flow.

When I stopped my car outside the house I was surprised that none should come out to greet me. Maka had sent word of my coming; all should have been in readiness. But I was forced to use my whistle.

There was no stir. I became angry; I told my bullies to stay where they were, and myself burst in the door.

The house was a sturdy stone affair of one floor, set against the side of the mountain, a short distance above the flume. I looked about the interior in surprise; for not a soul was in sight in any of the compartments. There were signs that people had been there but a few moments before. I called it strange, for I had seen no one leave the house as I approached.

At last, as I was inspecting the eating place, I noted a small door let into the outer wall. It was open; and by squeezing I managed to get through. I found that it let into a long, dark passage.

I followed this, going steadily down a flight of stairs, and all of a sudden bumped into an iron grating. At the same moment I saw that the passageway made a turn just beyond. By craning my neck and straining my eyes I could see a faintly lighted chamber just a few feet away.

And before my eyes could scarce make out the figures of some people in the middle of the place, a voice came to my ear.

"Hail, Strokor!" it said. And great was my astonishment as I recognized the tones of Edam, the young dreamer whom Maka had brought to my house.

"Edam!" I cried. "What do ye here? Come and open these bars!"

He made no reply, save to laugh in a way I did not like. I shook the grating savagely, so that I felt it give. "Edam!" I roared. "Open this grating at once; and tell me, where is Ave?"

"I am here," came another voice. I stopped in sheer surprise, to peer closer and to see, for the first time, that it was really the dreamer and the chit, these two and no more, who sat there in the underground chamber. They seemed to be sitting in some sort of a box, with glass windows.

"Ave, come here!" I spoke much more gently than to Edam; for my heart was soft with thoughts of her. "It is thy lord, Strokor, the emperor, who calls thee. Come!"

"I stay here," said she in the same clear voice, entirely unshaken by my presence. "Edam hath claimed me, and I shall cleave to him. I want none of ye, ye giant!"

FOR a moment I was minded to throw my weight against the barrier, such was my rage. Then I thought better on it, and closely examined the bars. Two were loose.

"Ave," said I, contriving to keep my voice even, although my hands were busy with the bars as I spoke. "Ave—ye do wrong to spite me thus. Know ye not that I am the emperor, and that these bars cannot stand before me? I warn ye, if I must call my men to help me, and to witness my shame, it will go hard with ye! Better that ye should come willingly. Ye are not for such as Edam."

"No?" quoth the young man, speaking

up for the chit. "Ye are wrong, Strokor. We defy thee to do thy worst; we are prepared to flee from ye at all costs!"

I had twisted one of the bars out of my way without their seeing it. I strove at the next as I answered, still controlling my voice, " 'Twill do ye no good to flee, Edam, ye know that. And as for Ave— she shall wish she had never been born!"

"So I should," she replied with spirit, "if I were to become thy woman. But know you, Strokor, that Ave, the daughter of Durok, would rather die than take the name of one who had spurned her, as ye did me!"

So I had; it had slipped my mind. "But I want thee now, Ave," said I softly, preparing to slip through the opening I had made. "Surely ye would not take thine own life?"

"Nay," she answered, with a laugh in her voice. "Rather I would go with Edam here. I would go," she finished, her voice rising in her excitement, "away from this horrible world; away from it all, Strokor, and to Jeos! Hear ye? To Jeos! And—"

But at that instant I burst through the grating. Without a sound I charged straight for the pair of them.

And without a sound they slipped away from my grasp. Next second I was gazing stupidly at the rushing, swirling water of the flume.

And I saw that they had been sitting in the cabin of a tiny boat, and that they had got away!

There was an opening into the outer air; I rushed through, and stared in the growing twilight down the black furrow of the flume. Far in the distance, and going like a streak, I spied the glittering glass windows of the little craft. Once I made out the flutter of a saucy hand.

"We shall get them when they reach the valley!" I shouted to the men. Then I reached for my tube, and sighted it on the lower end of the flume, far, far below, almost too far away to be clear to the naked eye.

In an incredibly short time the craft reached the end. It traveled at an extraordinary rate; perchance 'twas weighted. I marveled that its windows could stand the force of the air. And I scarce had time to fear that the twain should be destroyed on that upturned spillway before it was there.

And then an awesome thing happened. As the boat struck the incline it shot upward into the air at a steep slant. Up, up it went. My heart jumped into my mouth; for surely they must be crushed when they came down.

But the craft did not come down. It went on and on, up and up; its speed scarcely slackened; 'twas like that of a shooting star. And in far less time than it takes to tell it, the little boat was high up among the stars, going higher every instant, and farther away from me. And suddenly the sweat broke cold on my forehead. For dead ahead, directly in line with their travel, lay the bluish white gleam of Jeos.

So great was my rage over the escape of the dreamer with my woman, at first I felt no sorrow. Later, after days and days of search in and about the basin, I came to grieve most terribly over my loss. When I came home to the palace, I was well-nigh ill.

In vain did I make the most generous of rewards. The whole empire turned out to search for the missing ones, but nothing came of it all. Yet I never ceased to hope, especially after my talk with Maka.

"Aye," he said, when I questioned him, "it is barely possible that they have left this world for all time. I have calculated the speed which their craft might have attained, had it the right proportions. And, in truth, it might have left the spillway at such a speed that it entirely overcame the draw of the ground.

"But I think it was a slim chance. It is more than likely that Ave shall return."

Was I not the fitter man? Surely Edam's purposes could not succeed; Jon would not have it so. The woman was mine, because I had chosen her. And she must come back to me, and in safety, or I should tear Edam into bits.

But as time went on and naught transpired, I became more and more melancholy.

Life had become an empty thing; it had been empty enough before I had craved the girl, but now it was empty with hopelessness.

After a while I got to thinking of some of the things Maka had told me. The more I thought of the future, the blacker it seemed.

True, there were many other fine women; but there had been only one Ave. No such beauty had ever graced this world before. And I knew I could be happy with no other.

Now I saw that all my fame had been in vain. I had lost the only woman that was fit for me, and when I died there would be naught left but my name. Even that the next emperor might blot out, if he chose.

It had all been in vain!

"It shall not be!" I roared to myself, as I strode about my compartment, gnawing at my hands in my misery. And in just such a fit of helpless anger the great idea came to me.

No sooner conceived than put into practice. I will not go closely into details; I will relate just the outstanding facts. What I did was to select a very tall mountain, located almost on the equator, and proclaimed my intention to erect a monument to Jon upon its summit. I caused vast quantities of materials to be brought to the place; and for a year a hundred thousand men labored to put the pieces together.

When they had finished, they had made a mammoth tower, partly of wood and partly of alloy. It was made in sections, so that it might be placed, piece upon piece, one above another high into the sky.

It was an enormous task. When it was complete I had a tower as high as the mountain itself erected upon its summit.

And next I caused section after section of the long, iron, pole-to-pole rod, which had tricked Klow, to be hauled up into the tower. I was only careful to begin the process from the top and work downward. I gave word that the last three sections be inserted at midday on a given day.

And at that hour I was safe inside a non-magnetic room.

I know right well when the deed was done. There was a most terrific earthquake. All about me, though I could see nothing at all, I could hear buildings falling. The din was appalling.

At the same time the air was fairly shattered with the rattle of the lightning. Never have I heard the like before. The rod had loosed the wrath of the forces above our air!

And as suddenly the whole deafening storm ended. Perchance the rod was destroyed by the lightning; I never went to see. For I know, the electricity split the very ground apart. But I gazed out of a window in the top of my palace, and saw that I had succeeded.

Not a soul but myself remained alive.

None but buildings made of the alloy were standing. Not only man, but most of his works had perished in that awful blast. I, alone, remained!

I, Strokor, am the survivor! I, the greatest man; it was but fit that I should be the last! No man shall come after me, to honor me or not as he chooses. I, and no other, shall be the last man!

And when Ave returns—as she must, though it be ages hence—when she comes, she shall find me waiting. I, Strokor, the mighty and wise, shall be here when she returns. I shall wait for her forever; here I shall always stay.

The stars may move from their places, but I shall not go!

For it is my intention to make use of another secret that Maka taught me. In brief—

(The record ends here. It may be that Strokor left the machine for some trivial reason, and forgot to finish the story. At all events, it is necessary to refer to the further discoveries of the expedition in order to learn and understand the outcome of it all.)

Part III
The Survivor

PROVIDED with a sledge-hammer, a crowbar, and a hydraulic jack, and even with drills and explosives as a last resort, Jackson, Kinney, and Van Emmon returned the same day to the walled-in room in the top of that mystifying mansion. The materials they carried would have made considerable of a load had not Smith removed enough of the weights from their suits to offset their burden. They reached the unopened door without special exertion, and with no mishap.

They looked in vain for a crack big enough to hold the point of the crowbar; neither could the most vigorous jabbing loosen any of the material. They dropped that tool and tried the sledge. It got no results; even in the hands of the husky geologist, the most vigorous blows failed to budge the door. They did not even dent it.

So they propped the powerful hydraulic jack, a tool sturdy enough to lift a house, at an angle against the door. Then, using the crowbar as a lever, the architect steadily turned up the screw, the mechanism multiplying his very ordinary strength a hundredfold. In a moment it could be seen that he was getting results; the door began to stir. Van Emmon struck one edge with the sledge-hammer, and it gave slightly.

In another minute the whole door, weighing over a ton, had been pushed almost out of its opening. The jack, overbalanced, toppled over. They did not readjust it, but threw their combined weight upon the barrier.

There was no need to try again. With a shiver the huge slab of metal slid, upright, into the space beyond, stood straight on end for a second or so, then toppled to the floor.

And this time they heard the crash.

For, as the door fell, a great gust of wind rushed out with a hissing shriek, almost overbalancing the men from the earth. They stood still for a while, breathing hard from their exertion, trying in vain to peer into the blackness before them. Under no circumstances would either of them have admitted that he was gathering courage.

In a minute the architect, his eyes sparkling with his enthusiasm for the antique, picked up the electric torch and turned it into the compartment. As he did so the other two stepped to his side, so that the three of them faced the unknown together. It was just as well. Outlined in that circle of light, and not six feet in front of them, stood a great chair upon a wide platform. And seated in the chair, erect and alert, his wide open eyes staring straight into those of the three, was the frightful, mountainous form of Strokor, the giant, himself.

For an indeterminable length of time the men from the earth stood there, speechless, unbreathing, staring at that awful monster as though at a nightmare. He did not move; he was entirely at ease, and yet plainly on guard, glaring at them with an air of conscious superiority which held them powerless. Instinctively they knew that the all-dominating voice in the records had belonged to this Hercules. But their instinct could not tell them whether the man still lived.

It was the doctor's brain that worked first. Automatically, from a lifelong habit of diagnosis, he inspected that dreadful figure quite as though it had been that of a patient. Bit by bit his subconscious mind pieced together the evidence; the man in the chair showed no signs of life. And after a while the doctor's conscious mind also knew.

"He is dead," he said positively, in his natural voice; and such was the vast relief of the other two that they were in no way startled by the sound. Instantly all three drew long breaths; the tension was relaxed; and Van Emmon's curiosity found a harsh and unsteady voice.

"How under heaven has he been preserved all this time? Especially," he added, remembering, "considering the air that we found in the room?"

The doctor answered after a moment, his reply taking the form of advancing a step or two and holding out a hand. It touched glass.

For the first time since the discovery, the builder shifted the light. He had held it as still as death for a full minute. Now he flashed it all about the place, and they saw that the huge figure was entirely encased in glass. The cabinet measured about six feet on each of its sides, and about five feet in height. But such were the squat proportions of the occupant that he filled the whole space.

A slight examination showed that the case was not fixed to the platform, but had a separate bottom, upon which the stumplike chair was set. Also, they found that, thanks to the reduced pull of the planet, it was not hard for the three of them to lift the cabinet bodily, despite the weight of almost a thousand pounds. They let the tools lie there, discarded as much weight as they could, and proceeded to carry that ages-old superman out into the light.

Here they could see from an examination of his mammoth cranium and extraordinary expression, that he was as highly developed as the greatest men on earth. It was the back of his head, however, so flat that it was only a continuation of his neck, or, rather, shoulders, that told where the flaw lay. That, together with the hardness of his eyes, the cruelty of his mouth, and the absolute lack of softness anywhere in the ironlike face or frame. All this condemned the monster as inhuman.

It was not easy to get him down the two flights of stairs. More than once they had to prop the case on a step while they rested; and at one time, just before they reached that curious heap of rubbish at

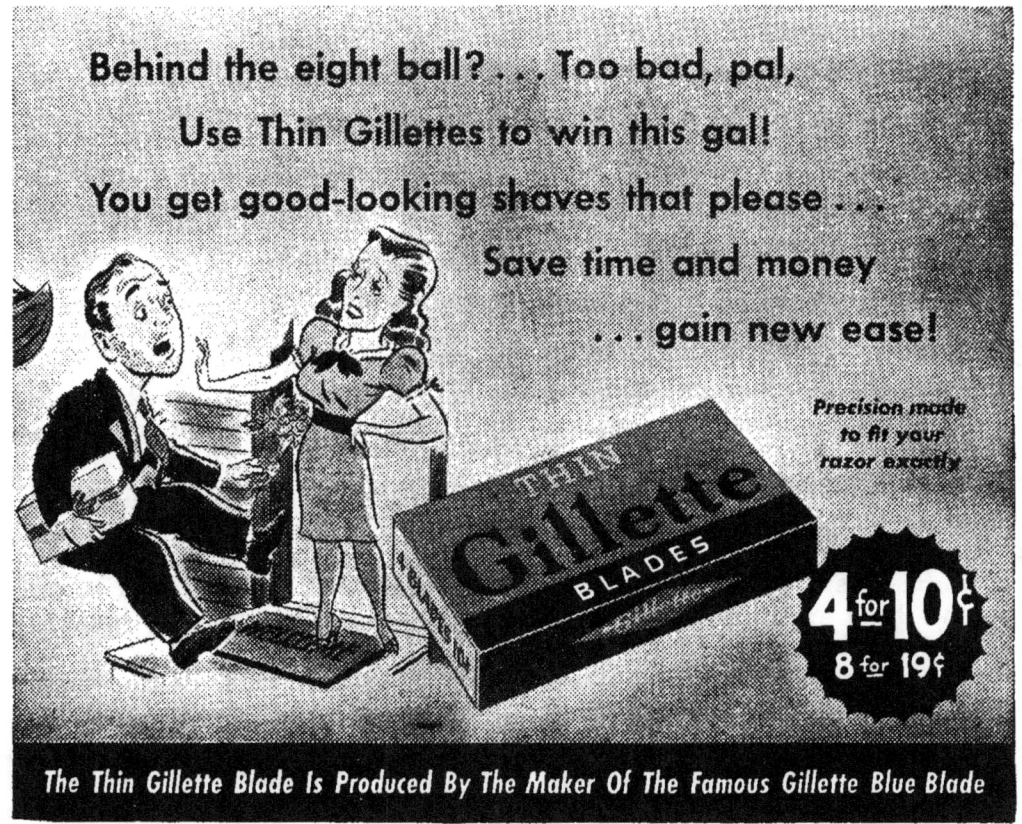

the foot of the upper stairs, Jackson's strength gave way and it looked as though the whole thing would get away from them.

Once at the bottom of the lower flight, the rest was easy. Within a very few minutes the astonished face of the engineer was peering into the vestibule. He could hardly wait until the airtight door was locked before opening the inner valves. He stared at the mammoth figure in the case long and hard; and from then on showed a great deal of respect for his three friends.

Of course, at that time the members of the expedition did not understand the conditions of Mercury as they are now known. They had to depend upon the general impression they got from their first-hand investigations; and it is remarkable that the doctor should have guessed so close to the truth.

"He must have made up his mind to outlast everybody else," was the way he put it as he kicked off his suit. He stepped up to the cabinet and felt of the glass. "I wish it were possible, without breaking the case, to see how he was embalmed."

His fingers still rested on the glass. Suddenly his eyes narrowed; he ran his fingers over the entire surface of the pane.

"That's mighty curious!" he ejaculated. "This thing was bitter cold when we brought it in! Now it's already as warm as this car!"

Smith's eyes lit up. "It may be," he offered, "that the case doesn't contain a vacuum, but some gas which has an electrical affinity for our atmosphere."

"Or," exclaimed the geologist suddenly, "the glass itself may be totally different from ours. It may be made of—"

"Good Heavens!" shouted the doctor, jerking his hand from the cabinet and leaping straight backward. At the same instant, with a grinding crash, all three sides of the case collapsed and fell in splinters to the floor.

"Look out!" shrieked Jackson. He was staring straight into the now unhooded eyes of the giant. He backed away, stumbled against a stool, and fell to the floor in a dead faint. Smith fumbled impotently with a hammer. The doctor was shaking like a leaf.

But Van Emmon stood still in his tracks, his eyes fixed on the Goliath; his fingernails gashed the palms of his hands, but he would not budge. And as he stared he saw, from first to last, the whole ghastly change that came, after billions of years of waiting, to the sole survivor of Mercury.

A glaze swept over the huge figure. Next instant every line in that adamant figure lost its strength; the hardness left the eyes and mouth. The head seemed to sink lower into the massive shoulders, and the irresistible hands relaxed. In another second the thing that had once been as iron had become as rubber.

But only for an instant. Second by second that huge mountain of muscle slipped and jellied and actually melted before the eyes of the humans. At the same time a curious acrid odor arose; Smith fell to coughing. The doctor turned on more oxygen.

IN LESS than half a minute the man who had once conquered a planet was reduced to a steaming mound of brownish paste. As it sank to the floor of the case, it touched a layer of coarse yellow powder sprinkled there; and it was this that caused the vapor. In a moment the room was filled with the haze of it.

And thus it came about that, within five minutes from being exposed to the air of the sky-car, that whole immense bulk, chair and all, had vanished. The powder had turned it to vapor, and the purifying chemicals had sucked it up. Nothing was left save a heap of smoking, grayish ashes in the center of the broken glass.

Van Emmon's fingers relaxed their grip. He stirred to action, turned to Smith.

"Here! Help me with this thing!"

Between them, they got the remains of the cabinet, with its gruesome load, into the vestibule. As for the doctor, he was bending over Jackson's still unconscious form. When he saw what the others were doing, he gave a great sigh of relief.

"Good!" He helped them close the door. "Let's get away from this cursed place!"

The outer door was opened. At the same time Smith started the machinery; and as the sky-car shot away from the ground he tilted it slightly, so that the contents of the vestibule was slid into space. Down it fell like so much lead.

The doctor glanced through a nearby window. and his face brightened as he made out the distant gleam of another planet. He watched the receding surface of Mercury with positive delight.

"Nice place to get away from," he commented. "And now, my friends—home!"

But the others' eyes were fixed upon a tiny sparkle in the dust outside the palace, where the vestibule had dropped its load It was the sun shining upon some broken bits of glass. The glass which, for untold ages, had enclosed the throne of the Death-lord.

THE SPIRIT-BOATS

WITHIN the many-chambered tomb
For Tut-ankh-Amen built,
Among the alabaster jars,
The faience and the gilt,
Were placed the spirit-boats designed
To bear his soul away
To happy shores by Horus blest
With everlasting day.

Pink shallops far more fit to hold
Young Loves perfumed and curled
Than navigate the dreary dark
And haunted underworld,
Light fairy vessels that should rock
On waters laced with foam,
By sunny isles or emerald woods
Where Pan was wont to roam.

No doubt the ancient monarch hoped
On blue Egyptian nights
To steer his bark to mundane parts
And taste of old delights,
Between the lotus-lilies drift
Along the star-lit Nile,
And play the sistrum for his queen
While basking in her smile.

Behold! above the dusky hills
The new moon's silver boat
Upon its bright celestial way
Serenely certain float.
Who knows? Mark Antony its course
From sky to earth may guide,
To visit once again the scene
Where Cleopatra died.

—By Minna Irving.

Lights

By PHILIP FISHER

Author of "The Devil of the Western Sea." "Beyond the Pole," etc.

Hazard on the high sea and a ghostly warning that the eyes of one sailor only could see

I

THERE had never been any question of Carey's seamanship. Officers who knew had testified to that. The captain himself had declared so to the court. And he had added further the unsolicited opinion that he knew no officer he would more fully trust to keep safe position when the destroyer division was making twenty-five knots in close column.

Furtive glances flickered between the officers grouped about the green baized wardroom table. A disagreeable duty, this trying a brother at arms. The judge advocate himself hesitated. Then, pushing aside a thought not entirely complimentary to naval regulations, he sighed almost audibly and put another question.

Captain Kennart shook his head with grim decision.

"No," he said emphatically. "Carey never used the stadimeter. Always judged the distance with his naked eye."

A member of the court cleared his throat. Another tapped the table top with his pencil. The judge advocate sighed within himself again.

"That's all," he said finally.

Carey's counsel nodded. The president of the court looked inquiringly at his confrères. Each shook his head in turn.

The president made the routine admonition regarding silence and Captain Kennart left the room.

Lieutenant, junior grade, Warren Carey relaxed somewhat in his seat. He had felt that his captain would do his best by him. He thrilled with a growing faith in his fellow man at this positive evidence that despite what had occurred the captain bore no grudge. Yet had Captain Kennart given testimony inspired by an active hate, he could have found no fault.

Hope again grew in his breast. These officers about him, too, he had shopped and partied with all over the China coast. The admiral had ordered them on this court. A regulation duty. They were to ascertain facts, impartially weigh them, give judgment in accordance with navy law. This they would do, Carey knew. Yet when one's fate is to be settled by real men, mercy ever tempers justice. Real men can understand.

A fluttering breath escaped Carey, nevertheless.

He dared not succumb to optimism. Between him and these others, all other men indeed, he still sensed something inexplicable, as if he were befogged in vibrations of a different plane. He could not see this clouding envelope. It was a thing to be felt, but not by a normal perceptive faculty. He wondered if he really differed in any strange way from ordinary men. It appeared almost that he did.

He shuddered slightly in recollection of that night on the lower Yangtze when he, and only he, had seen those lights. Every man who had been on the bridge when the thing had occurred had sworn to having seen not a single light. He, Carey, witness at the captain's own trial, had been alone in the affirmative. He had not been told this of course. Yet instinctively he knew it must be so. That night they had declared themselves. Before the court they assuredly had done the same thing.

Another witness was summoned.

Through the haze of strange introspection Carey heard fragments of his testimony.

To think that this companion of many an upper Yangtze rice-bird hunt, this doctor who had brought him through the dengue fever down in Cavite, should now have to vouch for him in a general court. To think—could something about him really be different from other men? Was he—gifted? Why had it been given to him, and him only, to see what had been withheld from the sight of all other men on the ship—those lights? Or was he prone to temporary hallucination such as his captain pityingly had hinted in an endeavor to extenuate his—Carey's—crime? And was the medico now—

"No." The doctor's voice rose. "I have fished, hunted, shopped, seen the sights with Carey, and doctored him, for the last year and a half. He is not insane."

Carey's heart leaped in gratitude at the man's vehement assertion. The medico, too, was a man!

But—insane!

Surely the court had understood the captain's hint. Not by any possible chance could they bring that dread judgment of his case. Never!

And yet—he, and only he, had been the man to see. And then, that trouble with the captain. Carey shook his head. Surely he had not been even temporarily mad. Persons laboring under mental delusions promptly forgot, he had heard, the vagaries of their period of aberration. And too clearly could he still recall those lights, still envision that horrid struggle on the destroyer's bridge. From the first order he had given the man at the wheel every incident was indelibly impressed on his memory, and with a clarity not to be confuted. Even to the final catastrophe and the terror inspired by the crew. No, no, the medico was quite right. He, Carey, was not insane.

Yet, somehow, he was the only one.

Dimly the doctor's voice drifted again through the cloud.

"No, sir." He was answering the judge advocate's question. "I tested Carey's eyes when he went up for full lieutenant just before we sailed from the Philippines.

They were perfect then. And I examined them yesterday again. His eyes are perfect now."

Carey quivered slightly. If it wasn't his eyes what could it be?

The captain had declared that he was a trustworthy seaman; the medico swore that he was neither insane nor visually defective. Then what? He had seen.

And ever since the thing had occurred he had been in this daze. He could not understand.

THE judge advocate put another question.

The doctor answered with promptness and certitude.

"Yes, I have heard of such cases. They are not of uncommon occurrence. I have heard them discussed in many a wardroom. Last spring, when the division was proceeding from Manila to Lingayen Gulf for torpedo practice there happened an instance of it. I was on the flagboat, leading the column. It was during the first watch. I was on the bridge, and the captain and navigator were there with the officer of the deck.

"We had just rounded Cape Bolinao and expected to pick up the light across the gulf. We were all peering dead ahead —there's always a little rivalry to sight a light first. The division commander ordered one-third speed until we got a bearing on that light. Then he was going to turn column right and go down the gulf and anchor off Dagupan.

"For half an hour every man on the bridge gazed straight ahead and strained to see the light we knew must show up. Suddenly one of the men on the lookout sang out that he saw it. He pointed almost due west, about a point on the port bow. We all strove to make it out. The lookout insisted it was there. Then one after another we saw it. It was an occulting light, and we could even discern its pulsations and check its rate. The column swung south at standard speed.

"Ten minutes later we had to change course several degrees to westward to avoid going on the beach. The next day we received a radio to the effect that that light had not been in order for two nights. Yet we had seen it. We had expected it to be there, and our straining eyes had actually envisioned the thing. It's a common enough occurrence, as I said before. The eye often sees what we want it to see."

The members of the court nodded understandingly. The judge advocate made a pertinent query.

"Is it really the eye that sees this specter of a light that doesn't exist?"

The doctor shook his head.

"I would say not," he answered slowly. "In my estimation it is not the eye that sees it at all. It's the brain behind the eye. The brain knows that the light ought to be seen and deludes itself into the belief that it actually does see it. No, it's the brain in such a case rather than the eye."

"But in the defendant's case," came the logical question, "there was no such expectation. How do you account for that?"

The doctor shrugged his shoulders. Carey moved uneasily in his chair.

That was the very question that had troubled him ever since that night a week ago. He had not expected to see the things that so clearly impressed themselves on his vision. He had not even been thinking about such a thing. The lower reaches of the Yangtze had few enough lights; and sparse were ships that ran the river at night. His own destroyer had attempted it solely because ordered down from Chefoo for emergency missionary protection upstream. For above Hankow was a local uprising led by a Taoist priesthood. The river gunboats were five hundred miles farther up stream, and turtle slow. The destroyer, though north in Pechili Gulf, could reach the threatened area first. So they had entered the river's upper channel at night.

No, he had not expected to see a thing. And yet of the half dozen men on the bridge he had, and only he. The medico had just stated that such hallucination

was of the brain rather than the eye. Could it have been his brain—his alone? The fog closed in upon Carey again. He found it hard to think.

"In the defendant's case," he felt more than heard the doctor say, "I find no precedent. I can simply testify that he is a steady man, entirely sane, and has perfect eyesight. And yet I do believe that he was dead certain that he saw those lights. And as certain, too, that the others did not. What he saw must have been a delusion of the mind, yet of a mind that was normal. Such things also do occur. Yet his eyes are perfect, and he is as balanced mentally as any officer here."

Carey's hands bit into each other.

His captain was for him. And now the medico.

And yet—and yet? What could the court do? He had committed a crime for which in olden days he might have hanged. And his excuse for the offense was what? Simply that he had seen something that no other man had seen. The mere fact that the catastrophe he saw coming overwhelmed them on the very heels of the captain's interference could have but little weight with a court that must decide his fate on tangible fact.

And yet—good Heaven, it must be excuse enough! He had seen the lights, the captain had interfered, disaster had followed. It would not have closed upon them had the captain let him alone. Surely the court must understand that. He had explained it all so carefully, in minutest detail, when his counsel had put him on the stand as witness in his own behalf.

The doctor was dismissed. The court was cleared.

II

CAREY had the freedom of the ship. For a moment he felt that the fresh breeze sweeping from the rice paddies of the lower Whampoo and the Yangtze beyond would clear his head and give a little friendly stimulation. Then he recalled that other officers would be topside. Friends they all were, indeed. But Carey did not desire brotherly companionship just now, nor did he care to feel the pitying glances of old shipmates. He wanted to be alone; to think; to go over again the events of the past week; of that night. He turned down the passageway to the stateroom assigned him since the disaster. Now that he was away from the atmosphere of the court he already felt better.

The doctor had said that his eyes were normal. He had also declared that his brain was as rational as that of any officer on the court—a fine thing and a daring one for a destroyer medical officer to say. He must have meant it, must have wanted to strongly impress the court with his earnestness and his belief. Carey drew a breath of relief.

Good eyes, good mind. The chill fog that in fear for the latter had penetrated his very being, gradually began to dissipate.

How clearly it all came back.

He had been officer of the deck. The captain had snatched a hasty meal from the food brought up by his Filipino boy to the emergency cabin on the bridge. The navigator had plotted changes of course, and was below finishing off his coffee with the other officers.

A half hour remained of the second dog watch. Carey had been going over some points he wished to impress upon the chief boatswain's mate when he took the eight o'clock reports. A tear in the awning canvas where it stretched tight over the freezing apparatus on top of the ice locker just abaft the bridge was one of these.

The awning was beginning to flap, and this night Carey demanded silence on the bridge. He could sense better, then, any variation in the hum of the forced draft blowers. And in the currents of the lower Yangtze all things must be anticipated. The officer of the deck must know as soon as the fire-room watch that something was going wrong. Must have the fo'c's'le gang ready to let go the anchor even before word of the lost steam came through the voice tube.

He stood on the starboard side of the bridge, near the rack of tubes, leaning on the sill of the open port. Fleet sparks from the captain's pipe indicated his almost identical position near the engine room telegraphs to port. Carey was almost tempted to call the boatswain's mate at once to have that awning repaired. He had all but turned to give the order when his eye caught something yet dim in the distance.

For a minute or more he gazed steadily at the object. Then, from where they were hanging on one of the searchlight directing wheels on the bulkhead of the emergency cabin, he took up his binoculars. Faintly through the glass he could make out that there were three lights instead of one.

He softly called the starboard lookout. "Do you see any lights about three points on the bow?" he asked. "Pretty far off?"

The lookout stared into the blackness of the night, blinking as the damp breeze bedewed his eyelashes. Then he shook his head. "No, sir."

"Try the glass," Carey suggested.

The lad shook his head as before.

"Don't see a thing, sir."

"Certain of it?" demanded Carey.

"Absolutely, sir," was the answer.

CAREY remembered all this with extreme clearness—every detail. Lying on the bunk in his stateroom, he found himself living over again that fifteen-minute period in which so much had happened.

He had taken the binoculars from the lookout, and ordered him back to his post. Then he glanced at the clock on the emergency cabin bulkhead just behind the man at the wheel. This was a matter of habit. There was nothing to record. He had not expected to see any lights, anyway. And the flapping of the canvas over the ice locker did not disconcert him now. It had become part of the normal respiration of the ship, and Carey decided that he would not disturb the boatswain's mate about it until the eight o'clock reports.

He turned back to his open port, but discovered the captain staring out into the blackness, charging his pipe with one of the patent fillers he had bought from the Greek in Chefoo. He paused tentatively at his elbow, undecided whether to stay there or assume the captain's former position near the annunciators.

Then something urged him to remain. The captain acknowledged his presence with a grunt.

"Did you see something?"

Carey nodded rather hesitantly.

"Thought I did, sir. Looked to me like a ship's light off to starboard."

The captain lifted his binoculars and focused them in the direction Carey had indicated. The latter raised his own glass. He recalled that he gave an exclamation of surprise.

"The lights are there, sir, all right. Seem nearer now, too."

"Humph! I don't make anything out," grunted the captain.

Carey stepped back of him and leveled an arm over his shoulder with the edge of his hand up, as in aiming.

"About two points on the bow, sir. Left a trifle, captain. There—that's it. See them now, sir?"

Intently the captain gazed, slowly changing focus with his forefinger on the adjusting wheel. Then he dropped the glass.

"Don't see a thing, Carey."

He bent to gain the protection of the bulkhead, and a match scratched, then glowed over his pipe.

"That's funny," Carey answered, somewhat mystified.

He wondered if perhaps his last look at the light-flooded chart had left dancing gleams on the retina of his eye. He carefully wiped his eyes with his handkerchief, and cleaned the binoculars with a bit of lens paper. Then raised them again—and started.

"But the lights are close now, captain." He lowered his glass slightly. "Why, I can see them with my naked eye! Right there, sir." He leveled his arm again.

"Hanged if I can see 'em, Carey. But this river breeze blurs everything. Let's try your glass."

Carey ducked from under the leather strap and handed the binoculars over. The captain rapidly found focus, then shook his head again.

"Not a thing, not a thing. Better have your eyes examined, young fellow."

"But they're holding steady, captain!" Carey expostulated. "A ship as clear as day. Heading from starboard across our course. I can see her masthead and port running light. And cabin lights topside." Suddenly he swung to the wheelsman. "What's your compass?"

"Right on, sir. Two forty-eight."

"Come on two sixty," Carey ordered.

"What's that?" demanded the captain.

"Get the time of that change, quartermaster," snapped Carey. Then in answer to the captain: "Shifting course a bit to right, sir. She's got the right of way, and there's no use taking any chances."

"Who's got the right of way?" the captain demanded again.

"That ship, sir—"

"Dammit, Carey, your eyes must have gone bad. There's no ship in sight."

"But, Captain Kennart—"

The captain turned sharply to the wheelsman.

"Back on your former course!" To the quartermaster: "Get that time." He swung back to the open port, and snapped for the lookouts. Sensing something unusual in the very atmosphere, the whole bridge force was now tensely on the alert. "Do you lads see anything ahead—lights?"

All hands intently stared out into the blackness of the night.

Their opinion was unanimous. "Not a thing, sir."

Carey gave a cry of alarm. "Captain!" He turned savagely on the man at the wheel. "Fifteen degrees right. On the jump now!"

The captain's suddenly livid face glared in the glow of the binnacle light.

"Dammit, sir, get off the bridge!" he cried peremptorily. To the wheelsman:

"Back to your former course. Snap into it! You're taking your orders from me now. Lively!"

Carey recalled how the men had looked at each other in consternation. He recalled his own utter dismay. For the first time in his career he was ordered off the bridge. That ship—lights looming up now not a cable length away. Holding steadily on the same angle—collision sure! And he, officer of the deck, when the life of his ship was a matter of seconds and every one blind but him, ordered below. Good Heaven! It meant shipwreck; the captain was bound for destruction. Mad! He resolved on one last frantic appeal.

"But Great God, captain—it's on our very bows! We'll hit sure! We'll—"

The captain turned on him with an oath. Then as Carey stood his ground the captain's face became hard and grim. A deadly implication chilled in the ice-level tone his voice held.

"Mr. Carey, consider yourself under arrest. You're either mutinous or mad. This will be reported when we finish the business up river and return to Shanghai. Get out!"

The lights were within a hundred yards, Carey saw. He was ordered off in disgrace. The captain was mad himself. The whole bridge force had gone mad. That ship—

His answer was literally forced from him. "By Heaven, sir, I will not leave!" he cried in utter desperation.

And he leaped to the annunciators and jerked the signals for both engines to full reverse. Then jumped for the steering gear, shoved the man aside, and madly spun the wheel to starboard.

With an oath the captain seized him, cried to the lookout to drag him below. A struggle ensued. The ship throbbed as the power of thirty thousand horses strove to stop its forward rush. Carey remembered the cloud of horror and impotence that almost overcame him. His one thought was for the ship, and of the vessel even now across their knifelike stem.

He recalled his last hopeless words, forgetful of naval discipline and the men about.

"The lights! Too late! Too late! Captain, you damn fool—"

And then the crash had come.

III

LYING in the bunk, the racking shock of it was a physical blow again. Carey recalled sickeningly his own release —too late. The startled outcries of the men; the intermittent raucous honking of the general alarm some one had retained command enough to switch on from the bridge. The shrill piping of the boatswain's mate, his bellowing roar of: "All hands abandon ship!"

And then the siren's scream.

His station in such an emergency was in charge of No. 2 life raft. Later he found himself clinging to this bobbing float, mind and body benumbed by the whispering waves of the swirling Yangtze.

Rescue. Court martial.

The captain for the loss of his ship. He himself for mutinous insubordination.

And yet—he had seen those lights.

A fog gathered about him again.

IV

PULSATIONS beat upon his brain. Dimly he recognized them as rapid footsteps in the passageway outside his room. He aroused somewhat as his door was flung open and a shipmate burst in upon him. Blinking, he noted that the newcomer was excited to an extreme.

"News, by thunder, news for you, Warren! The admiral says he's going to quash every court martial that came out of the wreck. News from the divers down the river just came up, and set him all in a daze. He's pacing the deck now. We did not hit an uncharted rock last week, Warren. We tore our bottom out on the hulk of the Kew Li, whose boilers blew up, and only two men left to tell the tale. And what gets the admiral, Warren, is that you swore you saw those lights on the night of the wreck, but the Kew Li went down four months ago!"

The Conquest of
the Moon Pool

By A. MERRITT

Author of "The Metal Monster," "The Face in the Abyss," etc.

Dr. Goodwin presses further into the labyrinth of the Moon Pool, to discover a fantastic subterranean empire

Part II

What happened before:

Following the strange and inexplicable disappearance of Mr. David Throckmartin's wife, his associate, Dr. Stanton, and his wife's maid, Thora Helverson, in the uncanny depths of the Moon Pool, Throckmartin implored Dr. Walter T. Goodwin to rescue them. Shortly after he saw Throckmartin himself snatched from the deck of their ship by a weird entity of living light— the dread Dweller of the Moon Pool.

Determined to rescue the four victims, Goodwin sails to the island of Nan-Matal, where lies the entrance to the cavern of the Moon Pool.

While proceeding toward the island of Nan-Matal, and the cavern in which was the Moon Pool, in the little sailing vessel, *Suwarna*, on the way he rescued Olaf Huldricksson from an abandoned vessel. Olaf told them that a "sparkling devil" had come down the path of the moon and taken his wife and his little daughter.

On learning Dr. Goodwin's mission, Olaf consented to join him. With Larry O'Keefe of the Royal Air Force, whom they picked up from his wrecked hydroplane the next day, they landed on Nan-Matal.

The full of the moon was past, but by means of light condensers Dr. Goodwin managed to focus the moon rays in sufficient strength to cause the rock door to the Moon Pool to open. Scarcely had it done so when Olaf, shrieking, rushed through the portal. A rifle cracked. The next moment a figure catapulted out of the shadows, and in a second O'Keefe and the stranger were struggling on the threshold of the Moon Door.

They rolled past the opened slab, Dr. Goodwin following.

The great rock door swung to, and they found themselves imprisoned in the lair of the Dweller.

CHAPTER VII

THE MOON POOL

"LARRY!" I cried, turning to O'Keefe, "the stone has shut! We're caught!"

O'Keefe took a brisk step toward the barrier behind us. There was no mark of juncture with the shining walls; the slab fitted into the sides as closely as a mosaic.

"It's shut all right," said Larry. "But if there's a way in, there's a way out. Anyway, Doc, we're right in the pew we've been heading for, so why worry?" He grinned at me cheerfully, and although I could not accept his light-hearted view of the situation, I felt a twinge of shame for my momentary panic. The man on the floor groaned, and O'Keefe dropped swiftly to his knees beside him.

"Von Hetzdorp!" he said.

At my exclamation he moved aside, turning the face so I could see it. It was clearly German, and just as clearly its possessor was a man of considerable force and intellectuality.

The strong, massive brow with orbital ridge unusually developed, the dominant, high-bridged nose, the straight lips with their more than suggestion of latent cruelty, and the strong lines of the jaw beneath a black, pointed beard all gave evidence that here was a personality beyond the ordinary. The hair was closely cropped on the square head, and the short, stocky body with its deep chest and abnormal length of torso as compared to the legs, indicated extraordinary vitality.

Unscrupulous, I thought, looking down upon him, remorseless, crafty, and with a brain as unmoral as is science itself.

"Couldn't be anybody else," said Larry. "He must have been watching us over there from Chau-ta-leur's vault all the time. When he saw that we had the slab open I suppose he figured that now we had picked the chestnuts out of the fire, he'd better collect 'em all for himself. So he took a pot shot at me first, and meant to get you and Olaf next. But his aim was bad —too good, rather—and when he saw what

he'd done he took a crazy chance."

The man on the corridor's floor stirred, and swiftly O'Keefe ran practised hands over his body; then stood erect, holding out to me two wicked-looking magazine pistols and a knife. "He got one of my bullets through his right forearm, too," he said. "Just a flesh wound, but it made him drop his rifle. Some arsenal, our little German scientist, what?"

I opened my medical kit and knelt beside Von Hetzdorp—if indeed it was he. The wound was a slight one, and Larry stood looking on as I bandaged it.

Golden-eyed Lakla stood looking down at the sleeping Larry, and all about her were other eyes. . .

"Got another one of those condensers the Heinie here broke?" he asked me suddenly. "And do you suppose Olaf will know enough to use it?"

And then it dawned upon me that O'Keefe could not have heard, as I had, the Norseman race into the moon door's passage before the door had closed! I arose swiftly.

"Larry," I answered, "Olaf's not outside! He's in here somewhere!"

His jaw dropped.

"Didn't you hear him shriek when the stone opened?" I asked.

"I heard him yell, yes," he said. "But I didn't know what was the matter. And then this wildcat jumped me—" He paused and his eyes widened. "Which way did he go?" he asked swiftly. I pointed down the faintly glowing passage.

"There's only one way," I said.

"Watch that bird close," hissed O'Keefe, pointing to Von Hetzdorp—and pistol in hand stretched his long legs and raced away. I looked down at the German. His eyes were open and he reached out a hand to me. I lifted him to his feet.

"I have heard," he said. "We follow, quick. If you will take my arm, please, I am shaken yet, yes—" I gripped his shoulder without a word, and the two of us set off down the corridor after Larry. Von Hetzdorp was gasping, and his weight pressed upon me heavily, but he moved with all the will and strength that was in him.

A S WE ran I took hasty note of the tunnel. I saw that its sides were smooth and polished, and that the light seemed to come not from their surfaces, but from far within them—giving to the walls an illusive aspect of distance and depth; rendering them spacious in a peculiarly weird way. The passage turned, twisted, ran down, turned again. It came to me that the light that illumined the tunnel was given out by tiny points deep within the stone, sprang from the points ripplingly and spread upon their polished faces. Involuntarily I stopped to look more closely.

"Hurry," gasped Von Hetzdorp. "Explain that later—etheric vibration—set up in that composition—stones really etheric lights—stupendous! Hurry!"

Through his panting speech broke a cry from far ahead. It was Larry's voice. "Olaf!"

I gripped Von Hetzdorp's arm closer and we sped on. Now we were coming fast to the end of the passage. Before us was a high arch, and through it I glimpsed a dim, shifting luminosity as of mist filled with rainbows. We reached the portal and I drew myself up short, almost tripping the German. For what I was looking into was a chamber that might have been transported from that enchanted palace of the Jinn King that rises beyond the magic mountains of Kaf.

It was filled with a shimmering, prismatic lambency that thickened in the distances to impenetrable veils of fairy opalescence. It was a shrine of sorcery!

Before me stood O'Keefe, and a dozen feet in front of him, Huldricksson, with something clasped tightly in his arms. The Norseman's feet were at the verge of a shining, silvery lip of stone within whose oval lay a blue pool. And down upon this pool staring upward like a gigantic eye, fell seven pillars of fantom light—one of them amethyst, one of rose, another of white, a fourth of blue, and three of emerald, of silver and of amber. They fell each upon the azure surface, and I knew that these were the seven streams of radiance, within which the Dweller took shape —now but pale ghosts of their brilliancy when the full energy of the moon stream raced through them.

Then Huldricksson bent and placed on the shining silver lip of the Pool that which he held, and I saw that it was the body of a child! He set it there so gently, bent over the side and thrust a hand down into the water. And as he did so he stiffened strangely, moaned and lurched against the little body that lay before him. Instantly the form moved, and slipped over the verge into the blue. Rigid with horror, I watched Huldricksson recover himself and throw his body over the stone, hands clutching, arms thrust deep down. And then I heard from his lips a long-drawn, heart-shriveling cry of pain and of anguish that held in it nothing human!

Close on its wake came a cry from Von Hetzdorp.

"*Gott!*" shrieked the German. "Drag him back! Quick!"

He leaped forward, but before he could half clear the distance, O'Keefe had leaped, too, had caught the Norseman by the shoulders and toppled him backward, where he lay whimpering and sobbing. And as I rushed behind the German I saw Larry lean over the lip of the Pool and cover his eyes with a shaking hand; saw Von Hetzdorp peer down into it with real pity in his cold eyes; heard him murmur, "*Das armes Kind! Ach! das armes Kleine Mädchen!*"

THEN I stared down, myself, into the Moon Pool, and there, sinking, sinking, was a little maid whose dead face and fixed, terror-filled eyes looked straight into mine; and ever sinking slowly, slowly— vanished! And I knew that this was Olaf's Freda, his beloved "*yndling*" whose mother had snatched her up from the *Brunhilda's* deck when the Dweller had wrapped its awesome, coruscating folds about her, and had drawn her, the child still in her arms, along the moonbeam path to where we stood.

But where was the mother, and where had Olaf found his babe?

Simultaneously, it seemed, we straightened ourselves, the three of us, and looked into each other's faces; each of us, yes, even Von Hetzdorp, shaken to the heart. The German was first to speak.

"You have nitroglycerin there, yes?" he asked, pointing toward my medical kit that I had gripped unconsciously and carried with me during the mad rush down the passage. I nodded and drew it out.

"Hypodermic," he ordered next, curtly; took the syringe, filled it accurately with its one one-hundredth of a grain dosage, and leaned over Huldricksson, who, with

arms held out rigidly, was fighting for breath as though a great weight lay on his chest. He rolled up the sailor's sleeves halfway to the shoulder. The arms were white with that same strange semitranslucence that I had seen on Throckmartin's breast where a tendril of the Dweller had touched him. His hands were of the same whiteness —like a baroque pearl. Above the line of white, standing out like marble on the bronzed arms, Von Hetzdorp thrust the needle.

"He will need all his heart can do," he said to me.

Then he reached down into a belt about his waist and drew from it a small, flat flask of what seemed to be lead. He opened it and let a few drops of its contents fall on each arm of the Norwegian. The liquid sparkled and instantly began to spread over the skin much as oil or gasoline dropped on water does, only far more rapidly. And as it spread it seemed to draw a sparkling film over the tainted flesh and little wisps of vapor rose from it.

The Norseman's mighty chest heaved with agony, and I could see the over-stimulated heart beating in a great pulse in his throat. He strove to rise to his feet, but his weakness was too great. His hands clenched. The German gave a grunt of satisfaction at this, dropped a little more of the liquid, and then, watching closely, grunted again and leaned back. Huldricksson's labored breathing ceased, his head dropped upon Larry's knee, and from his arms and hands the whiteness swiftly withdrew.

Von Hetzdorp arose and contemplated us, almost benevolently.

"He will all right be in five minutes," he said. "I khow. I do it to pay for that shot of mine, and also because we will need him. Yes." He turned to Larry. "You have a poonch like a mule kick, my young friend," he said. "Some time you pay me for that shot, eh?" He smiled; and the quality of the grimace was not exactly reassuring. Larry looked him over quizzically.

"You're Von Hetzdorp, of course," he

said. The German nodded, betraying no surprise at the recognizition.

"And you?" he asked.

"Lieutenant O'Keefe of the Royal Flying Corps," replied Larry, saluting. "And this gentleman is Dr. Walter T. Goodwin."

Von Hetzdorp's face brightened.

"The American botanist?" he queried. I nodded.

"Ach!" cried Von Hetzdorp eagerly; "but this is fortunate. Long I have desired to meet you. Your work, for an American, is most excellent; surprising—"

Huldricksson interrupted him. The big seaman had risen stiffly to his feet and stood with Larry's arm supporting him. He stretched out his hands to me.

"I saw her," he whispered. "I saw mine Freda when the stone swung. She lay there, just at my feet. I picked her up and I saw that mine Freda was dead. But I hoped—and I thought maybe mine Helma was somewhere here, too. So I ran with mine *yndling*, here—" His voice broke.

"I thought maybe she was not dead," he went on. "And I saw that." He pointed to the Moon Pool. "And I thought I would bath her face and she might live again. And when I dipped my hands within, the life left them, and cold, deadly cold, ran up through them into my heart. And mine Freda she fell." He covered his eyes, and dropping his head on O'Keefe's shoulder, stood, racked by sobs that seemed to tear at his very soul.

CHAPTER VIII

THE FLAME-TIPPED SHADOWS

VON HETZDORP nodded his head solemnly as Olaf finished.

"*Ja!*" he said. "That which comes from here took them both—the woman and the child. *Ja!* They came clasped within it and the stone shut upon them. But why it left the child behind I do not understand."

Larry was watching him, in his eyes incredulous indignation and amazement.

"You, too, try to tell me that something carried a woman and a child from a ship hundreds of miles away, through the air over the seas to here?" he cried, an edge of contempt in his voice. "Something that Dr. Goodwin has said is made of—moonshine—carried a strong woman and a child. How do you know?"

"Because I saw it," answered Von Hetzdorp simply. "Not only did I see it, but hardly had I time to make escape through the entrance before it passed whirling and murmuring and its bell sounds all joyous. *Ja!* It was what you call the squeak close, that."

"Wait a moment," I said, stilling Larry with a gesture. "Do I understand you to say that you were within this place?"

Von Hetzdorp actually beamed upon me.

"*Ja*, Dr. Goodwin," he said, "I went in when that which comes from it went out!"

I gaped at him, stricken dumb. Into Larry's bellicose attitude crept a suggestion of grudging respect. Olaf, trembling, watched silently.

"Dr. Goodwin and my impetuous young friend, you," went on Von Hetzdorp, "it is time that we have an understanding. I have a proposition to make to you, also. It is this; we are what you call a bad boat, and all of us are in it. *Ja!* Also in this troublous water we find ourself we need all hands, is it not so? Let us put together our knowledge and our brains and resource," he looked wickedly at O'Keefe, "and pull our boat into quiet waters again. After that—"

"All very well, Von Hetzdorp," interjected Larry angrily, "but I don't feel very safe in any boat with somebody capable of shooting me through the back."

Von Hetzdorp waved a deprecating hand.

"It was natural," he said; "logical, yes. Here is a very great secret, perhaps many secrets to Germany invaluable. You are an enemy of Germany, although why as an Irishman you should be I do not know."

I considered the German's proposition. After all, what else was there to do? He was undoubtedly a man of resource and courage, and, as he said, possessed of special information regarding the phenomena I had come to seek. What good would there be in—disposing of him? But how much could he be trusted? Larry echoed my thoughts:

"In effect, Goodwin, the professor's proposition is this," he said: "He wants to know what it is that's going on here, and he knows he can't do it by himself. Also he knows we have the drop on him. We're three to his one, and we have all his hardware and cutlery."

There was almost a twinkle in Von Hetzdorp's eyes. As Larry ended he bowed.

"It is not just as I would have put it, perhaps," he said, "but in its skeleton he was right. Nor will I turn my hand against you while we are still in danger here. I pledge you my honor on this!"

I glanced at Larry half doubtfully and back at the German. Then I thrust out a hand to him. He gripped it, dropped it, and thrust his to Larry. The Irishman hesitated then with a laugh, took it.

"But I'll just keep the guns, professor," he said. Von Hetzdorp bowed again.

"Now," he said, "to prove my good faith I will tell you what I know. Something I knew of what was occurring here before I was sent"—he corrected himself hurriedly —"before I came. I found the secret of the door mechanism even as you did, Dr. Goodwin. But by carelessness, my condensers were broken. I was forced to wait while I sent for others, and the waiting might be for months. I took certain precautions, and on the first night of this full moon I hid myself within the vault of Chau-ta-leur. There is"—he hesitated—"there is a something there also which I do not quite understand that—protects. But I did not know this when I first hid myself, nein! All I thought was that I could see from there and perhaps come through."

AN INVOLUNTARY thrill of respect for the man went through me at the manifest heroism of this leap of his in the dark. I could see it reflected in Larry's face.

"I hid in the vault," continued Von Hetzdorp, "and I saw that which comes from here come out. I waited long hours. At last, when the moon was low, I saw it return—ecstatically—with a man, a native, in embrace enfolded. It passed through the door, and soon then the moon became low and the door closed. I had found it difficult, and had it not been for whatever it is of protection there in the vault—" He hesitated again, perplexedly.

"The next night," he went on, "more confidence was mine, yes. And after that which comes had gone, I looked through its open door. I said, 'It will not return for three hours. While it is away, why shall I not into its home go through the door it has left open?' So I went—even to here. I looked at the pillars of light and I tested the liquid of the Pool on which they fell, and what I found led me to believe the shape of light emerged from there."

I started. Evidently then, he did not know just how the Dweller materialized from the Pool. He saw my movement and interpreted it correctly.

"You know how it comes?" he asked eagerly.

"Yes," I answered. "Later, I will tell you."

"I analyzed that liquid," he went on, "and then I knew I had been right in one phase at least of my theory. That liquid, Dr. Goodwin, is not water, and it is not any fluid known on earth." He handed me a small vial, its neck held in a long thong.

"Take this," he said, "and see."

Wonderingly, I took the bottle; dipped it down into the Pool. The liquid was extraordinarily light; seemed, in fact, to give the vial buoyancy. I held it to the light. It was striated, streaked, as though little living, pulsing veins ran through it. And its blueness even in the vial, held an intensity of luminousness.

"Radioactive," said Von Hetzdorp. "Some liquid that is intensely radioactive; but what it is I know not at all. Upon the living skin it acts like radium raised to the nth power and with an element most mysterious added. The solution with which I treated him," he pointed to Huldricksson, "I had prepared before I came here, from information I had of what I might find. It is largely salts of radium, and its base is Loeb's formula for the neutralization of radium and X-ray burns. Taking this man at once, before the degeneration had become really active, I could negative it. But after two hours I could have done nothing." He paused a moment.

"Next I studied the nature of these luminous walls. I concluded that whoever had made them, knew the secret of the Almighty's manufacture of light from the ether itself. Colossal! *Ja!* But the substance of these blocks confines an atomic —how would you say?—atomic manipulation, a conscious arrangement of electrons, light-emitting, and perhaps indefinitely so. These blocks are lamps in which oil and wick are—electrons drawing light waves from ether itself! A Prometheus, indeed, this discoverer! *Hein!* Hardly had I concluded these investigations before my watch warned me to go. I went. That which comes forth returned, this time empty-handed.

"And the next night I did the same thing. Engrossed in research, I let the moments go by to the danger point, and scarcely was I replaced within the vault when the shining thing raced over the walls, and in its grip the woman and child. Then you came, and that is all. And now, what is it you know?"

Very briefly I went over my story. His eyes gleamed now and then, but he did not interrupt me.

"A great secret! A colossal secret!" he said at last. "We cannot leave it hidden."

"The first thing to do is to try the door," said Larry, matter of fact.

"There is no use, my young friend," said Von Hetzdorp mildly.

"Nevertheless we'll try," said Larry.

We retraced our way through the winding tunnel to the end, but soon even O'Keefe saw that any idea of moving the slab from within was hopeless. We returned to the Chamber of the Pool. The pillars of light were fainter, and we knew that the moon was sinking. On the world outside before long dawn would be break-

ing. I began to feel thirst, and the blue semblance of water within the silvery room seemed to glint mockingly as my eyes rested on it.

"*Ja!*" said Von Hetzdorp, reading my thoughts uncannily. "*Ja!* We will be thirsty. And it will be very bad for him of us who loses control and drinks of that, my friend!"

Larry threw back his shoulders as though shaking a burden from them.

"We're four able-bodied men up against a bunch of moonshine and a lot of dead ones. Buck up, for Heaven's sake!"

"Do you suggest that we poonch our way out?" asked Von Hetzdorp mildly.

"Forget that, professor," answered Larry almost testily. "I suggest that we look around this place and find something that will take us somewhere. You can bet the people that built it had more ways of getting in than that once-a-month family entrance. Doc, you and Olaf explore the left wall; the professor and I will take the right."

He loosened one of his automatics with a suggestive movement.

"After you, professor," he said politely. And I knew that despite the German's apparent frankness and docility he did not trust him.

Nor did I. And how much did Von Hetzdorp really know? I wondered, as the Norseman and I started off. Clearly more than he had told us; and from whence had come the information that had been detailed enough to enable him to prepare an antidote for the exact effects the touch of the Moon Pool produced? So, wondering, I walked with Olaf, and then soon forgot my perplexity in the contemplation of that greater wonder which I was observing.

THE chamber widened out from the portal in what seemed to be the arc of an immense circle. The shining walls held a perceptible curve, and from this curvature I estimated that the roof was fully three hundred feet above us. It occurred to me that perhaps the Chamber of the Pool was shaped like half a hollow sphere, an inverted bowl. As we silently passed on, I was confirmed in this belief, for clearly we were circling. If I were right, the circumference of the place, reckoning the radius at three hundred feet, must be one thousand eight hundred feet, or a little less than a third of a mile.

The floor was of smooth, mosaic-fitted blocks of a faintly yellow tinge. They were not light-emitting like the blocks that formed the walls. The radiance from these latter, I noted, had the peculiar quality of thickening a few yards from its source, and it was this that produced the effect of misty, veiled distances. As we walked, the seven columns of rays streaming down from the crystalline globes high above us waned steadily; the glow within the chamber lost its prismatic shimmer and became an even gray tone somewhat like moonlight in a thin cloud.

Now before us, out from the wall, jutted a low terrace. It was all of a pearly rose-colored stone, and above it, like a balustrade, marched a row of slender, graceful pillars of the same hue. The face of the terrace was about ten feet high, and all over it ran a bas-relief of what looked like short trailing vines, surmounted by five stalks, on the tip of each of which was a flower. Behind the vines ran a design of semiglobes from which branched delicate tendrils. I did not recognize the carved flowers; they were, I thought, some symbolization in which the true form of the original had been lost.

How then could I have known the incredible thing which these stones pictured! We passed along the terrace. It turned in an abrupt curve. I heard a hail, and there, fifty feet away, at the curving end of a wall identical with that where we stood, were Larry and Von Hetzdorp. Obviously the left side of the chamber was a duplicate of that we had explored. We joined. In front of us the columned barriers ran back a hundred feet, forming an alcove. The end of this alcove was another wall of the same rose stone, but upon it the design was much heavier.

We took a step forward, and then stopped, every muscle rigid. There was a gasp of terrified awe from the Norseman, a guttural exclamation from Von Hetzdorp. For on, or rather within, the wall before us, a great oval began to glow, waxed almost to a flame, and then shone steadily out as though from behind it a light was streaming through the stone itself!

Within the roseate oval two flame-tipped shadows appeared, stood for a moment, and then seemed to float out upon its surface. The shadows wavered; the tips of flame that nimbused them with flickering points of violet and vermilion pulsed outward, drew back, darted forth again, and once more withdrew themselves. And as they did so the shadows thickened, and suddenly there before us stood two figures!

One was a girl—a girl whose great eyes were golden as the fabled lilies of Kwan-Yung that were born of the kiss of the sun upon the amber goddess the demons of Lao-tse carved for him; whose softly curved lips were red as the royal coral, and whose golden-brown hair reached to her knees.

The second was a gigantic frog—a woman frog, head helmeted with carapace of shell around which a fillet of brilliant yellow jewels shone; enormous round eyes of blue circled with a broad iris of green; monstrous body of banded orange and white girdled with strand upon strand of the flashing yellow gems; six feet high if an inch, and with one webbed paw of its short, powerfully muscled forelegs resting upon the white shoulder of the golden-eyed girl.

CHAPTER IX

"I'D FOLLOW HER THROUGH HELL!"

MOMENTS must have passed as we stood in stark amazement, gazing at that incredible apparition. The two figures, although as real as any of those who stood beside me, unfatomlike as it is possible to be, had a distinct suggestion of—projection.

They were there before us—golden-eyed

girl and grotesque frog-woman—complete in every line and curve. And still it was as though their bodies passed back through distances. As though, to try to express the well-nigh inexpressible, the two shapes we were looking upon were the end of an infinite number stretching in fine linked chain far away, of which the eyes saw only the nearest, while in the brain some faculty higher than sight recognized and registered the unseen others.

It crossed my mind that so we three-dimensional beings might appear to those dwellers in the hypothetical two-dimensional space we use to help us conceive the fourth dimension. And yet there was nothing of any metaphysical fourth dimension about them; they were actualities —real, breathing, complete.

The gigantic eyes of the frog-woman took us all in, unwinkingly. I could see little glints of phosphorescence shine out within the metallic green of the outer iris ring. She stood upright, her great legs bowed, the monstrous slit of a mouth slightly open, revealing a row of white teeth sharp and pointed as lancets; the paw resting on the girl's shoulder, half covering its silken surface, and from its five webbed digits long yellow claws of polished horn glistening against the delicate texture of the flesh.

But if the frog-woman regarded us all, not so did the maiden of the rosy wall. Her eyes were fastened upon Larry, drinking him in with extraordinary intentness. She was tall, far over the average of woman, almost as tall, indeed, as O'Keefe himself; not more than twenty years old, if that, I thought. Abruptly she leaned forward, the golden eyes softened and grew tender; the red lips moved as though she were speaking.

Larry took a quick step, and his face was that of one who after countless births comes at last upon the twin soul lost to him for ages. The frog woman turned her eyes upon the girl; her huge lips moved, and I knew that she was talking! The girl held out a warning hand to O'Keefe, and then raised it, resting each finger upon one of the five flowers of the carved vine close beside her. Once, twice, three times, she pressed upon the flower centers, and I noted that her hand was curiously long and slender, the digits like those wonderful tapering ones the painters we call the primitives gave to their Virgins.

Three times she pressed the flowers, and then looked intently at Larry once more. A slow, sweet smile curved the crimson lips. She stretched both hands out toward him again eagerly; and then I distinctly saw a burning blush rise swiftly over white breasts and flowerlike face.

And in that instant, like the clicking out of a cinematograph, the pulsing oval faded and golden-eyed girl and frog-woman were gone!

And thus it was that Lakla, the handmaiden of the Silent Ones, and Larry O'Keefe first looked into each other's hearts!

With their evanishment a spell was lifted from us. Olaf Huldricksson ran a hand over a brow from which tiny beads of sweat had sprung; Von Hetzdorp turned to me with an exclamation; Larry stood rapt, gazing at the stone.

"Eilidh," I heard him whisper; "Eilidh of the lips like the red, red rowan and the golden-brown hair!"

"Clearly of the *Ranadae*," said Von Hetzdorp, " a development of the fossil *Labyrinthodonts*: you saw her teeth, *ja?*"

"Ranadae, yes," I answered. "But from the *Stegocephalia;* of the order *Ecaudata*—"

"Upon what evidence do you base your theory that she was of the *Stego*—"

I think I never heard such complete indignation as was in O'Keefe's voice as he interrupted the German.

"What do you mean, fossils and Stego whatever it is?" he asked. "She was a girl, a wonder girl—a real girl, and Irish, or I'm not an O'Keefe!"

"We were talking about the frog-woman, Larry," I said, conciliatingly.

His eyes were wild as he regarded us.

"Say," he said, "if you two had been in the Garden of Eden when Eve took the apple, you wouldn't have had time to give her a look for counting the scales on the snake."

"But I took especial note of the girl, too, Larry," I pleaded mildly, "and she couldn't have been Irish. Now how could she?"

"Couldn't, eh?" he said. "But she was. Didn't you notice the sweet little tilted nose of her, an' the hair an' the eyes like the sunshine? She's a daughter of the old people, the *Taithada-Dainn*. I'm thinkin' that's who it was, anyway, that made this place on their way to Erin. Not Irish? A girl like that couldn't be anything else!"

He strode swiftly over to the wall. We followed. He sounded the stone. It did not ring hollowly—nor indeed had I expected it to, for the figures had shadowed themselves through the terrace, and had stood upon its surface. Larry paused, stretched his hand up to the flowers on which the tapering fingers of the golden-eyed girl had rested.

"It was here she put up her hand," he murmured. He pressed caressingly the carved calyxes, once, twice, a third time even as she had—and silently and softly the wall began to split. On each side a great stone pivoted slowly, and before us a portal stood, opening into a narrow corridor glowing with the same rosy lustre that had gleamed around the flame-tipped shadows.

O'Keefe leaped forward. I caught him by the arm. The far wall of the tunnel that had been revealed was not more than eight feet from where we were, and it ran, apparently, at right angles to the entrance. There was little of it to be seen, therefore, save the space just in front of us, and I will confess that my nerves were slightly shaken.

"What's the matter?" he asked.

"Wait," I answered. "Don't rush in there. Let us go together and carefully."

"Come, then, quickly," he said, curiously distrait. "I won't wait. I must follow. That's what she meant, you know."

"What she meant?" I echoed stupidly.

"What she meant when she pointed out the way to open the wall, of course," he said impatiently. "Don't you know that was why she pressed those flowers? She meant us—me—to follow her. Follow her? Why, I'd follow her through a thousand hells!"

Huldricksson stepped beside him. He set a great hand upon the Irishman's shoulder.

"*Ja!*" he rumbled. "That was no *Troldkvinde*, no black witch, that *Jomfru!* She was a white virgin, ja. Well I know that this is Trolldom, but she will help me find my Helma! You go, and Olaf Huldricksson's arm you have with you, always; ja, ready to hold or to strike. Come!"

His hand fell from Larry's shoulder and gripped the Irishman's own. I reached down and picked up my emergency kit.

"Have your gun ready, Olaf!" said Larry. With Huldricksson at one end, O'Keefe at the other, both of them with automatics in hand, and Von Hetzdorp and I between them, we stepped over the threshold.

A T OUR right, a few feet away, the passage ended abruptly in a square of polished stone, from which came the faint rose radiance of what Von Hetzdorp had called the "etheric lights." The roof of the place was less than two feet over O'Keefe's head. Behind us was the portal leading into the Chamber of the Pool.

We turned to the left to look down the tunnel's length, and each of us stiffened. A yard in front of us lifted a four-foot high, gently curved barricade, stretching from wall to wall. Beyond it was blackness; an utter and appalling blackness that seemed to gather itself from infinite depths and to be thrust back by the low barrier as a dike thrusts back the menacing sea threatening ever to overwhelm it.

The rose-glow in which we stood was cut off by that blackness as though it had substance; it shimmered out to meet it, and was checked as though by a blow. Indeed, so strong was the suggestion of sinister, straining force within the rayless opacity that I shrank back, and Von Hetzdorp with me. Not so O'Keefe. Olaf beside him, he strode to the wall and peered over. He beckoned us.

"Flash your pocket-light down there," he said to me, pointing into the thick darkness below us. The little electric circle quivered down as though afraid, and came to rest upon a surface that resembled nothing so much as clear, black ice. I ran the light across, here and there. The floor of the corridor was of stone, so smooth, so polished, that no man could have walked upon it; it sloped downward at a slowly increasing angle.

"We'd have to have non-skid chains and brakes on our feet to tackle that," mused Larry. Abstractedly he ran his hands over the edge on which he was leaning. Suddenly they hesitated and then gripped tightly.

"That's a queer one!" he exclaimed. His right palm was resting upon a rounded protuberance, on the side of which were three small circular indentations.

He pressed his fingers upon the circles. They gave under the pressure much, I thought, as an automatic punch does. O'Keefe's thrusting fingers sank deep, deeper, within the stone. There was a sharp click; the slabs that had opened to let us through swung swiftly together; a curiously rapid vibration thrilled through us, a wind arose and passed over our heads. A wind that grew and grew until it became a whistling shriek, then a roar and then a mighty humming, to which every atom in our bodies pulsed in rhythm painful almost to disintegration.

The rosy wall dwindled in a flash to a point of light, and disappeared.

Wrapped in the clinging, impenetrable blackness we were racing, dropping, hurling at a frightful speed—where?

And ever that awful humming of the rushing wind and the lightning cleaving of the tangible dark—so, it came to me oddly, must the newly released soul race through the sheer blackness of outer space up to that Throne of Justice, where God sits high above all suns!

I felt Von Hetzdorp creep close to me;

gripped my nerve and flashed my pocket-light; saw Larry standing, peering, peering ahead, and Huldricksson, one strong arm around his shoulders, bracing him. And then the speed began to slacken.

Millions of miles, it seemed, below the sound of the unearthly hurricane I heard Larry's voice, thin and ghostlike, beneath its clamor.

"Got it!" shrilled the voice. "Got it! Don't worry!"

The wind died down to a roar, passed back into the whistling shriek and diminished to a steady whisper.

"Press all the way in these holes and she goes top-high," Larry shouted. "Diminish pressure—diminish speed. The curve of this—dashboard—here sends the wind shooting up over our heads—like a windshield. What's behind you?"

I flashed the light back. The mechanism on which we were ended in another wall exactly similar to that over which O'Keefe crouched.

"Well, we can't fall out, anyway," he laughed. "Wish I knew where the brakes were! Look out!"

We dropped dizzily down an abrupt, seemingly endless slope; fell—fell as into an abyss—then shot abruptly out of the blackness into a throbbing green radiance. O'Keefe's fingers must have pressed down upon the controls, for we leaped forward almost with the speed of light. I caught a glimpse of luminous immensities, on the verge of which we flew; of depths inconceivable, and flitting through the incredible spaces—gigantic shadows as of the wings of Israfel, which are so wide, say the Arabs, the world can cower under them like a nestling. And then again the dreadful blackness.

"What was that?" This from Larry, with the nearest approach to awe that I had yet heard from him.

"Trolldom!" croaked the voice of Olaf.

"*Gott!*" This from Von Hetzdorp. "What a space!

"Have you considered, Dr. Goodwin," he went on after a pause, "a curious thing? Probably the moon was hurled out of this same region we now call the Pacific when the earth was yet like molasses; almost molten, I should say. And is it not curious that that which comes from the moon chamber needs the moon rays to bring it forth? And also that the stone depends upon the moon for operating? *Ja!* And last, such a space in mother earth as we just glimpsed, how else could it have been torn but by some gigantic birth, like that of the moon?"

I started; there was so much that this might explain—an unknown element that responded to the moon-rays in opening the moon-door; the blue Pool with its weird radioactivity, and the peculiar mystery within it that reacted to the same light stream—What is there at the heart of earth? What of that radiant unknown element upon the moon mount Tycho? Yes—and what if Tycho's enigma had itself come from earth heart? What miracles were hidden there?

CHAPTER X

THE END OF THE JOURNEY

THE car seemed to poise itself for an instant, and then again dipped itself, literally down into sheer space; skimmed forward in what was clearly curved flight, rose as upon a sweeping up-grade, and then began swiftly to slacken its fearful speed. I glanced at the illuminated dial of the watch on my wrist. It had been exactly twelve minutes since we had seen the roseate door fade into the blackness. But how far had we gone in those twelve minutes—scores of miles or hundreds of miles?—there was no knowing.

Far ahead a point of light showed; grew steadily; we were within it. Then softly all movement ceased.

It was then I noted that the car, for so I must call it, that had brought us to this place was shaped somewhat like one of the Thames punts. Its back must have fitted with the utmost nicety into the end of the passage upon which the inner doors of the Moon Pool Chamber had opened, for certainly when we stepped within it there had been no sign that it was other than part of the wall itself.

Where was its guiding mechanism? I could only conjecture that as the car moved away from the entrance there were slabs that slipped ingeniously into place, protecting those within from what would have been instant annihilating contact with the tunnel walls when the car ran close to them, or from pitching out when it skirted in the blackness, abysses such as that luminous green space that had sent each of our souls shivering back in awe.

The car rested in a slit in the center of a smooth walled chamber perhaps twenty feet square. The wall facing us was pierced by a low doorway through which we could see a flight of steps leading downward.

I glanced upward. The light streamed through an enormous oval opening, the base of which was twice a tall man's height from the floor. A curving flight of broad, low steps led up to it. And now it came to my steadying brain that there was something puzzling, peculiar, strangely unfamiliar about this light. It was silvery, shaded faintly with a delicate blue and flushed lightly with a nacreous rose; but a rose that differed from that of the terraces of the Pool Chamber as the rose within the opal differs from that within the pearl. In it were tiny, gleaming points like the motes in a sunbeam, but sparkling white like the dust of diamonds, and with a quality of vibrant vitality; they were as though they were alive. The light cast no shadows!

A little breeze came through the oval and played about us. It was laden with what seemed the mingled breath of spice flowers and pines. It was curiously vivifying, and in it the diamonded atoms of the light shook and danced.

Something flashed within the opening—fluttered and came to rest. A bird stood there regarding us; a bird as large as a pheasant, whose golden eyes were the color of the eyes of the maid of the rosy wall, and whose body was a floating, shimmering cloud of moonlight plumes as fairylike as those that veil the gigantic silver moths which guard, the fellahs say, the secret shrine of Isis in the desert beyond the second cataract, and whose touch brings madness.

For a moment it looked at us, then slowly floated like a shining cloud through the doorway. From without came a sudden sweet chiming as of tiny golden bells.

O'Keefe leaped over the low parapet to the floor; sprang to the portal; peered down.

"She sent that!" he said with conviction, turning to me. "She sent it to show the way!"

I caught a faint sardonic grin from Von Hetzdorp, stepped out of the car, the German following, and began to ascend the curved steps toward the oval opening, at the top of which O'Keefe and Olaf already stood. I hurried forward.

At first all that I could see was space. A space filled with the same coruscating effulgence that pulsed about me. I glanced upward, obeying that instinctive impulse of earth folk that bids them seek within the sky for sources of light. There was no sky. All was a sparkling nebulosity rising into infinite distances as the azure above the day-world seems to fill all the heavens. Through it ran pulsing waves and flashing javelin rays that were like shining shadows of the aurora; echoes, octaves lower, of those brilliant arpeggios and chords that play about the poles. My eyes fell beneath its splendor; I started outward.

And now I saw, miles away, gigantic luminous cliffs springing sheer from the limits of a lake whose waters were of milky opalescence. It was from these cliffs that the spangled radiance came, shimmering out from all their lustrous surfaces. To left and to right, as far as the eye could see, they stretched, and they vanished in the auroral nebulosity on high.

"LOOK at that!" exclaimed Larry. I followed his pointing finger. On the face of the shining wall, stretched between two colossal columns, hung an incredible veil; prismatic, gleaming with all the colors

of the spectrum. It was like a web of rainbows woven by the fingers of the daughters of the Jinni. In front of it and a little at each side was a semicircular pier, or better, a plaza of what appeared to be glistening, pale-yellow ivory. At each end of its half-circle clustered a few low-walled, rose-stone structures, each of them surmounted by a number of high, slender pinnacles.

"Of a hugeness, that!" It was Von Hetzdorp. "Have you considered that those precipices must from eight to ten miles away be, Dr. Goodwin? And, if so, how great must that so strange, prismatic curtain that we see so clearly be, eh? What hands could carve those columns between which it hangs? It is in my mind that we will carry back with us many new things, Dr. Goodwin—if we carry back at all," he concluded slowly.

We looked at each other, helplessly, and back again through the opening. We were standing, as I have said, at its base. The wall in which it was set was at least ten feet thick, and so, of course, all that we could see of that which was without were the distances that revealed themselves above the outer ledge of the oval.

"Let's take a look at what's under us," said Larry.

He crept out upon the ledge and peered down, the rest of us following. We stared in utter silence. A hundred yards beneath us stretched gardens that must have been like those of many-columned Iram, which the ancient Addite King had built for his pleasure ages before the deluge. And which Allah, so the Arab legend tells, took and hid from man, within the Sahara, beyond all hope of finding—jealous because they were more beautiful than his in paradise. Within them flowers and groves of laced, fernlike trees, pillared pavilions nestled.

The trunks of the trees were of emerald, of vermilion, and of azure-blue, and the blossoms, whose fragrance was borne to us, shone like jewels. The graceful pillars were tinted delicately. I noted that the pavilions were double—in a way, two-storied — and that they were oddly splotched with circles, with squares, and with oblongs of opacity. I noted, too, that over many this opacity stretched like a roof.

Yet it did not seem material; rather was it—impenetrable shadow!

Down through this city of gardens ran a broad, shining green thoroughfare, glistening like glass and spanned at regular intervals with graceful, arched bridges. The road flashed to a wide square, where rose, from a base of that same silvery stone that formed the lip of the Moon Pool, a Titanic tower of seven terraces; and along it flitted objects that bore a curious resemblance to the shell of the nautilus. Within them were human figures. And upon tree-bordered promenades on each side walked others.

Far to the right we caught the glint of another emerald paved road.

And between the two the gardens grew sweetly down to the hither side of that opalescent water across which were the radiant cliffs and the curtain of mystery.

Thus it was that we first saw the city of the Dweller; blessed and accursed as no place on earth, or under or above earth has ever been—or, that force willing which some call God, ever again shall be!

"*Gott!*" whispered Von Hetzdorp. "Incredible!"

"Trolldom!" gasped Olaf Huldricksson. "It is Trolldom!"

With the three of us close behind, Larry marched toward the entrance through which the white bird had floated.

Was Throckmartin out there in that strange place, I wondered—Throckmartin and his bride, Stanton and Thora—and Olaf's wife? And how would we find them? In what state? Was the Dweller not malign? A weird, inexplicable messenger carrying those on whom it set its seal to some unearthly paradise?

But, whatever it was, I had found the place I aimed for.

Somewhere here, I was convinced, were my lost friend and those he loved.

CHAPTER XI

PRIESTESS OF THE SHINING ONE

"YOU'D better have this handy, Doc." O'Keefe paused at the head of the stairway and handed me one of the automatics he had taken from Von Hetzdorp.

"Shall I not have one also?" rather anxiously asked the latter.

"When you need it you'll get it," answered O'Keefe. "I'll tell you frankly, though, professor, that you'll have to show me before I trust you with a gun. You shoot too straight—from cover."

The flash of anger in the German's eyes turned to a cold consideration.

"You say always just what is in your mind, Lieutenant O'Keefe," he mused. "*Ja*—that I shall remember." Later I was to recall this odd observation, and Von Hetzdorp was to remember, indeed.

In single file, O'Keefe at the head and Olaf bringing up the rear, we passed through the portal. Before us dropped a circular shaft, into which the light from the chamber of the oval streamed liquidly; set in its sides, the steps spiraled, and down them we went, cautiously. The stairway ended in a circular well; silent, with no trace of exit. The rounded stones joined each other evenly, hermetically. Carved on one of the slabs was one of the five flowered vines. I pressed my fingers upon the calyxes, even as Larry had within the moon chamber.

A crack—horizontal, four feet wide—appeared on the wall; widened, and as the sinking slab that made it dropped to the level of our eyes, we looked through a hundred-feet-long rift in the living rock! The stone fell steadily, and we saw that it was a Cyclopean wedge set within the slit of the passageway. It reached the level of our feet and stopped. At the far end of this tunnel, whose floor was the polished rock that had, a moment before, fitted hermetically into its roof, was a low, narrow, triangular opening through which light streamed.

"Nowhere to go but out!" grinned Larry.

"And I'll bet Golden Eyes is waiting for us with a taxi!" He stepped forward. We followed, slipping, sliding, along the glassy surface. And I, for one, had a lively apprehension of what our fate would be should that enormous mass rise before we had emerged. We reached the end, crept out of the narrow triangle that was its exit.

We stood upon a wide ledge carpeted with a thick yellow moss. I looked behind, and clutched O'Keefe's arm. The door through which we had come had vanished! There was only a precipice of pale rock, on whose surfaces great patches of the amber moss hung; around whose base our ledge ran, and whose summits, if summits it had, were hidden, like the luminous cliffs, in the radiance above us.

"Nowhere to go but ahead, and Golden Eyes hasn't kept her date!" laughed O'Keefe—but somewhat grimly.

We looked down. At the left the green roadway curved, and, at least thirty feet below us, swept on. Far off to the right it swerved again and continued as the glistening distant ribbon we had seen from the high oval. Within its loop, like a peninsula, its foot bathed by the lake, lay the gardened city. What was beyond the road we could not see for, all along its outer side, it was banked with solid masses of high-flung verdure.

We walked a few yards along the ledge and, rounding a corner, faced the end of one of the slender bridges. From this vantage point the oddly shaped vehicles were plain, and we could see they were, indeed, like the shell of the Nautilus and elfinly beautiful. Their drivers sat high upon the forward whorl. Their bodies were piled high with cushions, upon which lay women half-swathed in gay silken webs. From the pavilioned gardens smaller channels of glistening green ran into the broad way, much as usual automobile runways do; and in and out of them flashed the fairy shells.

There came a shout from one. Its occupants had glimpsed us. They pointed; others stopped and stared; one shell turned and sped up a runway—and quickly over the other side of the bridge came a score of men. They were dwarfed—none of them more than five feet high, prodigiously broad of shoulder, clearly enormously powerful.

"*Trolde!*" muttered Olaf, stepping beside O'Keefe, pistol swinging free in his hand.

But at the middle of the bridge the leader stopped, waved back his men, and came toward us alone, palms outstretched in the immemorial, universal gesture of truce. He paused, scanning us with manifest wonder; we returned the scrutiny with interest. The dwarf's face was as white as Olaf's—far whiter than those of the other three of us; the features clean-cut and noble, almost classical; the wide set eyes of a curious greenish gray and the black hair curling over his head like that on some old Greek statue.

Dwarfed though he was, there was no suggestion of deformity about him. The gigantic shoulders were covered with a loose green tunic that looked like fine linen. It was caught in at the waist by a broad girdle studded with what seemed to be amazonites. In it was thrust a long curved poniard resembling the Malaysian kris. His legs were swathed in the same green cloth as the upper garment. His feet were sandaled.

My gaze returned to his face, and in it I found something subtly disturbing; an expression of half-malicious gaiety that underlay the wholly prepossessing features like a vague threat. A mocking deviltry that hinted at entire callousness to suffering or sorrow; something of the spirit that was vaguely alien and disquieting.

HE SPOKE, and to my surprise, enough of the words were familiar to enable me clearly to catch the meaning of the whole. They were Polynesian, the Polynesian of the Samoans which is its most ancient form, but in some indefinable way—archaic. Later I was to know that the tongue bore the same relation to the Polynesian of today as does that of haucer to modern English.

Huldricksson spoke Polynesian well, and understood it better than he spoke it; O'Keefe had a working smattering. Later I was to find the German was a master of it.

"From whence do you come, strangers, and how found you your way here?" said the green dwarf.

I waved my hand toward the cliff behind us. His eyes narrowed incredulously; he glanced at its drop, upon which even a mountain goat could not have made its way, and laughed.

"We came through the rock," I answered his thought. "And we come in peace," I added.

"And may peace walk with you," he said half-derisively, "if the Shining One wills it!"

He considered us again.

"Show me, strangers, where you came through the rock," he commanded. We led the way to where we had emerged from the well of the stairway.

"It was here," I said, tapping the cliff.

"But I see no opening," he said suavely.

"It closed behind us," I answered; and then, for the first time, realized how incredible the explanation sounded. The derisive gleam passed through his eyes again. But he drew his poniard and gravely sounded the rock.

"You give a strange turn to our speech," he said. "It sounds strangely, indeed—as strange as your answers." He looked at us quizzically. "I wonder where you learned it! Well, all that you can explain to the Afyo Maie." His head bowed and his arms swept out in a wide salaam. "Be pleased to come with me!" he ended abruptly.

"In peace?" I asked.

"In peace," he replied. Then slowly, "With me, at least."

"Oh, come on, Doc!" cried Larry. "As long as we're here let's see the sights. *Allons mon vieux!*" he called gaily to the green dwarf. The latter, understanding the spirit, if not the words, looked at O'Keefe with a twinkle of approval.

He stood aside and waved a hand courteously, inviting us to pass. We reached the bridge again; he spoke two words to his men, who immediately lined up on each side of the arch, watching us as we walked between them with that same suggestion of expectant, malicious derision that I found so disquieting in their leader. We crossed. At the base of the span one of the elfin shells was waiting.

"Free ride in the subway patrol," whispered O'Keefe, grinning.

Beyond, scores of the shells had gathered, their occupants evidently discussing us in much excitement. The green dwarf waved us to the piles of cushions and then threw himself beside us. The vehicle started off smoothly, the now silent throng making way, and swept down the green roadway at a terrific pace and wholly without vibration, toward the seven-terraced tower.

WE TURNED abruptly and swept up a runway through one of the gardens, and stopped softly before a pillared pavilion. I saw now that these were much larger than I had thought. The structure to which we had been carried covered, I estimated, fully an acre. Oblong, with its slender, vari-colored columns spaced regularly, its walls were like the sliding screens of the Japanese. I had little time to note them, nor, to my regret, to satisfy my very eager curiosity as to the character of the trees and the beautiful bowering blossoms.

The green dwarf hurried us up a flight of broad steps flanked by great carved serpents, winged and scaled. He stamped twice upon mosaicked stones between two of the pillars, and a screen rolled aside, revealing an immense hall, scattered about with low divans on which lolled a dozen or more of the dwarfish men, dressed identically as he.

They sauntered up to us leisurely; the surprised interest in their faces tempered by the same inhumanly gay malice that seemed to be characteristic of all these people we had as yet seen.

"The Afyo Maie awaits them, Rador," said one.

So the green dwarf's name was Rador.

He nodded, beckoned us, and led the way through the great hall and into a smaller chamber whose far side was covered with the opacity I had noted from the aerie of the cliff. I examined the—blackness—with lively interest.

It had neither substance nor texture; it was not matter—and yet it suggested solidity; an entire cessation, a complete absorption of light; an ebon veil at once immaterial and palpable. I stretched, involuntarily, my hand out toward it, and felt it quickly drawn back.

"Do you seek your end so soon?" whispered Rador. "But I forgot that you do not know," he added. "On your life touch not the blackness, ever. It—"

He stopped, for abruptly in the density a portal appeared; springing out of the shadow like a picture thrown by a lantern upon a screen. Through it was revealed a chamber filled with a soft, rosy glow. Rising from cushioned couches, a woman and a man regarded us, half leaning over a long, low table of what seemed polished jet, laden with flowers and unfamiliar fruits.

About the room—that part of it, at least, that I could see—were a few oddly shaped chairs of the same substance. On high silvery tripods stood three immense globes, and it was from them that the rose glow emanated. At the side of the woman stood a smaller globe whose roseate gleam was tempered by quivering waves of blue.

"Enter Rador with the strangers!" a clear, sweet voice called.

Rador bowed deeply and stood aside, motioning us to pass. We entered, the green dwarf behind us, and out of the corner of my eye I saw the doorway fade as abruptly as it had appeared and again the dense shadow fill its place.

"Come closer, strangers. Be not afraid!" commanded the bell-toned voice.

We approached.

The woman, unimaginative scientist that I am, made the breath catch in my throat. Never had I seen a woman so beautiful as was Yolara of the Dweller city, and none of so perilous a beauty. Her hair was of the color of the young tassels of the corn and coiled in a regal crown above her broad, white brows. Her wide eyes were of gray that could change to a corn-flower blue and in anger deepen to purple. Gray or blue, they had little laughing devils within them, but when the storm of anger darkened them, they were no longer laughing.

The silken web that half covered, half revealed her did not hide the ivory whiteness of her flesh nor the sweet curve of shoulders and breasts. But for all her amazing beauty, she was sinister! There was cruelty about the curving mouth, and in the music of her voice. Not conscious cruelty, but the more terrifying, careless cruelty of nature itself. And she exhaled an essence of vitality that made the nerves tingle toward her and shrink from her, too, as though from something that was abnormal.

The girl of the rose wall had been beautiful, yes! But here beauty was human, understandable. You could imagine her with a babe in her arms, but you could not so imagine this woman. About her loveliness hovered something unearthly. A sweet, feminine echo of the Dweller was Yolara, the Dweller's priestess—and as gloriously, terrifyingly evil!

CHAPTER XII

THE JUSTICE OF LORA

AS I LOOKED at her the man arose and made his way round the table toward us. For the first time my eyes took in Lugur. A few inches taller than the green dwarf, he was far broader, more filled with the suggestion of appalling strength.

The tremendous shoulders were four feet wide if an inch, tapering down to mighty thewed thighs. The muscles of his chest stood out beneath his tunic of red. Around his forehead shone a chaplet of bright-blue stones, sparkling among the thick curls of his silver-ash hair.

Upon his face pride and ambition were written large, and power still larger. All the mockery, the malice, the hint of callous indifference that I had noted in the other dwarfish men were there, too—but intensified, touched with the satanic.

The woman spoke again.

"Who are you strangers, and how came you here?" She turned to Rador. "Or is it that they do not understand our tongue?"

"One understands and speaks it, but very badly, O Yolara," answered the green dwarf.

"Speak, then, that one of you," she commanded.

But it was Von Hetzdorp who found his voice first, and I marveled at the fluency, so much greater than mine, with which he spoke.

"We came for different purposes. I to seek knowledge of a kind, he"—pointing to me—"of another. This man"—he looked at Olaf—"to find a wife and child."

The gray-blue eyes had been regarding O'Keefe steadily and with plainly increasing interest.

"And why did you come?" she asked him. "Nay, I would have him speak for himself, if he can," she stilled Von Hetzdorp peremptorily.

When Larry spoke it was haltingly, in the tongue that was strange to him, searching for the proper words.

"I came to help these men, and because something I could not then understand called me, O lady whose eyes are like forest pools at dawn," he answered. And even in the unfamiliar words there was a touch of the Irish brogue, and little merry lights danced in the eyes Larry had so apostrophized.

"I could find fault with your speech, but none with its burden," she said. "What forest pools are I know not, and the dawn has not shone upon the people of Lora these many *sais* of *laya*. But I sense what you mean!"

The eyes deepened to blue as she regarded him. I saw Lugur shift impatiently and send a none too pleasant look at O'Keefe. She smiled.

"Are there many like you in the world from which you come?" she asked softly. "Well, we soon shall—"

Lugur interrupted her almost rudely and glowering.

"Best we should know how they came hence," he growled.

She darted a quick look at him, and again the little devils danced in her wondrous eyes.

"Yes, that is true," she said. "How came you here?"

Again it was Von Hetzdorp who answered—slowly, considering every word.

"In the world above," he said, "there are ruins of cities not built by any of those who now dwell there. To some of us above these places called, and we sought for knowledge of those wise ones passed on. We were seeking, and we found a passageway. The way led us downward to a door in yonder cliff, and through it we came here."

"Then you have found what you sought!" spoke she. "For we are of those who built the cities. But this gateway in the rock—where is it?"

"After we passed, it closed upon us; nor could we after find trace of it," answered Von Hetzdorp.

The incredulity that had shown upon the face of the green dwarf fell upon theirs; on Lugur's it was clouded with furious anger.

He turned to Rador.

"I could find no opening, lord," thus the green dwarf quickly.

And there was so fierce a fire in the eyes of Lugur as he swung back upon us that O'Keefe's hand slipped stealthily down toward his pistol.

"Best it is to speak truth to Yolara, priestess of the Shining One, and to Lugur, the Voice," he cried menacingly.

"It is the truth," I interposed. "We came down the passage. At its end was a carved vine, a vine of five flowers"—the fire died from the red dwarf's eyes, and I could have sworn to a swift pallor. "I rested a hand upon these flowers, and a door opened. But when we had gone through it and turned, behind us was nothing but unbroken cliff. The door had vanished."

I had taken my cue from Von Hetzdorp. If he had eliminated the episode of car and Moon Pool, he had good reason, I had no doubt; and I would be as cautious. And deep within me something cautioned me to say nothing of my quest; to stifle all thought of Throckmartin. Something that warned, peremptorily, finally, as though it were a message from Throckmartin himself!

"A vine with five flowers!" exclaimed the red dwarf. "Was it like this, say?"

He thrust forward a long arm. Upon the thumb of the hand was an immense ring, set with a dull-blue stone. Graven on the face of the jewel was the symbol of the rosy walls of the Moon Chamber that had opened to us their two portals. But cut over the vine were seven circles, one about each of the flowers and two larger ones covering, intersecting them.

"This is the same," I said; "but these were not there"—I indicated the circles.

The woman drew a deep breath and looked deep into Lugur's eyes.

"The sign of the Silent Ones!" he half whispered.

It was the woman who first recovered herself.

"The strangers are weary, Lugur," she said. "When they are rested they shall show us where the rocks opened."

I sensed a subtle change in their attitude toward us; a new intentness; a doubt plainly tinged with apprehension. What was it they feared? I wondered; and why had the symbol of the vine wrought the change? And who or what were the Silent Ones?

YOLARA'S eyes turned to Olaf, hardened, and grew cold gray. Subconsciously I had noticed that from the first the Norseman had been absorbed in his regard of the pair; had indeed never taken his gaze from them; had noticed, too, the priestess dart swift glances toward him.

Upon Olaf's face had been an early look of puzzlement, of uncertainty. Now this had changed to decision; clearly he had made his mind up about something. His gaze was fixed; he returned the woman's scrutiny fearlessly; a touch of contempt in the clear eyes—like a child watching a snake which he did not dread, but whose danger he well knew.

Under that look Yolara stirred impatiently, sensing, I know, its meaning.

"Why do you look at me so?" she cried.

An expression of bewilderment passed over Olaf's face.

"I do not understand," he said in English.

I caught a quickly repressed gleam in O'Keefe's eyes. He knew, as I knew, that Olaf must have understood. But did Von Hetzdorp?

I glanced at him. Apparently he did not. But why was Olaf feigning this ignorance?

"This man is a sailor from what we call the North," thus Larry haltingly. "He is crazed, I think. He tells a strange tale, of a something of white fire that took his wife and babe. We found him wandering where we were. And because he is strong we brought him with us. That is all, O lady whose voice is sweeter than the honey of the wild bees!"

"A shape of white fire?" she repeated eagerly.

"A shape of white fire that whirled beneath the moon, with the sound of little bells," answered Larry, watching her intently.

She looked at Lugur and laughed.

"Then he, too, is fortunate," she said. "For he has come to the place of his something of white fire. And tell him that he shall join his wife and child, in time; that I promise him."

Upon the Norseman's face there was no hint of comprehension, and at that moment I formed an entirely new opinion of Olaf's intelligence. For certainly it must have been a prodigious effort of the will indeed that enabled him, understanding, to control himself.

"What does she say?" he asked.

Larry repeated.

An expression of gladness spread over his face.

"Good!" said Olaf. "Good!"

He looked at Yolara with well-assumed gratitude. Lugur, who had been scanning his bulk, drew close. He felt the giant muscles which Huldricksson accommodatingly flexed for him.

"But he shall meet Valdor and Tahola before he sees those kin of his," he laughed mockingly. "And if he bests them, he shall meet me. After that—for reward—his wife and babe!"

A shudder, quickly repressed, shook the seaman's frame. The woman bent her supremely beautiful head.

"These two," she said, pointing to the German and me, "seem to be men of learning. They may be useful. As for this man"—she smiled at Larry—"I would have him explain to me some things. She hesitated. "What 'hon-ey of 'e wild bees-s' is?" She laughed sweetly, sinisterly. "And now—take them, Rador, give them food and water and let them rest till we shall call them again."

She stretched out a hand toward O'Keefe. The Irishman bowed low over it, raised it softly to his lips. There was a vicious hiss from Lugur; but Yolara regarded Larry with eyes now all tender blue.

"You please me," she whispered.

And the face of Lugur grew dark with passion.

We turned to go. The rosy, azure-shot globe at her side suddenly dulled. From it came a faint bell sound as of chimes far away. She bent over it. It vibrated, and then its surface ran with little waves of dull color. From it came a whispering so low that I could not distinguish the words, if words they were.

She spoke to the red dwarf.

"They have brought the three who blasphemed the Shining One," she said slowly. "Now it is in my mind to show these strangers the justice of Lora. Perhaps, they may learn wisdom from it. What say you, Lugur?"

The red dwarf nodded, his eyes sparkling now with a malicious anticipation.

The woman spoke again to the globe. "Bring them here!"

And again it ran swiftly with its film of colors, darkened, and shone rosy once more. From without there came the rustle of many feet upon the rugs. Yolara pressed a slender hand upon the base of the pedestal of the globe beside her. Abruptly the light faded from all, and on the same instant the four walls of blackness vanished, revealing on two sides the lovely, unfamiliar garden through the guarding rows of pillars. At our backs soft draperies hid what lay beyond; before us, flanked by flowered screens, was the corridor through which we had entered, crowded now by the green dwarfs of the great hall.

THE dwarfs advanced. Each, I now noted, had the same clustering black hair of Rador. They separated, and from them stepped three figures—a youth of not more than twenty, short, but with great shoulders of all the males we had seen of this race; a girl of seventeen, I judged, white-faced, a head taller than the boy, her long, black hair disheveled, and clad in a simple white sleeveless garment that fell only to the knees. And behind these two a stunted, gnarled shape whose head was sunk deep between the enormous shoulders, whose white beard fell like that of some ancient gnome down to his waist, and whose eyes were a white flame of hate. The girl cast herself weeping at the feet of the priestess; the youth regarded her curiously.

"You are Songar of the Lower Waters?" murmured Yolara almost caressingly. "And this is your daughter and her lover?"

The gnome nodded, the flame in his eyes leaping higher.

"It has come to me that you three have dared blaspheme the Shining One, its priestess, and its Voice," went on Yolara smoothly. "Also that you have called out to the three Silent Ones. Is it true?"

"Your spies have spoken, and have you not already judged us?" The voice of the old dwarf was bitter.

A flicker shot through the eyes of

Yolara, again cold gray. The girl reached a trembling hand up to the hem of her veils. She thrust it aside with her foot cruelly.

"Tell us why you did these things, Songar," she asked. "Why you did them, knowing well what your reward would be?"

The dwarf stiffened; he raised his withered arms, and his eyes blazed.

"Because evil are your thoughts and evil are your deeds," he cried. "Yours and your lover's, there." He leveled a finger at Lugur. "Because of the Shining One you have made evil, too, and the greater wickedness you contemplate—you and he with the Shining One. But I tell you that your measure of iniquity is full; the tale of your sin near ended! Yea, the Silent Ones have been patient, but soon they will speak." He pointed at us. "A sign are they—a warning—harlot!" He spat the word.

In Yolara's eyes, grown black, the devils leaped unrestrained.

"Is it even so, Songar?" her voice caressed. "Now ask the Silent Ones to help you! They sit afar, but surely they will hear you." The sweet voice was mocking. "As for these two, they shall pray to the Shining One for forgiveness, and surely the Shining One will take them to its bosom! As for you, you have lived long enough, Songar! Pray to the Silent Ones, Songar, and pass out into the nothingness —you!"

She dipped down into her bosom and drew forth something that resembled a small cone of tarnished silver. She leveled it, a covering clicked from its base, and out of it darted a slender ray of intense green light.

It struck the old dwarf squarely over the heart, and swift as light itself spread, covering him with a gleaming, pale film. She clenched her hand upon the cone, and the ray disappeared; thrust it back into her breast and leaned forward expectantly; so Lugur and so the other dwarfs. From the girl came a low wail of anguish; the boy dropped upon his knees, covering his face.

For the moment the white beard stood rigid; then the robe that had covered him seemed to melt away, revealing all the knotted, monstrous body. And in that body a vibration began, increasing to incredible rapidity. It wavered before us like a reflection in a still pond stirred by a sudden wind. It grew and grew, to a rhythm whose rapidity was intolerable to watch and that still chained the eyes.

The figure grew indistinct, misty. Tiny sparks in infinite numbers leaped from it—like, I thought, the radiant shower of particles hurled out by radium when seen under the microscope. Mistier still it grew. And then there trembled before us for a moment a faintly luminous shadow which held, here and there, tiny sparkling atoms like those that pulsed in the light about us. The glowing shadow vanished, the sparkling atoms were still for a moment— and then they shot away, joining those dancing others.

Where the gnomelike form had been but a few seconds before—there was nothing!

O'Keefe drew a long breath, and I was sensible of a prickling along my scalp.

Yolara leaned toward us.

"You have seen," she said. Her eyes lingered tigerishly upon Olaf's pallid face. "Heed!" she whispered. She turned to the men in green, who were laughing softly among themselves.

"Take these two, and go!" she commanded.

"The justice of Lora," said the red dwarf. "The justice of Lora and the Shining One under Thanaroa!"

Upon the utterances of the last word I saw Von Hetzdorp start violently. The hand at his side made a swift, surreptitious gesture, so fleeting that I hardly caught it. The red dwarf stared at the German, and for the first time I saw complete amazement upon his face.

He glanced at Yolara, found her intent in thought, and as swiftly as had been Von Hetzdorp's action, returned it. I thought I saw the latter make an answering sign.

"Yolara," the red dwarf spoke, "it would please me to take this man of wisdom to my own place for a time. The giant I would have, too."

The woman awoke from her brooding; nodded.

"As you will, Lugur," she said. She beckoned Rador.

As he led us out I saw from the corner of my eye Olaf following quietly the German and the red dwarf. And again I wondered.

And as, shaken to the core, we passed out into the garden into the full throbbing of the light, I wondered if all the tiny sparkling diamond points that shook about us had once been men like Songar of the Lower Waters—and felt my very soul grow sick!

CHAPTER XIII

THE ANGRY, WHISPERING GLOBE

OUR way led along a winding path between banked masses of feathery ferns whose plumes were starred with fragrant white and blue flowerettes, slender creepers swinging from the branches of the strangely trunked trees bearing along their threads orchidlike blossoms both delicately frail and gorgeously flamboyant. Like the giant mosses which I later saw in the caverned road to the Sea of Crimson, in our flight to the Silent Ones, I could not identify them.

A smaller pavilion arose before us, single-storied, front wide open. Upon its threshold Rador paused, bowed deeply, and motioned us within. The chamber we entered was large, closed on two sides by screens of gray; at the back gay, concealing curtains. The low table of blue stone, dressed with fine white cloths, stretched at one side flanked by the cushioned divans.

At the left was a high tripod bearing one of the rosy globes we had seen in the house of Yolara; at the head of the table a smaller globe similar to the whispering one. Rador pressed upon its base, and two other screens slid into place across the entrance, shutting in the room.

He clapped his hands; the curtains parted, and two girls came through them. Tall and willow lithe, their bluish-black hair falling in ringlets just below their white shoulders, their clear eyes of forget-me-not blue, and skins of extraordinary fineness and purity—they were singularly attractive. Each was clad in an extremely scanty bodice of silken blue, girdled above a kirtle that came barely to their very pretty knees.

The maidens returned our stares with interest, and now I noted that the uncanny deviltry written so large upon the faces of the dwarfs, limned so delicately upon that of Yolara, was here but a shadow. Present it certainly was, but tinctured, underlaid, with a settled wistfulness almost melancholy.

They gave me, I must admit, only a slight share of their attention; Larry the most of it. I lack nearly a foot of his height, my eyes are spectacled.

Their wistfulness fled; they laughed with little gleams of milky teeth—the laughter of careless youth—and Larry laughed with them. The green dwarf regarded all with his malice-tipped smile.

"Food and drink," he ordered.

They dropped back through the curtains.

"Do you like them?" he asked us.

"Some cuties!" said Larry. "They delight the heart," he translated for Rador.

The green dwarf's next remark made me gasp. "They are yours," he said.

The pair re-entered, bearing a great platter on which were small loaves, strange fruits, and three immense flagons of rock crystal—two filled with a slightly sparkling yellow liquid and the third with a purplish drink. I became acutely sensible that it had been hours since I had either eaten or drank. The yellow flagons were set before Larry and me, the purple at Rador's hand.

The girls, at his signal, again withdrew. I raised my glass to my lips and took a deep draft. The taste was unfamiliar but delightful.

Almost at once my fatigue disappeared. I realized a clarity of mind, an interesting exhilaration and sense of irresponsibility, of freedom from care, that were oddly enjoyable. Larry became immediately his old gay self.

Still there did not seem to be any of the characteristics of alcohol in the drink. The bread was excellent, tasting like fine wheat. The fruits were as unfamiliar as the wine, and seemed to have the quality of making one forget any desire for either flesh or vegetables. The green dwarf regarded us whimsically sipping from his great flagon of rock crystal.

"Much do I desire to know of that world you came from," he said at last— "through the rocks," he added mischievously.

"And much do we desire to know of this world of yours, O Rador," I answered.

Should I ask him of the Dweller; seek from him a clue to Throckmartin? Again, clearly as a spoken command, came the warning to forbear, to wait. And once more I obeyed.

"LET us learn, then, from each other." The dwarf was laughing. "And first, are they all like you—drawn out?" He made an expressive gesture. "And are there many of you?"

"There are—" I hesitated, and at last spoke the Polynesian that means tens upon tens multiplied indefinitely—"there are as many as the drops of water in the lake we saw from the ledge where you found us," I continued; "many as the leaves on the trees without. And they are all like us, but varyingly."

He considered skeptically, I could see, my remark upon our numbers.

"In Muria," he said at last, "the men are like me or like Lugur. Our women are as you see them. Like Yolara or like those black-haired two who served you." He hesitated. "And there is a third; but only one."

Larry leaned forward eagerly.

"Brown-haired with glints of ruddy bronze, golden eyed, and lovely as a dream, with long, slender, beautiful hands?" he cried.

"Where saw you her?" interrupted the dwarf, starting to his feet.

"Saw her?" Larry recovered himself. "Nay, Rador, perhaps I only dreamed that there was such a woman."

"See to it, then, that you tell not your dream to Yolara," said the dwarf grimly. "For her I meant and her you have pictured is Lakla, the handmaiden to the Silent Ones, and neither Yolara or Lugur. nay, nor the Shining One, love her overmuch, stranger."

"Does she dwell here?" Larry's face was alight.

The dwarf hesitated, glanced about him anxiously.

"If she does, Doc, we're going to beat it her way quick." Larry shot the words to me quickly.

"Nay," Rador was answering. "Ask me no more of her." He was silent for a space. "And what do you who are as leaves or drops of water do in that world of yours?" he said, plainly bent on turning the subject.

"Keep off the golden-eyed girl, Larry," I interjected. "Wait till we find out why she's taboo."

"Love and battle, strive and accomplish and die; or fail and die," answered Larry —to Rador—giving me a quick nod of acquiescence to my warning in English.

"In that at least your world and mine differ little," said the dwarf.

"How great is this world of yours, Rador?" I spoke.

He considered me gravely.

"How great indeed I do not know," he said frankly at last. "The land where we dwell with the Shining One stretches along the white waters for—" He used a phrase of which I could make nothing. "Beyond this city of the Shining One and on the hither shores of the white waters dwell the *mayia ladala*, the common ones." He took a deep draft from his flagon. "There are, first, the fair-haired ones, the children of the ancient rulers," he continued. "There are, second, we the soldiers; and last the *mayia ladala*, who dig and till and weave and toil and give our rulers and us their daughters, and dance with the Shining One!" he added.

"Who rules?" I asked.

"The fair haired, under the Council of Nine, who are under Yolara, the Priestess and Lugur, the Voice," he answered, "who are in turn beneath the Shining One!" There was a ring of bitter satire in the last.

"And those three who were judged?"—this from Larry.

"They were of the *mayia ladala*," he replied, "like those two I gave you. But they grow restless. They do not like to dance with the Shining One, the blasphemers!" He raised his voice in a sudden great shout of mocking laughter.

In his words I caught a fleeting picture of the race. An ancient, luxurious, close-bred oligarchy clustered about some mysterious deity; a soldier class that supported them; and underneath all the toiling, oppressed hordes.

"And is that all?" asked Larry.

"No," he answered. "Beyond the Lower Waters, over the Black Precipices of Doul are the forests where lie the feathered serpents and the secrets they guard. The Black Precipices of Doul are hard to pass, but none can pass through the feathered serpents. And there is the Sea of Crimson where—" he stopped abruptly, drank and set down his flagon empty. Whatever the purple drink might be, it was loosening the green dwarf's tongue and neither of us cared to interrupt him.

"It is strange, strange indeed to be sitting with two who have newly come from that land that we were forced from so many *sais* of *laya* agone," he began again, half musingly, gone upon another tangent. "For we too came from your world, but how long, long ago! I have heard that the waters swept over us slowly, but dragging, ever dragging our land beneath them. And we sought refuge in the secret heart of our land, refusing to leave her. And at the last we made our way here, where was the Shining One and where had been others before us who had left behind them greater knowledge than we brought—and that was no

little, strangers. And now the *laya* turn upon themselves. The tail of the serpent coils close to his fangs." He took a great drink of the yellow liquid; his eyes flashed.

And without warning the globe beside us sent out an almost vicious note. Rador turned toward it, his face paling. Its surface crawled with whisperings—angry, peremptory!

"I hear!" he croaked, gripping the table. "I obey!"

He turned to us a face devoid for once of its malice.

"Ask me no more questions, strangers," he said. "And now, if you are done, I will show you where you may sleep and bathe."

He arose abruptly. We followed him through the hangings, passed through a corridor and into another smaller chamber, roofless, the sides walled with screens of dark gray. Two cushioned couches were there and a curtained door leading into an open, outer enclosure in which a fountain played within a wide pool of polished green stone. Its opalescent column rose high, and from it fell sprays of shimmering, milky water.

"Your bath," said Rador. He dropped the curtain and came back into the room. He touched a carved flower at one side. There was a tiny sighing from overhead and instantly across the top spread a veil of blackness, impenetrable to light but certainly not to air, for through it pulsed little breaths of the garden fragrances. The room filled with a cool twilight, refreshing, sleep-inducing. The green dwarf pointed to the couches.

"Sleep!" he said. "Sleep and fear nothing. My men are on guard outside." He came closer to us, the old mocking gaiety sparkling in his eyes.

"But I spoke too quickly," he whispered. "Whether it is because the Afyo Maie fears their tongues—or—" he laughed at Larry. "The maids are not yours!" Still laughing he vanished through the curtains of the room of the fountain before I could ask him the meaning of his curious gift, its withdrawal and his most enigmatic closing remarks.

CHAPTER XIV

TROUBLE IS BREWING

"SOME stuff, that. green ray of Yolara's," said O'Keefe, deepest admiration in his voice. "Can you imagine what it would be like in a war—seeing the enemy all at once beginning to shake themselves to pieces? Wow!"

"It's easy enough to explain, Larry," I answered. "The effect, that is—for what the green ray is made of I don't know, of course. But what it does, clearly, is stimulate atomic vibration to such a pitch that the cohesion between the particles of matter is broken and the body flies to bits.

"The green ray set up in the dwarf that incredibly rapid rhythm that you saw and —shook him to atoms!"

All at once I was aware of an intense drowsiness. O'Keefe, yawning, reached down to unfasten his puttees.

"Lord, I'm sleepy!" he exclaimed. "What made Reddy take such a shine to the von?" he asked drowsily.

"Thanaroa," I answered, fighting to keep my eyes open. "When Lugur spoke that name I saw Von Hetzdorp signal him. Thanaroa is, I suspect, the original form of the name of Tangaroa, the greatest god of the Polynesians. There's a secret cult to him in the islands. Von Hetzdorp may belong to it. He knows it anyway. Lugur recognized the signal and despite his surprise answered it."

"The Heinie gave him the high sign, eh?" mused Larry. "How could they both know it?"

"The cult is a very ancient one. Undoubtedly it had its origin in the dim beginnings before these people migrated here," I replied. "It's a link—one—of the few links between up there and the lost past."

"Trouble then," mumbled Larry. "Hell brewing! I smell it. Say, Doc, is this sleepiness natural?" half incoherently.

But I myself was struggling now desperately against the drugged slumber pressing down upon me.

"Lakla!" I heard O'Keefe's murmur. "Lakla of the golden eyes—no, Eilidh—the fair!

"Good luck, old boy, wherever you're going." His hand waved feebly. "Glad—knew—you. Hope—see—you—'gain—"

His voice trailed into silence. Fighting, fighting with every fiber of brain and nerve against the sleep, I felt myself being steadily overcome. But before oblivion rushed down upon me I seemed to see upon the gray screened wall nearest the Irishman an oval of rosy light begin to glow, watched, as my falling lids inexorably fell, a flame-tipped shadow waver on it; thicken, condense. And there looking down upon Larry, her eyes great golden stars in which intensest curiosity and shy tenderness struggled, sweet mouth half smiling, was the girl of the Moon Pool's Chamber, the girl whom the green dwarf had named—Lakla. The vision Larry had invoked before the sleep which I could no longer deny had claimed him.

And did I see about and behind her a cloud of other eyes—not those phosphorescent saucers of the frog woman's enormous eyes—triangular—pools of shining jet flecked with little rushing, flickering ruby flames?

Closer she came—closer—the eyes were over us. Then oblivion indeed!

WHEN I awakened, it was with all the familiar homely sensation of a shade having been pulled up in a darkened room. I thrilled with a wonderful sense of deep rest and restored resiliency. The ebon shadow had vanished from above and down into the room was pouring the silvery light. From the fountain pool came a mighty splashing and shouts of laughter. I jumped over and drew the curtain. O'Keefe and Rador were swimming a wild race; the dwarf like an otter, outdistancing and playing around the Irishman at will. I plunged in.

Tiring at last, we swam to the edge and drew ourselves out. The green dwarf quickly clothed himself and Larry rather carefully donned his uniform.

"The Afyo Maie has summoned us, Doc," he said. "We're to—well, I suppose you'd call it breakfast with her. After that, Rador tells me, we're to have a session with the Council of Nine. I suppose Yolara is as curious as any lady of—the upper world, as you might put it—and just naturally can't wait," he added.

He gave himself a last shake, patted the automatic hidden under his left arm, whistled cheerfully.

"After you, my dear Alphonse," he said to Rador, with a low bow. The dwarf laughed, bent in an absurd imitation of Larry's mocking courtesy and started ahead of us to the house of the priestess. When he had gone a little way on the orchid-walled path I whispered to O'Keefe:

"Larry, when you were falling off to sleep, did you think you saw anything?"

"See anything!" he grinned, "I was hit by that sleep like a fly swatted by Goliath. But wait a minute—" He hesitated. "I had a queer sort of dream."

"What was it?" I asked eagerly.

"Well," he answered, slowly, "I suppose it was because I'd been thinking of—Golden Eyes. Anyway, I thought she came through the wall and leaned over me. Yes, and she put one of those long white hands of hers on my head. I couldn't raise my lids, but in some queerish way I could see her. Then it got real dreamish. She had eyes all about her; a whole little cloud of them—"

"Like these, Larry?" I asked. I drew a pencil from my pocket and sketched the high triangles of flame-flecked blackness I had seen in my own vision.

"How did you know that!" he cried, in utter amazement. Rador turned back toward us. I slipped the paper in my pocket.

"Later," I answered. "Not now. When we're alone."

But through me went a little glow of reassurance. Whatever the maze through which we were moving; whatever of menacing evil lurking there, the Golden Girl was clearly watching over us.

We passed the pillared entrance. In the great hall were the same green dwarfs, this time introduced to us by a variety of names. Each saluted, throwing the right hand high above the head. We went through a long, bowered corridor and stopped before a door that seemed to be sliced from a monolith of pale jade—high, narrow, set in a wall of opal.

Rador stamped twice and with those supernally sweet, silver bell tones, the door swung open.

TO BE CONTINUED

A bizarre story of one man's astral and earthly duality

Who Is Charles Avison?

By EDISON TESLA MARSHALL

NO ONE knew what was going on behind the high board fence at the Avison place, which was difficult to climb. Besides, Avison's stolid neighbors were reluctant to show so much curiosity.

But a few boys lived in the neighborhood who were not troubled by such a sense of decorum. The tallest of them boosted another of the "gang" until a pair of round eyes gazed between the pickets. However, the report that the spy made to the other boys—and later to his parents—was certainly far from enlightening.

He had seen the big house, of course, with its trim lawns and walks. And also he had seen another building that had been erected since the fence. It was built much like a garage, but didn't quite look like a garage either. Protruding out of it was the queerest thing—almost like a huge egg of blue steel, with slabs of heavy glass, and many encircling bands of iron.

It was some time after this that another boy, returning in the late dusk from his milk-delivery, had a story to tell that no one had ever quite believed. As he talked his face flushed and his eyes widened. He said something almost spherical in shape, dark except for lighted windows, had rolled up into the air above the fence, straight up unwaveringly, and had *kept on going!*

The boy had watched it till the haze of evening shut it from his sight, until it had vanished among the early stars.

"You imagined it, my son," said his father. But his mother noticed that her husband was perplexed.

"No, I didn't! I saw it as plain as I see you."

"Well," concluded the father, "we'll probably know what it was in the morning. But, dear," he added, turning to his wife, "that Avison is quite a scientist. The delivery-boy wandered into the wrong door at the Avison place one day, and he told me he went into the uncanniest-looking room he was ever in. A laboratory of some kind it was, with big machines of porcelain and steel and copper."

"And you know he wrote some sort of a scientific article just when he got out of college," supplemented his wife. "It caused quite a sensation among the scientists."

"That's right. It was about gravity, wasn't it? Let's see; that was four years ago. I had almost forgotten. He's a smart young chap all right."

"But why doesn't he go into business?" the woman protested. "He's been engaged for almost a year now to that Cole girl, you know, and if something should happen to him——"

"Oh, well, he's probably pretty careful. And you're sure you didn't imagine it, son, or dream it?"

"I'm sure, sir!" replied the boy.

Nor had he dreamed or imagined it. And had Charles Avison wished he could have surprised even more the scientific world. But he wished to wait.

It was true he had been engaged to Agnes Cole for twelve months. In truth, she was mightily afraid of an accident to the young scientist. Even Avison had confessed to the danger in this latest experiment of his.

The afternoon before the Vulcan ascended, Avison had spent with Agnes. They had had a long talk, in which he told her much of his plan, but little of the danger. But there was a chance, he said, that he would not be at hand to marry her on the June day selected.

She had tried to dissuade him.

"I must go," he said. "You can't imagine how much it means. But I'm sure nothing will happen. Oh, I'll come back all right! My trial flight was a wonderful success."

His great, dark eyes glowed at the thought of it.

"Goodby, dearest!"

They had kissed and she had cried.

Then from the porch of her home she had seen the strange, dark bubble of a thing float away into the skies.

A FEW nights later the farmers, thirty miles from Avison's home, might have observed a few spots of light hovering in the air over the wide field of a deserted farm. They might have discerned the light-spots dart back and forth, then down, then up a way, and then descend to earth. But it is not recorded that any man was awake to see.

Charles Avison unscrewed the round door of the Vulcan and crept out. Instantly the light died from its windows. At first he could not stand, but staggered twice and fell in a heap under the curved side of the machine. He lay a little while, then flashed his light about and into the door of a great, deserted barn, in front of which his machine had alighted.

He climbed to his feet and steadied himself. After a little while he thrust his shoulder against the dark sphere and rolled it as silently as a great snowball into the high doorway. Then he glanced at his watch.

"Not far from morning," he said.

He walked unsteadily toward the road.

Avison congratulated himself on his nearness to home. A few hours before, when he had awakened from unconsciousness, he had been over water. He had risen from the bottom of the sphere, where he had fallen, with swimming head and drumming ears, and, getting his bearings, had guided the machine toward home. His light was failing when he was still thirty miles away, however, so he had thought it safer to descend.

His experiment had been a success!

Then he began to wonder what had occurred in that brief period of unconsciousness. And was it so brief? His watch had said 3.40 just before he had fainted and 4.35 just after he had awakened. But had it been one hour or twenty-five? His ears still rang; he walked drunkenly.

He sat down in a fence-corner to await daylight. He saw the stars—his companions, he called them—begin to dim as a wide ribbon of grayish blue showed above the eastern horizon. He saw this ribbon widen still more, and soon he could detect the lines of his hands. At his feet were flowers, wet with dew.

Avison lighted a cigar, but he could hardly see the smoke in the bluish dawn. But before the fire in it became too warm for his fingers it was daylight.

He arose and looked about. He knew the place—he had driven along the road many times in his car. He knew the great barn where he had housed the Vulcan, the long line of straggly telephone-poles, the spinelike row of poplars beside the creek.

Just thirty miles to home and Agnes! He would start to walk to the nearest railway station. Some friend in a car would probably pick him up.

But somehow—Avison did not know how or what or why—something, everything did not seem natural. He could not be mistaken in the place; the trees, the farms, the houses, even the fence-posts were familiar. But that queer, haunting feeling of unfamiliarity remained; he could not shake it off. It must be that he had not yet completely recovered from his fainting.

He started along the road. He laughed when he saw a deep rut that had once broken a spring of his car. Here was the muddy spot where a tiny creek seeped across the highway. Here was the bridge, with its familiar hole where Octavius, his favorite horse, always shied.

The ringing in his ears had gone now; he walked perfectly straight. His head no longer swam. But the feeling of alienation was as marked as ever.

Avison became a little frightened, even though he knew the road perfectly. He tested his knowledge. Soon he would arrive

at the crossroads, where the lane turned off toward the old Fair Grounds. Yes! He came to the place just where he thought it would be.

But why was it that everything was the same and yet different? He knew even the ruts of the road and the crack in the telephone post where the lightning had once struck. He knew the quiet fields of grain, the pretty farm-homes, the horses in the fields. Yet he felt—he knew it now—that something was terribly different.

He saw the farmers on their way to the dairy barns. He heard the windmills creaking, and the call of the hired men as they hitched their teams to the farming implements. The world about him was commonplace and ordinary, just as always on a late spring morning in the country. But he could not shake off the illusive feeling.

He tried to; he tried to think of other things. He whistled and smoked again, but found it useless.

He heard an automobile behind him—the commonplace *honk!* of the horn and the *chug* of the engine! A touring car, bearing only a driver, came up to him. The car stopped as Avison waved his arm.

"Can you give me a lift?" the scientist called.

"Sure."

Avison took a seat beside the driver, and looked at him searchingly.

"You're Johnston, aren't you?" he asked as the car started.

"Yes, but I don't remember you," the other man said.

"My name is Avison—Charles Avison."

Johnston looked at him quickly.

"Are you Charles Avison?" he asked. "I have heard of you many times."

He stretched out a gauntleted hand and found his companion's thin, long-fingered one.

"We can't be far from Smithford, can we?" Avison asked.

Smithford was a little town but a few miles from his home.

"About fifteen miles," replied the

driver. "And what are you doing along this road at this hour, may I ask?"

"Taking a morning walk," replied Avison.

THE road was becoming more familiar. He knew many of the names that he saw on the mail-boxes. He knew the dog that barked from the gateway of a farmhouse—a dog that had always barked at him. But yet he was perplexed and bewildered by the lingering sensation of unfamiliarity.

After ten miles the automobile slowed. "I have to turn here," said Johnston. "Which way are you going?"

"Straight on, I guess; and thank you."

Avison hopped out of the slowly moving car, and started again down the dusty road. He began to wonder why Johnston had not recognized him; they had passed each other several times. Avison put his hands to his face. He felt several days' growth of hair.

Of course, that was the reason. He needed a shave very badly on the day of his ascent, and in the five days at least that he was in the air a black growth had covered his cheeks and chin. And his face felt thinner; the bones protruded.

Soon he passed a farmhouse—one where he had often stopped for a meal while quail hunting. So he entered the gate; he was hungry for a warm breakfast again. He knew the dog that came to meet him, and patted its furry head. The old woman at the doorway did not recognize him.

He told her what he wanted, and she led him to the kitchen. He washed in a basin at the back and looked at himself in the glass.

No wonder the others had not known him! His face was much thinner; great, dark bags hung beneath his eyes.

Who would have thought that the days in the air could have been such a physical strain? His white, hollow cheeks and wide, black eyes, in contrast to the black hair, shocked him. No wonder he remained unknown to Johnston and the woman.

During the meal he asked but one question, and it was a peculiar one.

"What's the date?" he asked.

The old woman looked up quickly.

"Twenty-fourth," she replied.

Avison had gone up on the sixteenth. He had been two days unconscious!

And still the brooding strangeness perplexed and bewildered him.

Again he was out on the road. He picked up another ride soon, and when he came to Smithford, he took off the grease-stained clothes he had worn on the air journey. He laughed at himself in the suit he had just bought. In bad need of a hair-cut and shave, and in different clothes, he wondered if Agnes would know him.

The small town was at the end of his walk. He could take the train from there to his home. He walked about the town. Although he was well known there and many people looked at him interestedly, none came up to speak to him. He laughed to himself over the fact that even an old friend did not know him.

The train—the slow old train in which he had so often ridden—pulled in an hour later. By now it was noon; the Avison place was scarcely a half-hour's ride away. He remembered the worn-out plush on the seat of the cars, the conductor who punched his ticket. But always something was not quite the same.

"The trip has affected my mind," he said at last.

He could almost scream at the harassment of it all. He could not analyze or place his finger on the difference, but it was there, it was everywhere! The change of circumstance brooded about him and haunted him and made him grip his hands. His eyes widened at the thought of it.

Was he asleep? Or hurt?

Or dead?—*Dead!* Anything was possible to him now.

What if he *were* dead?

Then he laughed at himself for being a fool. The laugh was hysterical; the train newsie eyed him suspiciously. He pinched himself on the arm, and the hurt was real. But something had changed him, or changed the world in which he lived.

The train stopped at last at Avison's own town, at the outskirts of which stood his own house. Agnes lived here, too. Half-frightened, Avison wondered whether Agnes would know him.

"But it would be good sport if she didn't!"

So he dropped into a second-hand store and traded his trim cap for an old, battered hat. This he pulled down over his eyes, and started down the quiet street. Some boys stared at him as he passed, but no one spoke in recognition. A dog that he knew slunk away from him.

Even the town was different!

Yes! The stores and the people and the fountains and the sparrows in the streets and the signs were all the same in every physical particular. But there had been change, and Avison swore at himself.

A T a street-corner he saw a group of men talking quietly. Although they glanced at him, they did not speak to him. And yet he knew every one of them!

As he passed he heard his name mentioned. He paused a minute as if to stare across the street.

"I knew it would happen some time," old Felix Barnes was saying. "I've told him so a hundred times. But he would go on making experiments. It's a good thing his mother isn't alive. It would about kill her."

"And they say Agnes Cole is just prostrated," said another of the group.

Agnes Cole! Avison listened more attentively.

"The funeral procession ought to start soon," said another.

A ghastly feeling of sickness rose in Avison. He clenched his hands.

"How did it happen, anyway? Does anybody know?" asked a youth. "I just got back to town, and this is the first I've heard of it."

From under his arm Barnes drew a folded newspaper, which he opened slowly.

"Here's the account—as much as any one knows," he explained. "Avison went up on the sixteenth for a four-day trip according to Miss Cole. He had some scheme for beating gravity, mind you. Think of that—beating gravity!"

"Poor fellow!" murmured the youth.

"Well, they found his machine wrecked to pieces just outside of town yesterday. Every bone in his body was broken. I heard the crash myself when the machine fell."

Panic-stricken, Avison turned away. He pinched himself again. His eyes were wide, he knew. His scalp twitched. At a newsstand he bought a paper, and feverishly read of his own death.

The machine, said the account, was broken to pieces. The name plate, on which appeared the word

Vulcan

had been found, however.

Wildly Avison grasped at every possibility that came to his mind. Coincidence, of course. But what a devilish one! Some aviator had been killed, so badly crushed that even his own family had mistaken his identity. Avison must hurry out to his home and tell his family that he lived. He must tell Agnes, too.

But *was* he alive?

He cursed himself as a fool for letting the question come to his mind. But what did he know of the region and state of death? His eyes widened even more at the thought of it.

But it couldn't be that—it couldn't! He pricked his chest with a pin. Then he pricked his hand till he brought blood.

He came in sight of the old church where he had gone to Sunday school as a boy, and where his father had gone before him. The old ivy-grown church, with its sleepy belfry and its quiet lawn. Out in front were many carriages and automobiles. The sound of singing came up to him—a funeral dirge.

Avison hung back. He was afraid to go on to that church.

What if the body in the coffin should be his?

He cursed himself again, and slowly went on. But he *must* see the dead man before the coffin was closed! He began to walk swiftly.

He climbed the steps and entered the church doors. It was filled with his own friends. The sexton looked at him, but did not recognize him. Timidly he sat down, just beside an acquaintance. The man was weeping quietly.

The service was nearing its close when Avison entered. Almost at once the white-haired old parson said that those who wished might look again at the body.

The people stood up, the young scientist with them. Agnes in black, her face tear-stained, was in front. Near her stood his sister, weeping. He dared not approach them. There was his uncle—all of his cousins. Slowly and wearily the train of people began to walk past the long coffin of black. Avison followed them.

"What if it is?" he whispered. "What if it is?"

He gripped himself and resolved to keep his control. He came slowly up.

And the pall-bearers saw a young man at the end of the line—one who looked familiar, and yet whom they thought they did not know; one who needed a shave and wore a ridiculous suit of clothes—clench his hands until the nails nearly tore the flesh, and go white as the flowers banked about the coffin.

Avison rushed to the open air. Then he pressed his hands to his lips to suppress a scream.

"*It is I!*" he moaned. "*It is my own body!*"

And winding away out of the town, the funeral procession had started for the graveyard.

CONSIDERING everything, Avison kept his self-control well. He resolved that he would not go insane. That there had been some monstrous coinci-

dence. That the smooth face in the coffin was not his own. But this reflection was the only thing that preserved his sanity.

That day passed, and that night, and still the young man did not sleep. He had secured a room in the hotel, and he tried to forget, in the smoke of many strong cigars. That a ghost could smoke cigars! In the morning he slept a little.

That day his beard was longer than ever, and this, together with the thinness of his face, disguised him perfectly. At ten he caught a train for a near-by city. There he could think it out, away from Agnes and his mourning relatives, to whom he felt a deadly fear of identifying himself.

In the city he secured a hotel room, and again tried to think. He was baffled, bewildered, afraid. The strangeness of everything remained, but not in such a marked degree as in his home town.

"A coincidence," he kept repeating. "It *must* be! It can't be anything else!"

After a few days he began to think of his science again. What if he *were* taken for dead? He himself knew now that he was alive and well. He ate heartily at the hotel grill; he saw an occasional movie.

But yet he could not go back to the Avison place nor to Agnes—at least until the memory of the familiar face in the coffin had faded from the minds of those at home. He shut it out of his own mind.

Then he thought of his machine out in the great deserted barn. They had found the wreck of the dead man's machine, and machines do not have ghosts. He felt more himself every day. Finally he remembered that an observatory in connection with a great university was situated just outside the city. So one day he had his beard and mustache trimmed, put on a large pair of dark glasses, and went out to talk to the head of the astronomy department.

"I am Vunden, of Heidelberg," he told Gray, the old astronomer, "and I would like a position. The money part of it is of no importance to me."

This did not surprise Gray. He knew many men on the faculty who worked only for the love of it. He questioned the young man, whose knowledge of the stars he found amazing. So Gray procured "Vunden" a position on a low salary, and Avison went to work again at his old love. It was only for a little while, he thought, until he could straighten out things a little better in his mind. The work might make him forget; at least it would end the monotony of idleness.

But it came about that he was not long at the observatory. A few weeks after he obtained his position there came an eclipse of the sun. That noon, as Avison stared into the eye-piece of the telescope, he saw for an instant at the edge of the dark rim of the moon a new planet. The significance of it struck Avison squarely between the eyes.

He sat back, staring into space for a few seconds, then started up with raised arms. Gray, the old astronomer, found him laughing and crying hysterically.

"What's the matter, Vunden?" he demanded.

"Matter? Matter! Great Heavens!" began Avison excitedly. Then he calmed himself. "I have made the greatest discovery in the scientific world. I have made two of them, in fact! But this one is the greatest in the history of astronomy! Look through the telescope!"

"What is it?" questioned Gray as he adjusted the glass.

"Look!" Avison rasped.

Gray glanced a moment at the tiny orb. The moon hid it as he watched.

"A new planet!" The old man was staggered. "Why has it never been seen before?"

His face flamed.

"I can tell you why! It is in perpetual eclipse by the sun just opposite from us. The once or twice a year it is not eclipsed, probably on account of the eclipse of the earth's course around the sun, it is too near the sun to be seen. Don't you understand? Don't you?"

"But why—"

"Oh, I will tell you everything, soon. But first tell me this: Along the twentieth of May was there a kind of meteoric disturbance—a comet?"

"How came you not to notice that? A meteor swept very near the earth. But tell me—"

"No. Let me go. I won't explain now. I can't. But I will write to you in a day or so."

Then as he hurried out: "To think that I should find out the truth at last!"

IT WAS only a day or so later that Vunden disappeared as if from the face of the earth. But a mimeograph copy of a strange letter came to every great scientist in the nation. And one letter, the original, came to one recipient who was not a scientist at all. Agnes Cole.

It made many a gray-haired astronomer shake his head unbelievingly. But Agnes understood. The communication read:

To Agnes and to the Scientific Men of the World:

I do not expect you to believe what I have written here, but I only ask that you investigate and you will then learn that what I say is true. And I, Charles David Avison, of There, not of Here —but an equal in mind, ability, and genius of the Charles David Avison who died for science, Here, of whom you already know—I swear to you that it is the truth.

If you do not believe, it is no matter. For even now I feel that perhaps I am doing wrong to add to the knowledge of the world wherein I do not belong.

Understand first that there are two earth worlds. In order that you may not confuse them, I will call the one in which I now am Here. The other is There.

Both were thrown off from the sun as spiral nebula at the same instant. Here went one direction, and There the other. Both being of the same size, gravity overcame the centrifugal force at exactly the same distance in space from the sun.

The two cooled the same time, of course, their oceans formed coincidentally, and the first germs of life appeared upon There at the identical instant that they appeared Here.

I have already told you enough to enable you to understand what occurred. There is no fate or chance in life—everything is cause and effect, cause and effect.

So as life developed There, its exact counterpart developed Here. For every caveman There, one was Here—his exact counterpart in appearance. Everything that he did or thought or felt, the caveman Here did or thought or felt at the same time. And so it was through the ages.

When I, Charles David Avison, was born There, Charles David Avison was born Here. When he began to love, I began to love. When he made that greatest discovery of all ages—the S waves which, conducted through a certain substance, will render it immune to the attraction of gravity, I made it There. Together we built spherical machines, and at the same second christened them the Vulcan.

I will not tell here of my discovery, but will leave it for some one else to make. One who belongs on this Here of yours. Your world has had its Avison; my world still awaits the benefits accruing from the discoveries of its own Avison.

On the same day we each made trial flights, I There on that far-away counterpart world, and he Here. A few months later, on the sixteenth of May, we left our worlds. He left Here and I left There, and each of us floated away toward the stars.

Each of us had air for many days and food enough. But then for the first time something happened There that did not happen Here. For the first time the dualism was broken.

A meteor came near There when one did not come Here. My Vulcan was attracted to it by gravity, and before I could throw the S waves into the metal covering to render us immune, I was sweeping after it at a terrific pace, faster than our finite minds can conceive. I became unconscious then. Why, I do not know.

And I see now what happened. The meteor carried me across that infinite expanse to a point where the gravity of this world began to grip me. I began to fall.

I remember now that when I wakened the sea was below me. I remember that I threw on the S waves just in time, and floated down to safety.

I do not know how the other Charles Avison of Here fell to his death. I know that his machine was as good as mine, for the laws of cause and effect ordered it so. I can only attribute his fall to some influence on this meteor, this monstrous disturber out of space. The meteor probably never struck the earth. It might now be buried deep in the cold surface of the moon.

I have no place in this world of yours; I am a stranger here. In fact, I have no place anywhere now, for my counterpart is dead. If I stay here the old dualism will be broken still more, and our two worlds would soon become most different places. It is broken, anyway, now. For there is a man's body beneath the grass of Here, that is not There.

When you get this I will have boarded my Vulcan and will have started out into that strange, wonderful maze of worlds.

Perhaps I will go home—or perhaps to a new world. Perhaps I will not get anywhere. But I do not care. I would die out there among the stars, or perhaps on their unknown surfaces, the greatest voyager that the worlds have ever known.

The Gravity Experiment

By J. U. GIESY

Author of "Palos of the Dog-Star Pack," etc.

There were no rules in Patrolman McGuiness' manual for enforcing the Law of Gravity

"Whu-roo!" He gave vent to a full-toned Irish shout of amazed comprehension, and continued his progress aloft

"**M**EOUW!" The sound was one of feline protestation, a sort of outraged plaint, uttered in the accents of a snarling rage.

"Goodness! Was that Fluffy?" exclaimed Miss Nellie Zapt to her fiancé, Bob Sargent, with whom she was sitting in the dusk, back of the vines on the porch of her father's house.

"Sounded like her voice, at any rate," Bob agreed.

"Meouw! Psst! Zit!"

Nellie started to her feet and stood slenderly poised as a fresh outburst of something suspiciously like inarticulate profanity drifted to her ears. And then she laid hold of her companion.

"Come along, there's something wrong," she urged, and dragged him to his feet.

She darted into the house intent on learning what had evoked the outcries so vociferously emitted by her pet, and Sargent followed very much as he had been following her for something like a year. She was a dainty, glowing creature, and Bob was all tangled up in her feminine charms. So he kept close now as with a tapping of quick little heels on polished wood she entered the living-room of the house via the entrance hall.

And then Nellie paused. She stared at the figure of a small man with spectacles on the bridge of a high, thin nose, and iron-gray whiskers. He stood with back-tilted head, beside a small tin pail deposited on the table in the center of the room.

"Father!" Miss Zapt gasped.

And Sargent also exclaimed. "Good Lord!"

"Eh?" Xenophon Xerxes Zapt, "Unknown Quantity Zapt," as his associates sometimes called him because of the double "X" in his name, the celebrated investigator of the unknown in science, lowered his head and jerked it around in the direction of his daughter's voice. There was the atmosphere about him of a small boy apprehended in some prank. He put out a hand and laid it on the little tin pail. "Did you speak, my dear?" Out of near-sighted blue eyes, he peered at his radiant offspring who had drawn herself up in an indignant fashion.

"I did," said Miss Zapt firmly. "I suppose you're responsible for that?"

She lifted a graceful arm and pointed overhead, as indeed she very well might, considering that she pointed at the wildly gyrating form of a superb Angora cat.

One would hardly expect to find a Persian Angora flattened, with no visible means of support, against the ceiling of a room, as this one certainly was. She hung there threshing with frantic legs at the impalpable air, with a motion not unlike a rather desperate effort at swimming. Then she spun herself about in a circle, marked by a rapidly alternating head, from which gleamed yellow eyes and a twitching bushy tail. Her behavior was little short of hysteria.

"Meouw!" she voiced her troubled state once more as she heard her mistress's voice.

With poor tact Sargent chuckled. "Seems to have got the Angora's angora," he began.

Miss Zapt gave him a withering glance.

"Never mind, Fluffy pet," she called encouragement to the glaring creature that had temporarily given over its efforts and rested with back pressed against the ceiling.

And then she bore down on the little man who had once more lifted his eyes to the animal above him. "I suppose this is another of your detestable experiments," she went on in a voice half tears and half rage. "What have you done to my cat?"

"Nothing, nothing—about the seventy-fifth of an ounce." Professor Zapt fumbled in his pocket for notebook and pencil, opened the former and touched the latter to his lips.

"Father!" Miss Zapt seized both book and pencil. She stamped her foot.

"Eh? Oh, yes, yes—exactly." Xenophon Xerxes glanced into her flushed face. "As a matter of fact I have done nothing to your pet, my child. Nothing at all worth mentioning, that is. Indeed, as you will note I have even exercised extreme caution. I have closed the windows, and the ceiling, of course, prevents her further ascension. But if you refer to her present position—"

"It is rather unusual, don't you think, professor?" said Bob. "Now if she were a flying squirrel—"

"Exactly," Xenophon Zapt cut him short. "The term flying-squirrel is a misnomer, however, Robert. The animal so-called is incapable of sustaining itself for any considerable time in the air. As to the former part of your remark, however, hers is indeed a most unusual position. It is that which proves the complete success of my experiment. You are now witnessing one of the marvels of the ages—voluntary levitation. The rediscovery of one of the lost secrets of the ancients. The means by which—"

Abruptly Nellie caught up the little pail. "I suppose your lost secret's in this?"

And swiftly Xenophon Zapt put out a hand to retrieve what she had seized. "Nellie," he commanded sternly, "replace that receptacle where you found it. As you surmise, it contains a substance of incalculable value. The first practical preparation of Zapt's Repulsive Paste."

"Wha-a-at!" Sargent crossed to gaze into the little bucket his fiancée was holding. "Does look sort of repulsive," he agreed after a glance at the mess in the bottom of the pail. "But—you mean this stuff is responsible for Fluffy's sudden elevation in life?"

"Exactly." Professor Zapt nodded. "The animal is not injured except in her feelings, I assure you. I merely rubbed a very small portion of the paste into the fur on the under side of her body, and she assumed the position you are now privileged to behold. I am sure that in later years you will be glad to recall this evening, to remember that you were the first to witness the reapplication of those principles once before known to our race. You—"

"Just at present," his daughter interrupted, "I'm far more interested in knowing whether, having sent her up there, you intend letting her remain until she starves to death."

"Eh?" Professor Zapt frowned. "Starves? Why, certainly not. Having demonstrated to our satisfaction the efficacy of this latest addition to science, we may consider the test as ended. If Robert will obtain a stepladder from the basement, and you will procure some water in order that we may wash off the paste—"

"Sure," Bob said, and departed on his errand. Nellie went with him as far as the kitchen.

PROFESSOR ZAPT shook his head in depreciative fashion, retrieved his notebook and pencil from the table where Nellie had cast them, and began jotting down certain memoranda. His thin lips moved as his pencil traced its way across a page. "The seventy-fifth part of an ounce," he muttered.

Above his graying head glared a very much disgruntled cat. It was not the first time her mistress's father had made her the subject of some experiment.

Sargent and Nellie reappeared in due season. Bob set up his ladder and mounted to the rescue. Below, Nellie waited with a basin of warm water and a soft cloth in her hands.

"Lay her on her back," Professor Zapt advised as Sargent descended with the Angora clinging desperately to him. "That way she will not present any tendency to rise. The paste does not affect anything beneath it, but merely what is superimposed. That is the secret of its adaptability."

"Exactly," Bob said, grinning, and got down upon his knees.

Nellie knelt beside him. Together they administered to the resentful cat. While Bob held her, Nellie applied water to the body of her pet and dried her fur with the cloth. Fluffy glared, but submitted to superior force.

"Steady," said Bob at last, and turned her over. He removed his restraining hands, and in a flash she vanished through the door into the hall.

Xenophon watched the entire performance, his blue eyes glowing behind their lenses. He nodded as she disappeared. He rubbed his hands together as Bob rose and assisted Nellie to her feet. "A very satisfactory experiment," he declared; "a very satisfactory experiment indeed."

"If you don't let Fluffy alone"—Nellie turned on him— "I'll—I'll pack up and leave home." For years, since her mother's death, she had taken care of the little man's temporal wants and managed the house, but there were times when his complete attention to his scientific pursuits and his lack of attention to everything else,

got badly on her nerves. And now her violet eyes were winking, and her red mouth quivered.

"Any time you feel like that, I'll see you have another to go to," Bob suggested as she paused, with a little catch in breath.

"Ahem!" Xenophon Xerxes Zapt glared. He did not approve so wholly of Bob as did his daughter. "Do not make any premature preparations, Robert," he said, after a rather tense interval in which Nellie blushed. "The animal is not injured, as you yourself have seen, and as Nellie will realize in time. The main difficulty against which scientists have to contend in these days of self-interest is the conventional attitude of the average mind.

"Human beings are prone to allow some purely personal view-point to overshadow the major object to be attained. In the present instance it is consideration for a cat. It is permitted to obscure the fact that through her use we have demonstrated the rediscovery of the means by which the Egyptians built the Pyramids."

"What? By Jove!" Sargent opened his eyes in wonder as the point struck home. "You really mean that, professor?"

"Exactly," said Xenophon Zapt benignly, and stroked the graying whiskers on either side of his chin.

"But if that's the case," Bob began quickly, and came to a tonguetied pause.

"It is the case, Robert."

"I know—but—" Sargent floundered. "If it is, why couldn't you have proved it just as well with a book or a rock or a box?"

For an instant the professor's blue eyes twinkled. "I suppose I could have done so, Robert," he replied, "but, as a matter of fact, I took the first object at hand when I was ready to make the test. I—er—that is, I didn't give the matter any further thought.

"My mind was focused on the larger point, the demonstration which proves beyond question that Zapt's Repulsive Paste will revolutionize the commercial world. By means of it we shall be able to accomplish marvels heretofore quite beyond

any engineering scope. We shall, by insert-
ing definite quantities of the paste between
the object to be transported and the earth,
be able to move enormous buildings, nullify
the weight of tremendous loads, alter the
entire present-day conception as apper-
taining to weight."

"I don't doubt it," Bob agreed in actually enthusiastic fashion. "Lord, professor,
it's simply wonderful when you explain
it; and it's already sent Fluffy to the ceiling, and moved Nellie to tears."

"You beast," said Miss Zapt; but she
smiled.

Her father frowned. "My chief objection
to you, Robert, is the somewhat bizarre
sense of humor which induces you to approach matters of weight in a light mood.
If you would refrain from undue levity,
there are times when I would be inclined
to appreciate your otherwise not unin-
telligent apprehension of the results of
scientific investigation."

"I beg your pardon, sir," Bob apolo-
gized meekly. "What was it you were saying about the Pyramids?"

"The world has long marveled how they
were built, how it was possible to transport
and place in their walls monoliths of such
enormous size. The answer was suggested
some years ago, but never carried further,
so far as I am aware. It was reserved for
me to prove the truth of that suggestion
and give again to the world a substance
similar in effect at least to the one they
used.

"That substance you have seen in operation tonight. It is in principle a screen
for gravitation. Objects above it become
for the moment practically devoid of
weight; mere trifles light as air."

"You mean it cuts off the operation of
gravitation on anything above it?" Bob
asked. "Why, that's marvelous, professor."

"Exactly," Xenophon Zapt agreed.

"Dead or alive?"

"Animate or inanimate, as you have
seen." The professor rubbed his hands.
He eyed the stylish shoes his daughter's
fiancé was wearing. "For instance, Robert,
I could rub a certain amount on the soles

of your shoes, and you would walk a certain distance from the floor. Depending
upon the quantity employed in proportion
to your weight, you would rise slightly or
higher, as the centripetal force of the earth
revolutions threw you off.

"The entire action is capable of regulation by means of a calculation based upon
the weight of the object to be moved. If I
knew your exact weight I could cause you
to lose ponderability altogether. I could
even make you disappear. Still," he sighed,
"I presume Nellie would object to that
even more loudly than she protested my
use of the cat. However, as a matter of
scientific demonstration, it would be interesting, I think."

"Oh, very." Bob drew his modish foot-
wear well under the chair in which he was
sitting, and Nellie stiffened.

Xenophon Zapt arose. "I think I shall
go to my study now and write a brief
account of my experiment. Tomorrow I
shall begin the preparation of a large
amount of the powder which, blended with
water, constitutes the paste. I shall or-
ganize a company after a bit. If you wish,
Robert, I shall permit you to purchase a
reasonable amount of stock. Good night."

"Good night, sir. Thank you," said Bob,
and watched him disappear, a quaint little
figure in his loose slippers, his iron-gray
whiskers and his shapeless, flapping coat.

And after the professor was quite out
of sight, Bob turned to Nellie. "Lord! Do
you suppose he's really got it?" he remarked. "Something surely happened to
Fluffy, and after we washed off the paste
she was all right, and—I guess those old
wiseacres did know something in their day.
It makes a fellow feel funny—Egyptians
and Pyramids, and all those old things."

Five minutes later, while Professor
Xenophon Xerxes Zapt drew paper before
him and dipped his pen in ink, his daughter
and Sargent sat very close together on the
living-room couch.

TRUE to his promise, Professor Xenophon Xerxes Zapt spent the major
portion of the succeeding day mixing and

blending the ingredients of the powder which, when mixed with water, constituted the Repulsive Paste. He heaped it upon a tray and left it on a table in the upstairs room that he habitualy used as the scene of his scientific investigations—a room overlooking, from broad windows, the tree-shaded street.

And the succeeding morning he charged downstairs about ten and informed Nellie that he had nearly overlooked the fact that he meant to attend the meeting of a scientific body to which he belonged in a neighboring town. In considerable haste he arrayed himself in clean shirt and collar, the frock-coat, to which he consistently clung, and hat, and was on the point of departure for a train, when Nellie suggested that he had better wear his shoes, rather than the slippers on his feet. The professor acceding rather impatiently to the suggestion, the change of footgear was made and he departed. After that the day dragged past until four o'clock.

At that hour Bob Sargent, seated in the office where he dispensed legal advice to sundry clients, answered a ring on his phone.

"Oh, Bobby," came the voice of Miss Zapt; "come up to dinner. Dad's gone to one of his society meetings and he won't be home till rather late, and with all these recent burglaries and hold-ups in the city, I'm sort of nervous."

"Yes, you are," said Sargent with the chuckle, deriding the confession of Miss Zapt's timorous nerves.

"Yes, really, I am," she insisted. "You'll come, won't you, Bob?"

"I will," said Bob without hesitation. And he did.

Because he was in love, and a dinner with his sweetheart tête-à-tête is something no true lover in his senses will pass up. He arrived about six with a box of Nellie's favorite candy and anticipations of a pleasant evening, since Miss Zapt's experience as manager of her father's household had made a dinner under her supervision a thing not to be missed.

In this particular case anticipation proved no more than the precursor of realization. The dinner was a course affair of finely balanced quality, and the two young people rather dallied over it, from soup to cheese, as young people sometimes will, until a sudden deepening of the twilight sent Nellie to the window just as a peal of thunder reverberated sharply through the house.

"Goodness, it's going to rain cats and dogs, Bob!" she exclaimed. "The sky's as black as ink."

"Let 'er rain," said Sargent, content with a well-filled stomach and the society of the lady of his affections. "We've a good roof over our heads, so we should worry."

"I was thinking of father," Nellie explained and giggled as she recounted the professor's attempt to leave home without his shoes. "He's so absent-minded about little things. Mercy!"

A small cyclone seemed sweeping through the house, sending curtains eddy-

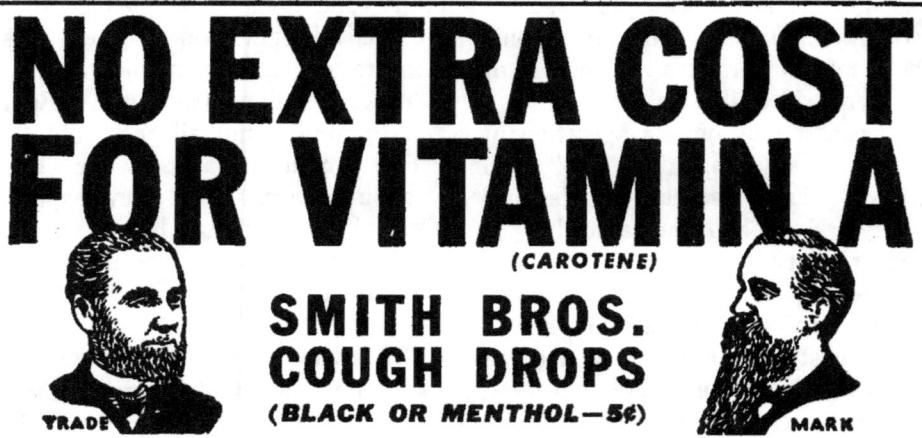

ing in flapping streamers, and doors banging as they were caught and slammed in the draft.

There followed a few moments of rapid effort in closing windows and making all secure, and then youth and maiden stood briefly watching the first dashing flurry of the summer shower, before they pulled down the shades and withdrew to a low-toned conversation, dealing as usual under similar conditions, quite largely with themselves.

Meanwhile, some distance up the street, a large and heavy-set figure sheltered itself as best it might beneath an arching tree, while waiting for the shower to pass.

It was that of Officer Dan McGuiness, patrolman on the beat that included the Zapt house. It wasn't a very exciting beat as a rule, but recently Danny had been nursing hopes. As Miss Zapt had said to Bob that afternoon, there had been a lot of burglaries of late and Danny really couldn't see why fate should not be kind and send one of the as yet unapprehended prowlers into his quiet street. He was thinking about it now as he listened to the patter of the rain among the leaves.

"Shure it would be a grand noght for a poorch-climber to git in his fancy wuruk," he soliloquized. "Th' wind an' th' rain would cover any noises he might be makin'. 'Tis th' sort of noight I'd consider as made to me order was I a burglar myself."

And the thought having taken hold upon him was with him still, as the shower swept on across the countryside, and the moon appearing, began to flirt with the dripping landscape from behind a veil of ragged clouds. It sent him on down the street with a wary eye for any burglarious-minded individual who might have been of the same opinion as himself.

Thus he came in time to a house, with a wide front porch, above which was an open window; and rising over the top of the porch as Danny watched, an object like a human head.

With a heart beginning to beat more quickly, McGuiness drew into the shadow of a tree and waited. He knew this house as the home of Professor Xenophon Xerxes Zapt, inhabited by the old man and his daughter. That open window and the head rising cautiously over the edge of the porch roof fitted in with the thoughts McGuiness had been entertaining. He thrust his club into its loop and felt for his revolver. He was convinced that at last he had been given his chance to prove himself.

The head kept on rising. It was followed by a crouching body, and a pair of legs. It became the figure of a man crawling on top of the porch toward the open window with the silent caution of stealth. Once it appeared to hesitate, to slip on the slanting surface, and then it again went on.

OFFICER McGUINESS had seen enough. He drew his gun and started at a heavy run for the gate in the fence before the house. And having reached it, he slipped through it without sound. He did not follow the walk, but tiptoed with burly caution over the dampened lawn, made his way quite close to the porch. Then and then only did he lift his voice in a heavy, authoritative summons:

"Coom out of ut, me poorch-climbin' beauty. What are ye doin' up there?"

For a moment the figure above him went flat. The flirtatious moon peeped out long enough to reval it sprawled on the rain-soaked shingles. And then, in most surprising fashion, it floated straight up into the air!

Danny McGuiness stared. Little by little while his breath came harshly, he tilted back his head to observe that most amazing ascent of a human body without apparent means or visible cause.

The man was swimming up as one might swim in water, to judge by the frantic threshing of his arms and legs. But— Danny had never heard of anyone's swimming in the air.

His eyes popped and his jaw dropped as his intended prisoner mounted twenty, fifty, seventy feet and paused, seemingly unable to go any higher. The policeman removed his helmet and scratched his head. The thing was beyond all precedent of experience, a defiance of natural law. A criminal accosted might vault a fence, or climb a wall, or even scale a building in an effort at escape; but to drop on his face and bounce into the air—and—stay there like a—like a kite! Danny put some of his bewilderment into a baffled mutter.

"He went up," he mumbled. "I ask, is ut a man, or a flea or a flyin' fish, devil take 'im. Coom down, I says, an' instead of realizin' th' disadvantages of his position, he rose straight up like a airyplane an' there he is."

And then remembering the dignity of the law and his own standing as a representative of its force, he addressed the figure above him: "Well, that's enough now. Yer quite a burd to judge by yer actions, but—come on down out of that, and light."

Above him the figure was still undergoing contortions beneath the moon and the broken clouds. As he spoke it rolled halfway over and started like a plummet for the earth. Out of it there broke a strangled exclamation of sheer instinctive terror. By a wild effort it again reversed its position and once more shot aloft.

"Up an' down," said Officer McGuiness. "Ye've foine control an' quite a lot of speed, an' that was a grand exhibition. But finish th' trip next time. I've seen enough of yer tricks."

There followed a breathless interval and then a gasping response, "I c-a-a-a-an't!"

"Huh?" Officer McGuiness began to feel the least bit annoyed. He began to entertain a suspicion that this night-hawk was making sport of a member of the police. At the least he was denying what Danny had actually seen with his own good eyes. "Ye can't, can't ye?" he remarked at length. "Well, th' way ut looked to me, ye started out all right."

"Yes, an' if I'd a kept on, you dub, I'd a broke my neck."

"Shmall loss an' ye'd had," said Danny, his anger rising at the other man's form of address. "An' 'tis not all noight I hov to stand here watchin' ye act like a bloomin' bat."

"Who's actin'?" It was a snarl that answered. "If you think I'm doin' this for my health, you got even less sense than th' average cop. I tell you—"

"That's enough. You don't need to tell me nuthin'." Officer McGuiness's outraged dignity came to his aid. "You're under arrest."

"Oh, am I?" Apparently the man in the air was inclined to dispute the patrolman.

"Ye are." Danny stood by his statement none the less.

"Then why don't you come up and get me?"

"Because I ain't no rubber ball." It was a taunt and nothing else, and Danny knew it, but he didn't know exactly what to do about it. He shifted his position, moving in until he stood close beside the porch.

It was a most amazing situation. He might call the fire department and get the extension-tower, but that would ruin the professor's lawn. He might shoot the defiant captive, and yet he doubted if such action on his part would be considered as justified. There might be a question as to whether or no a man's floating up in the air constituted resisting arrest.

He had been taught that an officer should always keep cool. Only it was hard to keep cool in the face of such an amazing situation. Once more he scratched his head and eyed the figure between himself and the moon. The odd thing was the fellow didn't go any higher or even try to swim off. That was another thing that Danny couldn't understand. In fact, he couldn't understand anything that had happened during the last fifteen minutes. The whole thing was a bit too much for his brain.

"How do you do ut?" he asked at length.

"I don't do it, you square-head." The flying man disclaimed all hint at a personal prowess.

"Oh, don't you?" A fine scorn crept into Danny's tones. "Then I should loike to know who does."

"I don't know, dang it," gibbered the other's voice. "You started it yourself, comin' up on me like you did. There was something on the roof, I tell you. I laid down in it when you yelled at me. I felt it, it was sticky. I got it on my clothes—"

"On th' roof?" Danny interrupted with a flash of understanding. He knew considerable about Xenophon Zapt. He had even been mixed up once or twice in his experiments, quite outside his own intent.

"Yes. It stuck to me when I laid down, an' it's keepin' me up here, I guess. If I lay on my face I'm all right, but I start fallin' as soon as I turn on my back. Here's some of the danged stuff, if you want a closer look." Something whistled through the air and hit the spot where Danny had been standing.

But Danny wasn't there. As the other man spoke he had ducked and stepped aside. And straightway he became conscious of two things at once. The man had sunk a trifle nearer the earth after throwing down whatever it was he had scraped from his clothing, and—there was something the matter with his, Officer McGuiness's foot.

It was exhibiting a most remarkable inclination to rise into the air despite Danny's efforts to keep it on the ground. It was throwing him off his balance. Instinctively he hopped sidewise to save himself from falling, landed his one sane foot in what might have been a mass of soft mud on the grass under the eaves of the porch, and became aware that it also had gone wild.

AT ONCE Officer Dan McGuiness found himself in a most bewildering case. He had large feet, powerful, tireless in the path of duty, and the soles of his shoes were of a large expanse. Yet, strangely enough now, those heavy feet seemed to have taken on a quality positively airy.

Strive as he would, they refused to remain on the grass. In desperation he tried a step and found himself unable to thrust either leg or foot downward to a contact with the earth. Still struggling against belief he repeated the endeavor with the other foot and found himself mounting to

the level of the porch roof. Then and then only did realization and acceptance of the situation come upon him.

"Whu-roo!" He gave vent to a full-toned Irish shout of comprehension and continued his progress aloft.

Inside the house as that shout woke the echoes of the night, Miss Zapt pricked her pretty ears. "Bob," she said sharply, "what was that?"

"Sounded like a yell or a battle-cry or something," Sargent made answer. "I've had a notion I heard voices outside for the past few minutes. Maybe I'd better find out."

He rose, and Nellie followed him into the hall. He opened the door and they both stepped out on the porch.

At first they saw nothing, and then a gruff voice drifted to them: "Lie shtill, ye spalpeen. Ye tould me to come an' git ye an', begob, I hov. Quit yer squirmin' or I'll bust yer bean wid me club."

"Bob!" Miss Zapt seized her companion's arm. She had recognized those stentorian tones: "That's Officer McGuiness. They—they must be on the roof."

"Probably." Sargent went down the porch steps before he lifted his eyes, and then he, too, gasped at what he beheld and his voice came a bit unsteady. "Good Lord, Nellie! Look at that!"

He lifted an arm and pointed to where Danny, treading air very much as a man treads water, was endeavoring to still the struggles of a human figure sprawled out weirdly with its face to the earth.

Miss Zapt took one glance at the spectacle above her and shrieked: "Bob—they'll be killed!"

There came the click of the gate and a little man with iron-gray whiskers and a flapping frock-coat came up the walk.

"Ahem," he said rather dryly, "just what is the meaning of so excitable a statement? Who will be killed, may I ask?"

"Officer McGuiness and — somebody else," Nellie stammered.

"Eh?" Professor Zapt stared, out of his near-sighted eyes. "Indeed? I fail to perceive any indications of an impending tragedy myself. Where are they?"

"There!" Once more Sargent pointed aloft.

"Huh?" The professor tilted back his head as Bob's arm rose. "Bless my soul!" he exclaimed and stared for at least fifteen seconds before he raised his voice in a question: "Officer McGuiness, exactly how did you get up there?"

Danny may have sensed the presence of those beneath him, but if so he had thus far given no sign. Now, however, he managed to snap the handcuffs on his man, tilted his head and shot a glance at the earth.

"An' is ut you, professor?" he replied. "Shure, an' if it is how I got up here yer askin' why I walked, though barrin' th' fact how I done ut I dunno, except that this poorch-climbin' beauty floated offen yer roof when I told him to come down, I stepped into somethin' on th' grass. An' then I found mesilf endowed wid th' ability of follerin' after, belike because of whativer it was I had got on me fate. An' 'tis not so much how I got up is troublin' me now, as how I shall git down wid th' burd I've caught."

"Remarkable — actually remarkable!" said Professor Xenophon Xerxes Zapt. "Officer, this is most amazing. Let me think—let me think." He made his way

to the porch steps and found himself a seat.

"If I moight be suggestin', sor, don't be thinkin' too long at present." Danny's voice came down in the tone of a plaint. "'Tis tiresome work 'entirely, this walkin' on air. 'Tis not an angel I am as yet, an' there is nothin' to sit on at all, at all, an' th' steady movement is tirin' on th' legs."

"Then stop it," said the other in a manner of impatience. "Keep your feet still and float." He began pulling at his graying whiskers as though minded to tear them out by the roots. Presently he hopped up, trotted a few steps down the walk, lifted his eyes to the laboratory windows and nodded. And then he turned to Bob and Nellie. "Did it rain here tonight?"

"It did," Bob declared.

"Wind—preceding the shower?"

"Lots of it at first."

"That explains it," said Xenophon Xerxes Zapt.

"Glad of it—" Bob began.

The professor gave him a glance. "If you will kindly let me finish my remarks. As I told you I would, I prepared a quantity of the Paste Powder the other day and left it when I departed this morning to catch a train. In my haste I forgot to close the windows. The wind blew the powder upon the roof and the rain con-

---

Coming in the Next Issue

On the Brink of 2000

By Garret Smith

New Year's Eve on the verge of the Twenty-first Century, and a young man's strange adventure, made possible by an invention which projects him into the lives of his friends and his enemies

The Red Germ of Courage

By R. F. Starzl

Dramatic intrigue on an interplanetary liner

verted it into the paste and washed some of it off on the lawn—"

"If yer quite done thinkin', professor, sor," Officer McGuiness interrupted, "would you moind tellin' me how to get down?"

"Eh?" Xenophon Zapt jerked up his head to view the patrolman and his captive. "Oh, yes—yes—certainly. That's simple. You have the substance merely on your feet?"

"Yes, sor."

"Then hold them up."

"Hould thim up? Hould thim up where?" Danny's tone was growing a trifle excited. "If I try houldin' up my fate, I'll be losin' my balance and breakin' my—"

"Exactly." Professor Zapt's voice grew crisp. "Take hold of your prisoner, bend your legs at the knees, so as to elevate the soles of your shoes and let gravity do the rest. Robert, go turn on the hose that we may wash the paste off the officer's feet when he reaches the ground. He's all mussed up."

Bob departed, running, on his errand. By the time he was back Danny had effected a landing and was kneeling on the grass with his captive stretched out on his back within reach.

WITHIN five minutes the paste was removed from McGuiness's feet and he stood erect.

"Shure, an' 'tis wonderful stuff, professor," he began after he had taken a deep breath of relief. "An' what moight you call th' same?"

"Zapt's Repulsive Paste," said the professor. "It robs anybody above it of weight."

"What do ye think of that now?" Officer Dan exclaimed. "But 'tis no more than th' truth yer spakin'. I've had an example of its effects myself. Oh, would ye!"

He broke off and sprang, snatching into the air to grip and drag back the form of his prisoner, who in the momentary distraction of conversation had managed to roll himself on his face.

Danny slammed him down none too gently, it must be confessed. "Lie there

now, ye human balloon," he admonished in a growl, "or I'll make ye more repulsive than any kind of paste ye ever saw. If ye think I'm going to let Spur Heel Eddie slip out of my fingers, once they grip him—"

"Spur Heel Eddie?" Sargent repeated in excitement. "McGuiness, is that right?"

"Roight ut is—dead roight, Mister Sargent," Danny chuckled. "Shure, an 'tis a foine noight's wuruk. He's the burd we've been sort of thinkin' was behindt all these here burglaries happenin' th' last two weeks."

"And you caught him trying to burglarize my house." Professor Zapt's fingers slipped inside his coat. They came out with something crisp. "Officer, let me express my appreciation of your fidelity to duty."

"Thank ye, sor." Danny deftly pocketed the "appreciation" without removing his watchful eye from Eddie. "As I was sayin', McGuiness niver shirks his duty, an' 'tis a foine noight's wuruk."

"I'll go in and telephone for the wagon," suggested Bob.

"Don't trouble, sor," said Danny. "Begorra, I'll be takin' him in myself."

Stooping, he rolled Eddie face downward, seized him securely by the slack of the trousers and started to walk with him across the grass.

"Ye'll notice that wid all this Repulsive Paste smeared on him, if I carry him loike this he hasn't any weight at all," he announced from the gate.

"Exactly. You're a man of intelligence, McGuiness." Xenophon Xerxes Zapt turned to enter his house. "Good night."

"Good night, sor," Officer McGuiness made answer.

"Good night," Bob echoed with a chuckle as he watched Eddie, literally held fast by the strong arm of the law, borne off down the tree-shaded street until he disappeared.

Professor Zapt whirled upon him. "The occasion is not one of levity, Robert," he remarked in decidedly acid tones.

"No, sir. Merely of levitation," said Bob.